JAMES BOND'S EVOLUTION:
FROM *CASINO ROYALE* TO *SPECTRE*

JAMES BOND'S EVOLUTION: FROM *CASINO ROYALE* TO *SPECTRE*

NADER ELHEFNAWY

TABLE OF CONTENTS

INTRODUCTION 1

1. THE ORIGINS OF JAMES BOND 5

2. THE NOVELS OF IAN FLEMING 23

3. THE JAMES BOND MOVIES, 1962-1967 51

4. OF OLD PATTERNS AND NEW 79

5. KEEPING UP WITH THE JONESES 95

6. TOPICALITY 113

7. DEEPER CHANGES? 127

8. REBOOT 139

9. THE POST-FLEMING JAMES BOND NOVELS 157

10. ODDS AND ENDS 173

CONCLUSION: WHERE TO, FROM HERE? 185

NOTES 189

SELECTED SECONDARY BIBLIOGRAPHY 195

INDEX 201

INTRODUCTION

When it comes to James Bond, there are fans of the books, and fans of the films, a pop cultural division which is underlain by a still deeper divide. On one side of it are those who judge the series by conventional, realistic dramatic standards—who prefer a Bond who is a three-dimensional human being with a past, baggage, vulnerabilities and limitations, who can and does screw up and get himself hurt, and whose adventures are grounded in something like the world we know. A dark, bitter, troubled, world-weary Bond setting about a rather nasty business.

On the other side are those who appreciate the series as an over-the-top fantasy, who enjoy the idea of a nearly superhuman Bond living it up as he leaps from one ultra-luxurious, gimmick and sex-packed adventure to the next, saving the world from cartoon supervillains on what can seem like a weekly basis, and making it all look like an incredible lark.

The vast majority of the books about the series are written from the standpoint of those who prefer the more realistic, "dark and gritty" version, which they often hold to be the "true" Bond from which all the rest represents a falling away. This book, however, is written with the recognition that the two visions of the character were never totally separate. The Fleming novels *did* favor the former, the great majority of the films the latter (at least, until the recent reboot). However, to a far greater degree than most observers seem to appreciate, the elements of the cinematic fantasy were gradually developed in the books so that by the time of *Dr. No*, *Goldfinger* and *Thunderball* it was not such a great distance from these books to what we see on the screen. At the same time, even the notoriously lightweight movies of the Roger Moore era acknowledged Bond's emotional scars, and the brutal, treacherous side of the business—as in *The Spy Who Loved Me*, where Bond acknowledges a sensitivity about his marriage, and his killing of Anya Amasova' lover.

In short, *both* are part of the series, and this book treats them as such, taking the view that there is something to be said for the lighter, more extravagant side of the series for which so many critics show disdain. Indeed, without it, it is inconceivable that the Bond franchise would ever have become the phenomenon that it is today. Certainly it is that lighter, more extravagant side that first captured my attention, and I have to admit that all these years later I still have a fondness for the over-the-top aspects at which so many "serious" fans turn up their noses.

Moreover, while I feel that both the films and the books each have their distinct interests and pleasures, there is enough interconnection—more than enough—for them to be worth discussing together, as I mean to discuss them both here. This is especially the case given this book's central concern: the evolution of James Bond, the character and the stories about him. To that end *James Bond's Evolution* them from their origin in an already lengthy tradition of spy and thriller writing, to Ian Fleming's development of them through his novels, to their adaptation into the films made by Albert R. Broccoli and Harry Saltzman's EON (Everything or Nothing) Productions during the 1960s, which more than anything else define his popular image. This book also traces the development of those films into the multi-decade franchise we know today, and the continuation of the Bond novels by a host of other writers working in the shadow and under the influence of those films.

In tracing these main lines of the franchise, this book is less concerned with the history of manuscripts, or film production, than it is with the actual books and films—the final results. Additionally, as its focus is the ways in which all these developed, its main interest in the books and films is in the ways in which they changed over time, rather than providing a comprehensive guide to the franchise's various branches (with which the book market and the Internet are already crowded). Still, this book pays some attention to marginalized aspects of the series, including the television version of *Casino Royale*, the non-EON films, and the novelizations of the books in Chapter Ten, "Odds and Ends," and in the concluding section, "Where To, From Here?" considers some of the turns the series might have taken—and might yet take.

1. THE ORIGINS OF JAMES BOND

It is typically the case that writers of fiction derive inspiration from a wide range of sources, mixing art and life, the personal and the historical in a single work. So is it with Ian Fleming's James Bond novels, which drew on everything from recent headlines (like the defection of Bogdan Stashinsky), to then-cutting-edge technological developments (like the intercontinental ballistic missile), to movie stars of the time (Tatiana Romanova, notably, resembling Greta Garbo).

However, in a consideration of the Bond novels, three elements warrant special notice, namely Ian Fleming's own life and experiences; the historical and cultural moment in which he was writing, post-World War II Britain; and the tradition of the British spy thriller prior to James Bond. Each is a considerable subject in its own right, but this chapter looks at the roles each of these played in the creation of James Bond.

James Bond and Ian Fleming

There seems to be no argument over how Fleming settled on the name "James Bond" for his protagonist. While at his Jamaican residence Goldeneye he simply noticed the name on the cover of a book he happened to have about the house, *Field Guide to Birds of the West Indies*—by American ornithologist James Bond—and decided, as he later wrote in a letter to his character's namesake that "this brief, unromantic, Anglo-Saxon and yet very masculine name was just what I needed."

However, Bond's background, personality traits and life experiences are another matter. Naturally real-life spies, generally British or employed by Britain, have often been discussed as models, with Sidney Reilly often named in such discussions. The majority of the subjects of such speculation, however, have been well-known World War II-era British spies, like William Stephenson, Dusan "Dusko" Popov and the Secret Service's then second-in-command, Wilfred Dunderdale. Many of these figures do present interesting parallels with Bond, like the luxurious tastes and flamboyance of Dunderdale who was known for, among other things, driving an armor-plated Rolls-Royce. Yet, the search for a single figure is fundamentally wrong-headed. Fleming himself described Bond as a composite of intelligence and military figures he met during the war, of which there were of course many given Fleming's special position as personal assistant to the head of British naval intelligence.

Moreover, while Fleming plucked ideas from this person here, that one there, any contribution from these other figures pales next to Fleming's use of his own life as a basis for Bond, the parallels between which go far beyond the most obvious ones of social class (each born a gentleman, more or less) and nationality (the Scottish Fleming making Bond half-Scot). Both men lost their fathers early in life, Fleming losing his in World War I at the age of nine, while Bond's father died in a mountain climbing accident while he was eleven. Bond also lost his mother in the same incident, and while this was not the case with Fleming, it may be said that in a sense he also lost his mother in the aftermath of his father's death. As Bruce A. Rosenberg and Ann Harleman Stewart wrote, Ian Fleming's "dead, hallowed father became an ideal his widow held up to her four sons . . . a sacred model that Ian could not possibly equal, much less surpass," as a result of which he "missed out on nearly all parental affection and encouragement."[1]

As would be expected given their privileged familial backgrounds, both men attended Eton, but did not go on to Oxbridge afterward. Both spent some of their youth in interwar Germany, and spoke German and French. Both were sportsmen who enjoyed diving and golf, and had an affection for the natural world—and even something of what might today be thought an ecological consciousness, which today surprises the more because of the "Tory" outlook they each shared. Both were Royal Navy officers who worked in intelligence during World War II and held the rank of Commander. Both traveled widely, and held a fondness for the Caribbean and in particular the Jamaica of which he made a second home. Both were involved with numerous women, but married only once, in middle age, and each fathered a son out of wedlock.

Even the differences suggest obvious inspirations. While Fleming was vague about Bond's exact age, in *Moonraker* he stated flatly that Bond was eight years away from the mandatory double-o retirement age of forty-five—and hence thirty-seven. In the year that novel was published, this made him precisely a decade younger than the forty-seven year-old Fleming, as if he simply decided to knock a decade off his own age.

That he would have so deliberately modeled the character on himself does not seem at all surprising. Andrew Lycett, among many, many others, has read as Fleming's fantasy image of himself, "the man of action he would have liked to have been," realizing

> Ian's frustrated urge to have been out in the field during the war [as] a full-time secret agent, rather than a . . . staff officer

sitting, office-politicking and dreaming in Room 39 of the Admiralty.[2]

Still, there was an element of irony in some of the fantasy. Much as Bond resembles Fleming, he is not the only character to do so. Fleming also shared a birthday with the greatest of his villains, Ernst Stavro Blofeld, also born on May 28, 1908. (Ironically, he also shared the year of his death with him, Blofeld also dying in 1964—in the pages of *You Only Live Twice*.) And of course, there were cases in which Fleming seemed to simply be "writing what he knows." Many have thought M a father figure, and seen parallels between him and Fleming's own father (addressed as "M" by some of those who knew him), but there is no question that M's club Blades was modeled on Fleming's own club, Boodle's. (*Moonraker* in fact contains a typo in which Fleming wrote Boodle's when he apparently intended to write Blades.[3])

Post-War Britain

As the details of Ian Fleming's biography attest, he lived through a tumultuous period in British history. The years in which he first put pen to paper—in the aftermath of World War II—were particularly consequential for British life, and there is no question that Fleming in his writing responded to those changes.

The World Turned Upside Down

At its nineteenth century height Britain was the world's greatest manufacturing, trading and financial power, possessor of the world's largest navy, and seat of history's vastest empire. The country's decline from that position of many-sided predominance set in well before the end of that century as industrial competitors caught up with and overtook it, as other nations converted their newfound wealth into military power, and colonialism became less politically tenable. Still, it remained possible to see Britain as the world's leading nation well into the twentieth century, even through World War I and the Great Depression.

The strain of World War II, however, accelerated the country's decline as a great power, while fully exposing it. The result was that while Britain was one of the "Big Three" Allies, by 1945 it was eclipsed in European and world affairs by the United States and the Soviet Union, undisputedly the world's leading economic and military powers by a long way.[4] Moreover, Britain's diminished, "third place" position was more than it could afford to keep up. The country was bankrupt, and its colonies were fast slipping away. Indeed, Britain itself relied on massive American loans to pay its way, while in place of its old policy of "splendid isolation" it was becoming enmeshed inside an American-led alliance system as its two former allies competed for dominance.

Fleming's plots reflected the country's straitened circumstances as Bond "policed the empire." In *Diamonds Are Forever*, he combated diamond smuggling out of Sierra Leone, a double-o-worthy mission because diamonds were so important to the country's dollar earnings—an oblique reference to Britain's precarious balance of payments. In "The Hildebrand Rarity," Bond is in the Seychelles, preparing a report on their suitability as a back-up base in case the Royal Navy had to pull out of the Maldives—as it had to pull out of so many other places in those years.

However, in line with the new political realities, Bond was less likely to be an imperial policeman in the narrow sense than a soldier of the Western alliance more broadly. Rather than Bond's undertaking a purely British mission, *Casino Royale* has him working with representatives of French counterintelligence and the Central Intelligence Agency, which is helping finance his effort to bankrupt and destroy Le Chiffre. Moreover, the rationale for going after Le Chiffre is the threat his labor organization is believed to pose not to Britain in any direct way, but rather France—significant because in the era of the North Atlantic Treaty Organization and the

Cold War, Britain's security was unprecedentedly bound up with the integrity of Western Europe against an attack from the east.

The emphasis endured in successive novels. Bond's American comrade Felix Leiter appeared in four later books, while the dependence on American intelligence cropped up even in novels where he did not make an appearance—like *You Only Live Twice*. To a lesser extent, so did the fact of the broader alliance, highlighted in differing ways in *From Russia with Love* (where the Soviet plot against Bond singled him out from a broader evaluation of Western intelligence), "A View to a Kill" (where Bond combats espionage in the vicinity of NATO's French headquarters), and *Thunderball* (where Britain's bombers are part of a broader NATO deterrent, and number foreign air force officers among their crews).

Additionally, even where the alliance was not referenced in such explicit ways, its Soviet enemy most certainly was. In six of the first seven novels—besides *Casino*, *Live and Let Die*, *Moonraker*, *From Russia with Love*, *Dr. No* and *Goldfinger*—Bond is up against Soviet agents. (*Diamonds Are Forever* is the only exception.) With *Thunderball* Bond's attention turned to SPECTRE, but the organization was happy to do business with the Soviets, as was certainly the case in *The Spy Who Loved Me*—a Soviet-contracted SPECTRE hit on a Soviet defector the reason why Bond was in the Western hemisphere in that novel. *You Only Live Twice* has for its principal villain Blofeld, but Bond is in Japan to secure an intelligence-sharing agreement with the Japanese government, with the Soviet threat presented as a principal justification for his efforts—and the book ends with Bond falling into the clutches of the Soviets, who brainwash him and send him to kill M in *The Man with the Golden Gun*. The attempt fails, and Bond is rehabilitated, but to redeem himself he has to assassinate Francisco Scaramanga—yet another gangster working for the Soviet bloc. Soviet activity also figures prominently in the short stories "A View to a Kill," "Risico,"

"Property of a Lady," "The Living Daylights" and even "007 in New York."

At the same time that the international order was changing in deep and fundamental ways, so was the social order in Britain itself. The national election of 1945 saw the election of a Labor government with a broad mandate for domestic reform. To that end it nationalized a substantial part of the British economy, empowered the labor unions and built up a welfare state. While this generally did not figure in the plots, this was an acknowledged part of the background from the start. In *Casino Royale* Bond, in one of his moments in which all seems relative, muses to Rene Mathis that though they are fighting Communism, "the brand of Conservatism we have today would have been damned near called Communism and we should have been told to go and fight that."

Shaken, Not Stirred

Given his particular generation, upper-class social background, self-described "hard" outlook and association with the national security state, it might be expected that Fleming responded to all this in a particular way—and by and large he does not surprise here. Fleming (and his "fantasy self" Bond) both regarded the decline of the British Empire with a dismay they did not hesitate to express, Bond in *You Only Live Twice* remarking that "the liberation of our Colonies may have gone too fast."[5]

They also tended to hope that this decline could be arrested, that Britain could continue to be a power and an empire in some fashion, with a great deal of hope pinned on a particular notion of British prowess, which is highlighted in the same novel. When Bond suggests the Japanese secret service share its intelligence with

Britain, the Japanese chief, Tanaka replies that his people had acquired

> an unsatisfactory opinion about the British people since the war. You have not only lost a great Empire, you have seemed almost anxious to throw it away with both hands.

An offended Bond admits that his country had been "bled pretty thin by a couple of world wars." However, he makes a case for Britain's value as an ally premised on the British being a people "who still climb Everest and beat plenty of the world at plenty of sports and win Nobel Prizes." The kind of economic and military power Britain once had may be lost and irrecoverable, but the nation—and certainly its elite—remains worthy, which is what Tanaka had been hoping to hear from Bond, and means to have Bond prove to him by assassinating Dr. Shatterhand. True to form, Bond completes the mission successfully.

Putting it another way, it seemed that the kinds of assets on which Britain could still draw were courage, adventurousness, individual prowess. In these novels intelligence is conceived as an area where those assets might compensate for Britain's material shortcomings. Indeed, the SMERSH chiefs are almost effusive in saying so in *From Russia with Love*:

> "I think we all have respect for [England's] Intelligence Service," General Vozdvishensky [said]. There were grudging nods from everyone present . . . "Their Secret Service is excellent . . . They have notable successes. In certain types of operation we are constantly finding that they have been there before us."

Moreover, the SMERSH chiefs acknowledge that the British achieve all this despite the meagerness of their resources, including the limited compensation commanded by devoted and excellent operatives, and the fact that the English "are not natural conspirators." Lest the reader miss the point, Vozdvishensky explicitly chalks it up to non-material, cultural factors, like "the Public School and University tradition. The love of adventure."

Britain's presumed superiority in the kinds of intangibles discussed here suggested certain possibilities. The most important was that the country might leverage such prowess to be more than simply another participant in the wide Western alliance, through its "special relationship" with the United States. As Harold Macmillan famously put it, Britain would play the role of Greece to America's Rome, lending its greater experience and sophistication to the richer but less cultivated Americans.

Casino Royale is a model of such a relationship in action, marrying the CIA's larger financial resources to the superior ability of the British to defeat their common foe. The Secret Service's Station S comes up with the plan, and their man Bond, because of his ability to handle himself in a casino (a mark of a "gentleman," with all that implied for his skills as a spy), executes it, with the help of the CIA's money (handed over in an envelope on which the words MARSHALL AID have been jokingly written). And just as American power props up Britain in its enterprises, as with the role of the *Manta* in recovering the stolen British warheads *Thunderball*, British prowess (M's hunch that the bombs are in the Bahamas, Bond's abilities in the field) play a key role in preventing SPECTRE from using those warheads to strike at American targets as much as British.

Of course, Fleming does not imagine some perfect harmony of interest between the two countries. It occurs to Bond in his first meeting with Leiter in *Casino Royale* that the American "held the interests of his own organization far above the mutual concerns of the North Atlantic Allies." Additionally, there are times when cooperation between the two countries' is imperfect, one nation withholding its assistance on an important matter (Bond is in Japan in *You Only Live Twice* because the U.S. has been less willing to share its intelligence on the Pacific region), or the two even working at cross-purposes (as in "007 in New York"). It also has to be admitted that the British, too, falter (the American reluctance to share intelligence in part a result of recent British spy scandals, blown out of proportion, but still real enough).

Nonetheless, on the whole the relationship works, to the benefit of both countries as they and their allies fight a Cold War presented in "orthodox" terms, and rather aggressive fashion. Certainly the early Cold War was a period in which the "red lines" were unestablished, and the conflict waged more aggressively than would later be the case, while the memory of the prior, "hot" war was very vivid. However, the over the top Soviet actions against the West—a nuclear missile attack on London in *Moonraker*, the robbery of Fort Knox in *Goldfinger*—assume an enemy which is not only aggressive, but fanatical and even blood-thirsty, so much so that in *From Russia with Love* Red Grant defects to the east specifically for a chance to glut himself with killing as a state executioner, and gets his wish. Indeed, writing of SMERSH in that novel Umberto Eco remarked that "the Soviet men are so monstrous, so improbably cruel that it seems impossible to take them seriously."[6]

The distaste for the Soviets, of course, was in part a distaste for Communism, an idea that like many conservatives Fleming interpreted very broadly, as his remark in *Casino Royale* about what Britain had at home demonstrated. And while his attitude seems relativistic as he muses to Mathis, he is not always so. In *Thunderball*, Bond disapproves the manner of his taxi driver—"this youth . . . [who] makes about twenty pounds a week, despises his parents, and would like to be Tommy Steele," a regrettable result of his having been "born into the buyers' market of the Welfare State, and into the age of atomic bombs and space flight" that did so much to define his books. Indeed, rather than an innovation of that era, the Bond novels can be read as an adaptation of an earlier tradition to it.

James Bond and the History of the Spy Story

When Fleming started writing *Casino Royale*, the spy story was already a half century old as a recognizable genre of popular fiction, with virtually all its essential ideas and formulas well-established by 1953. Moreover, Fleming wrote as an author quite well-acquainted with that vast body of prior work, much of which he consciously drew on.

In considering that body of work, and its influence on Fleming, it is useful to refer to critic Julian Symons' observation about there being

> two traditions in the spy story . . . The first is conservative, supporting authority, making the assertion that agents are fighting to protect something valuable. The second is radical, critical of authority, claiming that agents perpetuate, and even create, false barriers between "us," and "them."[7]

One might add that these two traditions fit more or less tidily with two other traditions within the field. One is the spy story as crowd-pleasing adventure—the tradition of Erskine Childers' *The Riddle of the Sands* (1904), of John Buchan's *The Thirty-Nine Steps* (1915), of H.C. "Sapper" McNeile's *Bulldog Drummond* (1920). The other is the spy story which emphasizes the human drama of espionage and its ambiguities, and which would conventionally be thought of as "literary"—the tradition of Joseph Conrad's *The Secret Agent* (1907), W. Somerset Maugham's *Ashenden* (1928), and Graham Greene's *The Quiet American* (1955). The conservative, orthodox sensibility predominates in the more adventure-oriented stories. By contrast, the more radical sensibility generally turns up in the more literary fiction—and increasingly predominates over it.

Given Fleming's Toryism, and the familiar image and wide popular success of the James Bond adventures, it can seem easy enough to class the James Bond novels in that first category of politically conservative adventure tales. Indeed, Symons judged Bond a "more sophisticated version of Bulldog Drummond," and the Fleming novels "the 'Sapper' pipe-dream converted to the mood of the fifties," and not without good reason.[8] Just like Drummond, Bond is a gentleman and sportsman ("an unbeatable production," Sapper tells us) who fought in the last war and finds himself unable to live as anything other than a "man of war." Like Drummond, he lives in an upscale London apartment, and is very particular about his tobacco.

Bond's adventures also have strong echoes of Drummond's, likewise pitting him against evil geniuses and their exotic and deadly cronies, weapons and creatures, as well as entangling him with good girls and bad. There is, too, the broader feel of the tale—the blend of gentility in manner with undisguised murderousness of intent in the meetings of hero and villain; the rounds of unconsciousness and capture and escape to which the hero is subject; and the protagonist's investigative style, which is heavily reliant on personal provocation in those genteel meetings.

Indeed, at the climax of *From Russia with Love*, Red Grant tells Bond that "No Bulldog Drummond stuff'll get you out of this one"—though true enough, what is recognizably Bulldog Drummond stuff *does* get him out of it. However, Sapper's novels hardly exhausted Bond's influences, even those explicitly acknowledged in the novels. The Drummond adventures drew on other, preceding books, among them those of John Buchan, whose hero Richard Hannay is notable, and worth bringing up here as having been a more fleshed-out, more thoughtful figure than the "happy warrior" that Drummond was. And while Drummond and Hannay were undeniably residents of what has come to be called "clubland," neither set of tales mixes espionage and glamour quite like Edward Phillips Oppenheim, who likewise came in for a mention in Fleming's novels (Gala Brand dismissing Bond and company as "just people that Phillips Oppenheim had dreamed up with fast cars and special cigarettes with gold bands on them and shoulder-holsters"). One can also point to smaller evidences of a whole host of other writers—Dennis Wheatley's bringing sex to clubland in his Gregory Sallust novels, or the echo of Sax Rohmer's Fu Manchu in Fleming's portrait of the villainous Dr. No.

More striking, however, is the fact that Fleming also drew heavily on that other, more critical, more literary tradition. Indeed, when describing the sorts of novels he aspired to write, he characterized them as "thrillers designed to be read as literature" of the kind written by Eric Ambler and Graham Greene.

Of course, there were limits to their influence on his work. The leftishness of a work like Ambler's *Background to Danger* (1937) or Greene's *Quiet American* were inconceivable in a Fleming novel. For that matter, the Bond novels could not go so far in the direction of parody and comedy as the books of Ambler and Greene often did, and certainly not in the same ways. Bond could not be made to seem quite as foolish as Ambler's heroes (whose unwittingly doing something massively stupid was usually what got the story going). Fleming was even less prone to make the British Secret Service seem quite as bumbling as Greene made it appear in *Our Man From Havana* (1959).

Quite the contrary, there is no question that the British government are "the good guys," the various adversaries Bond battles against "bad guys" like the operatives of the murderous SMERSH and the pure and simple gangsters of SPECTRE. Moreover, in those battles much is made of Bond's personal prowess, as time and again, in very different situations, he does his bit to save the day. And while he is to be taken as an outstanding British agent, the British Secret Service as a whole is held to be outstanding. This all seems to go double for the man at the very top of the heap, the seemingly all-seeing M. Even when Bond finds the old man's thinking eccentric (as when he sends him to Shrublands), or his reasoning dubious (as when he sends him to the Bahamas in that same novel), the old man's instincts always right in the end.

Still, something of their criticism manifested itself in Bond's sense of the ugliness of his work, something of Greene evident in Bond's more introspective, bleaker moments—thinking that perhaps destroying Le Chiffre was not the right thing as he recovers in hospital. (Bond muses that Le Chiffre was "serving a wonderful purpose . . . creating a norm of badness by which . . . an opposite norm of goodness could exist.") The novel subsequently dismisses such speculations as temporary weakness on the part of a run-down, injured man, but one cannot say the same of Bond's ambivalence about his mission in "Quantum of Solace," where his duty as a government agent requires him to fire-bomb a shipment of arms bound for anti-Batista rebels in Cuba, despite his distaste for Batista and corresponding sympathy for the rebels.

Additionally, the Bond novels had more than a little of those authors' humor, often at the expense of their protagonist. Like Ambler's heroes, Bond, formidable as he is, does time and again "make a fool of himself and fall headlong into a trap," starting with Le Chiffre's capture of him in *Casino Royale*. In one case, the influence of Ambler is underlined by a direct reference. In *From Russia with Love* Bond reads Eric Ambler's most celebrated work, *The Mask of Dimitrios* (1939) on an airline flight, evoking that novel's journey from Istanbul to Paris, which parallels the one Bond undertakes in this novel, trap and all. And if anything, Fleming's sense of Bond as really a rather ridiculous figure after all was displayed even more pointedly in the first quarter of *Thunderball*, dominated by his stay at the Shrublands spa, which in the end amounts principally to a long comedic sketch.

Hewing less closely to the thriller genre, but no less important, was Somerset Maugham's *Ashenden*. A collection of stories based on Maugham's real-life experiences in British intelligence, it depicts the titular hero's activities as a spy in Switzerland, Italy and Russia during World War I. Like the works by Ambler and Greene Maugham's stories show something of the cruelty and the bungling of real-life espionage in tales like "The Hairless Mexican," or "Giulia Lazzari," but are perhaps more remarkable for two other aspects.

One is that, in contrast with the normally individualistic spy story, Maugham acknowledged the reality of intelligence as an affair of large, bureaucratic organization in which the individual is apt to be

> no more than a tiny rivet in a vast and complicated machine . . . [who] never had the advantage of seeing a completed action. He was concerned with the beginning or the end of it, perhaps, or with some incident in the middle, but what his own doings led to he had seldom a chance of discovering.

As Maugham himself noted, this made the recounting of a spy's real-life experiences

> as unsatisfactory as those modern novels that give you a number of unrelated episodes and expect you by piecing them together to construct in your mind a connected narrative.

Moreover, the activities of both the machine and its rivets

> was as orderly and monotonous as a City clerk's. [Ashenden] saw his spies at stated intervals and paid them their wages; when he could get hold of a new one he engaged him, gave him his instructions . . . waited for the information that came through and dispatched it . . . kept his eyes and ears open;

and . . . wrote long reports . . . The work he was doing . . . could not be called anything but monotonous.

One result was that Maugham tended to push his hero's espionage-related activities into the background and concentrate on bits of drama that were at times almost completely unrelated to them. (*Ashenden*'s Russian episodes, for example, contain virtually no "secret agent stuff" of any kind.)

Fleming also acknowledged the reality of espionage as a big organization affair in his books, most obviously in the description of the British Secret Service in the early part of *Moonraker*. However, his consciousness of this reality also penetrated to the most basic premise of the novels, reflected in the way he reconciled the individualism of the clubland thriller with the reality of espionage as an affair of large, bureaucratic organizations: by making Bond a part of a unit directly responsible to the head of the service, and performing special tasks that have nearly nothing to do with the cultivation and running of agents that is the core of "human intelligence" work. Additionally, even if out in the field Bond is ever the individualist, giving the impression of a man working for an organization, or with an organization, rather than a *member* of an organization, back in London he inhabits a world of files and paperwork, much like any other government functionary—a fact which drives him to distraction when he has to endure it for very long.

Additionally, like Maugham, Fleming often used the tale of espionage as a backdrop to other sorts of dramas, most pointedly in "Quantum of Solace." That story depicts Bond not during his assignment, but after it, sitting with the British Governor in the Bahamas as he relates the story of a marriage gone bad—a scene strongly reminiscent of Ashenden's dinner with the British ambassador to Russia in "His Excellency." This is also the case in "The Hildebrand Rarity," where Bond gets caught up in a domestic drama and murder after checking out the Maldives for the Royal

Navy, and likewise *The Spy Who Loved Me*, the events of which happen while Bond is on his way home from a mission in Canada. Many critics also identify in Ashenden's boss "R" an inspiration for Fleming's M.

This all adds up to a veritable "Who's Who" of the history of the spy novel, one justifying a characterization of Fleming's novels as a distillation of the tradition. Still, there are elements clearly coming from outside it. Alongside Ambler and Greene, Fleming hailed American crime writers Dashiell Hammett and Raymond Chandler as writers of thrillers designed to be read as literature, and their influence would seem to have gone well beyond that broad affinity, or even Fleming's taste for including American gangsters in stories like *Diamonds*. Bond's oft-expressed cynicism, so unlike the cheerfulness of a Drummond; or the subtler handling of his upper-class background (his "backdoor semi-aristocratness" to paraphrase Kingsley Amis, as compared with the clubland types' plain old artistocratness), owes far more to the pavement-pounding private detectives from across the Pond than to anything native to his country's thriller tradition.

2. THE NOVELS OF IAN FLEMING

Fleming's own life and experiences, and his fantasies about the sort of life he might have had; the events of his era; and the long tradition of the spy novel; merged into the common stream of the James Bond stories. Still, they did not assume a fixed pattern at the outset. Rather, their shape evolved over time.

Indeed, it may be useful to think of his writing in terms of three different periods. The first (1953-1957), which began with *Casino Royale* and continued through the next four novels until *From Russia with Love*, can be thought of as "early Fleming" in which he tinkered with various approaches. The second (1958-1959), consisting of *Dr. No* and *Goldfinger*, can be thought of as "middle Fleming," in which Fleming drew on the elements of the early books (most pointedly, *Live and Let Die* and *Moonraker*) to establish the formula most associated with the adventures.

The third, "late Fleming," was already evident in the short story collection *For Your Eyes Only* (1960), but properly got underway with *Thunderball*, and continued through the remainder of his work, up to the novella "Octopussy." During this time Fleming made use of elements from his earlier books, and at times even made substantial use of the middle-period formula (as in *Thunderball* and

On Her Majesty's Secret Service). However, he was more prone to structure his novels in unconventional ways, and to stress character and theme. In particular while Fleming's books from the start utilized images of decay, decline and death, and suicide and betrayal, he emphasized these more than before. Indeed, the last five novels, from *Thunderball* to *The Man with the Golden Gun* can be regarded as a single saga of Bond's battle with Ernst Stavro Blofeld and its consequences, and with personal demons threatening to overwhelm him. Moreover, Bond's struggles appear less like the problems of just one man than they do a microcosm of a Britain with more doubtful prospects.

Enter 007

The story goes that in February 1952, anxious about his impending marriage to Anne Charteris, Ian Fleming settled down to write for three hours in the morning and produced about two thousand words of manuscript. Continuing the practice for a month, he completed the first James Bond novel, *Casino Royale*.

Casino Royale (1953)

Fleming's novel introduced James Bond to the world on the first page of the book, but even before introducing the character, it introduced a particular milieu, and a certain tone. The first paragraph reads:

> The scent and smoke and sweat of a casino are nauseating at three in the morning. Then the soul-corrosion produced by high gambling—a compost of greed and fear and nervous tension—becomes unbearable and the senses awake and revolt from it.

From these words one gets sophistication and luxury, but also a proneness to excess, and more than a hint of world-weariness and even decadence about the character. As the early chapters take him from one luxurious hotel, bar, casino to the next, and the hero indulges his famously particular tastes in alcohol, tobacco, food, cars, the hints become a fully fleshed-out portrait.

However, this is just one dimension of him, Fleming simultaneously introducing the reader to another. A veteran intelligence officer, Bond earned his double-o rating with two assassinations during the Second World War, and continued in the Secret Service into the Cold War.

The novel likewise introduces the familiar supporting cast—like Bond's boss M, gruff, old-fashioned, often narrow and humorless, and yet somehow the right man in the right place. There is Moneypenny, too. And of course there is also Bond's frequent CIA comrade, Felix Leiter, and the dynamic between them that was to become familiar—the special relationship in miniature.

Le Chiffre, of course, puts in only this one appearance, but established the pattern of the villains nonetheless. He is physically freakish, "sexually abnormal," and ethnically dubious, a man "of mixed blood," with "origins . . . complex and obscure," but generally lying "in an ethnic area that stretches from Central Europe to the Slav countries and the Mediterranean basin."[1] Naturally no gentleman, he is not above cheating at cards. Moreover, as would be the case with later villains, he runs a sophisticated operation, involving a large number of henchmen equipped with elaborate gadgetry (in this case a cane-gun with which Bond is nearly shot and a chain used to flip Bond's car), with both the team and its technology remarked by Bond, who can only envy him such resources.

Less obvious are the ways in which the novel's plot set a precedent for those of later books. The Secret Service calls on Bond to use his skill at baccarat to destroy Le Chiffre, a Soviet agent in a precarious position with his controllers because of his embezzling of his organization's funds. Le Chiffre's losing the game would deprive him of the money he needs to put back in its coffers, insure the Soviets kill him off. In the process they would damage the Soviet front organization (a trade union) of which he is chief, and also damage the French Communist and labor movements more broadly.

The struggle between the two men predictably turns violent before that point. However, Bond's role in that action is comparatively passive, consisting initially of his just sitting tight as the opposition tries to keep him from getting to that game. He subsequently survives two assassination attempts intended to prevent his winning the game (in one case, not by doing anything much at all; in the other, by falling back in his chair). Thus Bond is able to beat Le Chiffre at the table and take his money away—but then Bond sees Vesper being carried off by his thugs. Bond gives chase, winds up captured himself in what now seems to have been an obvious trap, and is then tortured by Le Chiffre, who wants him to return what he won at the table. Ultimately Bond is saved not by his own actions, but, ironically, by the agent of SMERSH who kills Le Chiffre as planned.

All of this concludes about two-thirds of the way through the novel, the remaining third of which deals with Bond's convalescence, and his involvement with Lynd, which it seems to him may be more than just another affair. However, it turns out that Lynd was working for the Soviets the whole time, and that her kidnap had been just a set-up, as she reveals in the note she leaves behind after her suicide. Bond is wounded by the knowledge of her betrayal, but at the same time, he commits himself to fighting the people who destroyed her—setting the stage for the battles to come against the SMERSH organization.

This all sounds rather idiosyncratic for a James Bond story. Nonetheless, it does establish the pattern for Bond's field work. Despite his being a full-time government agent, he tends not to practice conventional spycraft (of which little appears in the series), or even particular specialties in areas like burglary or assassination (like safecracking or sniping), but rather is utilized irregularly in capers involving varied, often unusual tasks. Additionally, while Bond's work may reveal secrets, the identity of the principal villain tends to be clear from the start, not just to the reader but to the Service, which points Bond in the bad guy's direction at the outset. Equally, the villain tends to know about Bond and what he is doing from early on—Le Chiffre alert to his intentions even before he arrived in the country.

Moreover, the conflict between the two men is time and again constrained in crucial ways by some aspect of the situation. While having Le Chiffre assassinated or arrested would be simplest, the conclusion that it would be preferable to have him bankrupted and killed by his SMERSH masters means that Bond must instead beat him at baccarat. Equally, Le Chiffre does not attempt to have Bond formally barred from the game, but instead to have him killed before he can arrive; to beat Bond at the table, or failing that, threaten him into backing off; or failing that too, forcibly recover his losses from Bond. Coming on top of the centrality of an actual game, this dynamic between the principals imbues the larger conflict with a game-like quality—and can seem to suggest that espionage (and even life more generally) may be best understood as one big game. This not incidentally stresses Bond's value as an agent. British gentleman and sportsman, games are his specialty.

This game-like aspect would be seen again, as would Bond's comparative passivity within this story (his being pointed at a target, his being maneuvered by people around him) and even the villains' getting the better of him (his foolishly walking into a trap). So would the typical result of his entrapment and capture, his subjection to brutal torture, and his convalescence afterward. Additionally, though it rarely reached the relativistic, mystical thinking about good and evil, God and the Devil, in which Bond indulges here, so would the ambivalence Bond expresses about his profession, and in particular the killings it requires him to commit. It was also not the last time that the novels treated Bond's broader outlook in an ironic fashion—or when, following the death of a close acquaintance, Bond felt himself steeled to continue in his actions.

The villainy of SMERSH, the depiction of labor unions as Soviet fronts, and the blending of "ordinary" criminality with espionage and affairs of state (Le Chiffre used his embezzled money to buy a chain of brothels just before these were outlawed), also feature in many a later Fleming plot. Even where the structure of the novel is concerned, the novel's opening with Bond in the middle of the action, then flashing back to how he got there, also set a precedent for later novels. And the element of comedy and parody makes an early appearance in the bungled attempt on Bond's life by the Bulgarian assassins early in the story.

Still, for all that the structure of *Royale*—with Le Chiffre merely trying to save himself rather than plotting any mayhem, the villain's early demise at other hands, Bond's being saved by SMERSH, the involved relationship with Vesper ending with her revelation of her betrayal and suicide—was hardly a basis for a formula for this or any other commercial series, and unsurprisingly *Live and Let Die* took quite a different tack.

Live and Let Die (1954)

The second James Bond novel saw its hero pitted against Harlem-based gangster Mr. Big, whose operations extend from the United States down into the British Caribbean.

Both countries having an interest in taking him down, M assigns Bond to work with the FBI and CIA in a joint operation intended to accomplish just that. Meeting his American counterparts in New York to that end, Bond is again working with Leiter, who takes Bond up to Harlem "for a look." What ends up happening is that they both get captured, and nearly killed, though it also does inspire Mr. Big's fortune-teller Solitaire to defect to his side. With the enemy in chase, he takes her by train to Florida—where Leiter, blundering again, gets fed to a shark. Bond avenges his friend, then is ordered to Jamaica, where, with the help of the trainer and guide assigned him, the Cayman Islander Quarrel, he is to blow up Big's yacht with a limpet mine. He gets captured again in the attempt, but not before he has planted the mine, which allows him to take down the enemy and wind up with the girl at the end.

In contrast with the story of the preceding book, this appears simple and uninventive. The movement of the plot is overly reliant on pointless or even blundering actions turning out fortuitously— the ill-conceived trip up to Harlem an excuse for some menace and violence, and for Solitaire to see Bond. And Solitaire and Bond's flight from New York seems principally an occasion for the glamour of the Silver Phantom, additional travelogue and a few more action scenes. It should be noted, too, that nothing that happens in the story is as personally involved for Bond as his recovery in the hospital after torture or his relationship with Vesper in the previous book.

Nevertheless, that simplicity, disjointedness and impersonality offered a better basis for replicable success than the more original, tighter plot of *Royale*. Here Bond gets a job, Bond goes and does the job, Bond finishes the job; during it he gets involved with a woman, but there is no sense that this is the romance to end all romances for him. And any agonies about what he is doing are short-lived. Thus he can go out on a new mission and meet a new girl in the next book.

Live also features many of the elements that would turn up again and again in later books—travel between multiple locations, shootouts, action scenes on a train and underwater, a big blow-up at the end, all of which have Bond dealing out violence rather than merely having it inflicted upon him. Additionally, while Le Chiffre is typical of the Bond villains in many respects, certain key features awaited the arrival of the six foot-four, football-headed, accidie-afflicted Mr. Big, who makes the first of the infamous Villain's Speeches (Le Chiffre having been too preoccupied with saving his own skin to offer up such a speech). Big's retreats also boast Gothic, even surreal touches (like the Boneyard nightclub with its moving wall, the use of voodoo by Big to control his followers, Henry

Morgan's cavern), and true to form, he also displays a taste for subjecting his captives to bizarre execution methods he explains as something more than a mere means to an end (his keel-hauling Bond and Solitaire a "scientific experiment" of sorts). For his part, Bond has some equipment of his own. The reader learns that he has steel toe caps in his shoes, and later on he takes a harpoon gun and the aforementioned limpet mine along on his attack on Big's yacht.

The novel is also notable for its choice of settings—the United States, and Jamaica. Fleming was to make heavy use of both locations in later novels, packing 007 off to America six times, Jamaica five times within the space of twenty-one tales. Meanwhile his trip to Jamaica is the first of what were to be many assignments Bond had "policing the colonies" Britain still had in its last years as an Empire.

That said, Fleming's affection for the Caribbean in general and Jamaica in particular is quite pronounced here, reflected in Bond's quickly forming a strong bond with Quarrel. Fleming's affection for America is more qualified, his treatment of the country comparatively ambivalent in this novel, as it was so often to be later. There is, on the one hand, America the Glamorous, seen in the luxurious hotels and cuisine and night life of New York Bond finds on arrival, and later the Silver Phantom train. However, the vistas he sees from the Phantom's windows, the stops in a Jacksonville diner and a Saint Petersburg retirement community sing "America the Tacky." Additionally, where Leiter was a genial figure helpfully topping off Bond's coffers in *Casino*, here he is taking a more active role in events—and it does not seem an accident that he makes a mess of things; it is his blundering that gets Bond and Leiter nearly killed in Harlem, and Leiter tortured and mutilated by that shark. (That episode ends Leiter's CIA career, though not his appearances in the books.) Leiter is simply in over his head playing the spy game, and so are his countrymen, Fleming seems to say—all the more so as some of his characters actually *do* say as much in later novels.

Moonraker (1955)

Important as the innovations of *Live and Let Die* were to prove to the creation of a Bond formula, Fleming did not immediately follow it up. *Casino Royale* was essentially unrepeatable, but *Moonraker* did use quite a few of its elements.

Just as in that first book Bond's skills as a card player are what initially bring him into contact with the wealthy Hugo Drax, like Le Chiffre a Soviet operative who infiltrated the West amid the confusion of post-World War Two Europe. The card game, in which the villain cheats, again turns out to be a prelude to another, deadlier game that has the two men maneuvering about one another while Drax goes about his plans. Once again, Bond plays that game with the help of a female partner in British government service (Gala Brand of the Special Branch). Again, Bond survives a bomb attack (an explosion on Dover Beach), and after that, sees his female partner kidnapped, drawing him into a car chase in pursuit. This results in Bond's being captured, after which he endures brutal torture (an attack with steam-hoses meant to flush him out, the heat of the rocket launch intended to kill him) at Drax's hands.

Nonetheless, *Moonraker* featured an important innovation in the mayhem planned by Drax. His program to build a ballistic missile for Britain actually turns out to be a cover for his plan to fire a missile at London, setting a precedent for plots involving the use of the most advanced technology to realize geopolitical aims. Related to this is the fact that, much more than the two previous novels, *Moonraker* is a "tale of detection" in which Bond, rather than being directed to take out a target, is asked to investigate what may be an innocuous if unfortunate incident—the shooting of a Ministry of Supply officer at Drax's facility.

The novel is also notable in its not beginning *in media res*, instead proceeding in a linear fashion from beginning to end. Indeed, like many of the later books, it starts with Bond in between missions, in this case practicing on the Service's indoor gun range. There is, too, what that scene on the range proves to be—the first stop on a broader tour of the Service's Regent's Park headquarters. In the course of that tour the book also establishes something of Bond's everyday reality as that of a typical senior civil servant, sufficiently specific that it gives numbers regarding his income—and his age. This was not repeated with the British Service, of course, but this broad picture view of an intelligence agency's workings did appear in later books.

Moonraker placed an unprecedented stress on something else, too, namely Bond's personal connection with M, both M's special reliance on his agent, and Bond's special loyalty to his boss. Bond initially played his card game with Drax not in the line of professional duty, but rather as a personal favor to his boss, at whose club Blades Drax's cheating had been noticed, and whose defeat was wanted as a relatively gentle way of dissuading Drax from the habit and avoiding the scandal that would have resulted if it became more widely known. Less important, but also noteworthy, is the role of Drax's henchman Krebs. While he is not one of the more memorable of the series' secondary villains, but a significant step in the direction of their emergence as important figures in their own right.

Finally, while *Moonraker* contained much that was already familiar from the previous books, and offered a few innovations of its own, it is notable for a feature that sets it apart from the rest of Fleming's novel. Just about everything within the tale happens in London, or in the vicinity of Drax's facility near Dover—confining the entirety of the tale to British soil in a way that not only never happened before in the series, and never happened again.

Diamonds Are Forever (1956)

In *Diamonds Are Forever*, Fleming turns back in the direction of *Live and Let Die*, troubles in a British colony (diamond smuggling in Sierra Leone) causing M to send Bond to America to fight the gangsters causing them—the Spang Brothers, of the Spangled Mob. Once more there is a good deal of travel and travelogue as Bond journeys to the States, once more he teams up with Leiter, once more he puts his skill with a gun to use, and once more the villains' eccentricities attain surreal levels—in the Spang's private Wild West town and miniature train. (And once more, the strain of working all of this into the narrative shows in a more disjointed book, the weaknesses of which are less well-concealed than in *Live*.)

However, in line with the pattern of *Moonraker*, *Diamonds* has a stronger investigative element, Bond's mission beginning with his infiltrating the diamond smuggling operation by posing as one of its couriers. The story also represents the first use of several elements which would afterward recur in the books. One is its opening not with James Bond's activities, but rather with a glimpse of the bad guys at work, the first chapter depicting the operation of the diamond pipeline. Another is Bond's operating on U.S. soil without the sanction of the U.S. government—while Leiter is working as a Pinkerton Detective. There is, too, the first appearance of the Italian Mafia in the novels, which here is depicted as uninvolved in espionage and subversion, but rather profit-minded gangsters pure and simple, with the Spangled Mob again mentioned by name in later works. Finally, the "Bond girl" of the book, Tiffany Case, presents a new sexual challenge to Bond in an apparent misandry resulting from sexual abuse, not the last time this theme was to appear.

From Russia with Love (1957)

After Bond's battle with the Spangs the books returned to their Cold War focus in *From Russia with Love*, where SMERSH, desirous of both a propaganda victory over the West and revenge against the secret agent who disrupted several important recent operations, concoct an elaborate plan to entrap Bond, scandalize him and kill him, and in the process damage the Service of which he is a part. For bait they use a file clerk whom they have instructed to claim that she has fallen in love with Bond from his photo, and is willing to defect to Britain with a sought-after decryption system if only Bond would collect her personally.

As might be guessed from the revenge plot directed against Bond personally (in which the game-like element is particularly strong), and the premise behind the bait, this particular installment of the Bond adventures was to prove almost as idiosyncratic (and unrepeatable) as *Casino Royale*. Still, it incorporated many ideas Fleming developed in previous books, in many cases extending them. In the first third of the book being taken up by the villain's plot, he considerably extends the practice *Diamonds* pioneered of beginning with the villains, and in the depiction of SMERSH's workings, going a big step beyond even the "inside look" he previously offered of the operations of the British Secret Service.

Similarly extending a prior theme is Bond's initial appearance in the flesh. This time 007 is not merely in between missions, but tormented by the idea that he is going soft—not as a result of convalescence after a mission that was too taxing, as in *Casino*, but the feeling that this man of war had not been taxed enough. ("The blubbery arms of the soft life had Bond round the neck and they were slowly strangling him" read the first words of his first scene.) There is, too, the idea of a girl being used to lure Bond into a trap, though it is a much more complex, larger-scale matter than was Vesper Lynd's kidnapping in the first adventure; and mention of Bond's distaste at cold-blooded killing, which leaves the Service's local stringer Kerim Bey taking out his Bulgarian opposite number Krilencu.[2]

Another, more novel feature appears in the division of the role of principal villain—in this case, between the plot's mastermind Rosa Klebb, and the assassin supposed to personally take Bond out, Red Grant (who is to do the job with a copy of *War and Peace* concealing a gun). Bond narrowly gets the upper hand over Grant and kills him instead on the train, so that he and Tatiana succeed in getting to Paris, but then Klebb personally makes one last attempt to kill Bond. She succeeds in stabbing him with a poisoned blade concealed in her shoe, and the story actually ends with Bond losing consciousness, the reader uncertain as to whether he is alive or dead.

Bond Lives?

Andrew Lycett has written that after *Diamonds Are Forever* Fleming felt "he had exhausted his inventiveness" with the series, as his work had already contained "'every single method of escape and every variety of suspenseful action.'"[3] While *From Russia with Love* is generally judged a much better book than *Diamonds* (and in the view of some, Fleming's best, period), and much of Fleming's best and most influential work still lay ahead of him, Fleming's sense of exhaustion and boredom with the series was real enough. The ambiguous close of *From Russia with Love*, as Andrew Lycett informs us, came out of Fleming's uncertainty about "whether to continue his hero's exploits in the future," with Bond's poisoning by Klebb a potential ending to the series.[4]

In the end Fleming decided that the poisoned blade only *nearly* killed Bond after all, later novels reflected his dissatisfaction with what he had been writing earlier. This would increasingly take the shape of an increased dramatic ambition, experiments in other genres, and plenty of sheer strangeness—as well as an increasing note of self-parody, beginning in the next year's *Dr. No*.

Dr. No (1958)

Dr. No begins with Bond having survived Klebb's attack, but not yet back in top form. Alert to Bond's condition, M sends him to Jamaica to check out the disappearance of two British agents stationed in the area—Regional Control Officer John Strangways and his number two, Mary Trueblood. The job is assumed to not be a very serious one (ran off with the girl probably, the chap), so that M seems to think it really just a government-sponsored vacation in which Bond can (yet again!) convalesce in the sun. Of course, that proves not to be the case. Fortunately, action is Bond's preferred form of therapy.

Where that action is concerned, there is much that had originally appeared in prior works, beyond the Jamaican setting, or for that matter, the character of Quarrel, or the deadly confrontations with undersea creatures. There is also the villain, who as in *Live and Let Die* is Soviet-backed, exploits local superstitions, and takes a quasi-scientific interest in how much punishment the human body can take, which results in his torture of Bond being something of an experiment. There is, too, something of *Moonraker*, in Bond's investigation into what turns out to be a murder (that of John Strangways) revealing foreign interference with a Western rocket program (Dr. No's sabotage of American rocketry) by a half-German fiend (the villainous No). And one can see something of Tiffany's past in Honeychile Rider's own personal history.

However, at a deeper level it can fairly be said that in *Dr. No* Fleming distilled much of what was best in the previous books, particularly the jet-setting action-adventure of *Live and Let Die*, and the detective work and high-tech conspiracy of *Moonraker* (complete with a rocket-minded, half-German villain), to create the Bond adventures as we have since come to think of them—even in their more parodic elements. This is, for example, the case with the villain of the piece, Dr. No, who stands out even among the rogue's gallery presented in the previous books. Described as six foot six, with a completely bald head and hooks projecting from the sleeves of the kimono that makes him seem to glide over the floor, he appears a "giant venomous worm wrapped in grey tin-foil." It is the case, too, with the details of the underwater aspect of the adventure—Bond this time contending not with sharks and barracudas, but with No's *pet giant squid*. And of course, there is the way in which Bond finishes off the villain, better-suited to the finale of a scatological comedy than a heroic epic—burying him under a pile of guano.

Goldfinger (1959)

A similar pattern is evident in Fleming's next, and longest, book, *Goldfinger*, though the repetition is more obvious here. Just like with Hugo Drax in *Moonraker*, Bond's association with Auric Goldfinger begins when an acquaintance who plays cards with him suspects him of cheating and wants Bond to help turn the tables on him. Fleming repeats the theme, at great length, in Bond's subsequent golf game with the titular character. The centrality of the smuggling of glamorous high value commodities (gold) to the plot, and the villain's association with American gangsters (including the Spangled Mob), recalls not just the diamond smuggling in *Diamonds Are Forever*, but also *Live and Let Die*, in which Mr. Big made use of gold coins from Henry Morgan's treasure hoard to fund Soviet spying in the U.S.. The same can be said for the book's American settings, and the help Bond gets from Leiter. Meanwhile, Pussy Galore's inaccessibility to men, and the trauma behind it, similarly recalls *Diamonds*' Case (and *No*'s Rider), while the theme of a wealthy Soviet agent in the West using a nuclear weapon against a high-profile target resembles Drax's plan to destroy London.

Just as in *Dr. No* one can find a note of self-parody in Fleming's reuse of these earlier elements, in Bond's attractiveness to women going so far as to have its effect on a lesbian, in the villain attempting the logistically mind-boggling feat of robbing Fort Knox. Still, the book contains three features worth remarking, all the more so as they all came up again in later Bond novels. The first is its opening with Bond having just completed an arduous field assignment unrelated to the main plot, in this case bombing the warehouse of a drug-runner in Mexico (only the first time Bond's missions would target the narcotics trade). The second is that rather than complaining about the villains' use of elaborate gadgets, as Bond himself makes do with more modest equipment, here he has a genuinely high-tech spy gadget of his own—the homing device he uses to follow Goldfinger's car in its travels about the continent. The third is the use of a Central European, specifically Swiss, setting in the earlier part of the narrative.

Enter SPECTRE

Fleming followed up *Goldfinger* with a short story collection, *For Your Eyes Only*, which contained five different pieces—"A View to a Kill," "For Your Eyes Only," "Risico," "Quantum of Solace" and "The Hildebrand Rarity." The first three pieces were briefer versions of the action-adventure tales the novels tended to offer. "A View to a Kill" took Bond back to France to fight Soviet agents. "For Your Eyes Only," like *Moonraker*, had Bond performing a mission in which M had a personal interest, namely avenging the murder of his friends the Havelocks, while being notable for extending the theme of Bond's operating independently in America. (He crosses the Canadian border to get to the Havelocks' killer, von Hammerstein, who resides in Vermont.) And "Risico" is notable for Bond's making an alliance with a criminal (Colombo) to take down a much more threatening enemy (Kristatos, smuggling drugs into the West on behalf of the Soviets).

However, the last two pieces were not action-themed, instead presenting a piece of domestic drama *after* Bond's completion of a mission. In "Quantum," following his destruction of a Castro-bound arms shipment, he listens to the Governor of the Bahamas tell him a story of an unhappy marriage; in "Hildebrand," following his report on the Seychelles, he rides aboard the yacht of the vile Milton Krest, who ends up murdered by one of the other passengers.

These two stories can be taken as a particularly clear reflection of Fleming's more literary aspirations, and desire to try something other than adventure thrillers. And while Fleming returned to writing novel-length action-adventures in in line with the emerging formula, those ambitions were increasingly evident in later work. The image of a run-down Bond is also bound up with a Britain presented as being in a more precarious position, an idea explicitly referenced in "The Hildebrand Rarity." After drinking more than he should have Krest pointedly tells Bond that "America, Russia and China . . . [were] the big poker game and no other country had either the chips or the cards to come into it" except when

> some pleasant little country . . . like England would be lent some money so that they could take a hand with the grown-ups. But that was just being polite like one sometimes had to be to a chum in one's own club who'd gone broke.

It is said that Krest was motivated by a "violent cruelty, a pathological desire to wound," but the nerve is there to be touched all the same. That Krest is an American—and indeed, is readable as a caricature of the stereotype of the Ugly American in his wealth, crassness, vulgarity and delight in abusing others.

Thunderball (1961)

The first new novel to appear after Fleming's short stories was *Thunderball*, which in its essentials can seem a conventional enough Bond adventure. In its sending Bond to the Bahamas; its centering on a nuclear threat originating in Britain's own deterrent (the villains hijacking a Royal Air Force bomber in this case); the targeting of the American rocket program (the first bomb's target being a rocket station on North-West Cay), and pairing Bond with Leiter again and involving Bond in fairly extensive underwater action; the story contains much that is familiar from prior works. Of course, the Special Executive for Counterintelligence, Terrorism, Revenge and Extortion (SPECTRE) makes its first appearance here, but its personnel are essentially Bond's old enemies—SMERSH agents, Italian gangsters—who mix crime with espionage like many of their predecessors.

Still, the novel extends many earlier ideas to the point of making them new. There is, for example, the abundant techno-military detail in Fleming's depiction of the bomber's hijacking and the subsequent hunt for it (which entails a submarine chase), with which little can be compared before the boom of the military techno-thriller in the late 1970s and 1980s. Additionally *Thunderball* is considerably more developed as a "tale of detection" than any of its predecessors, the hero following a lengthy and reasonably well-worked out chain of clues to the stolen weapons (rather than relying on a Talking Villain to reveal all).

From the standpoint of Fleming's larger body of work, however, this is less important than his amplification of a different theme—that of Bond's inter-mission decay. Once again Bond begins the tale worried that he has been going downhill after being without a mission for too long—and indeed he is in such a state that M packs him off to Shrublands spa to get clean. The episode, which comprises a quarter of the book, raises the element of irony and self-parody to a new height, as a regimen of "hot water and vegetable soup" amid the "ghastly daintiness and propriety" of Shrublands and its environs makes the rather hard, fast, "dirty" Tory wonder if he is not turning into a "soft, dreaming, kindly idealist." Subsequently his personal struggle with Red Lightning Tong member Count Lippe brings a good deal of indignity, Lippe tinkering with a spinal-traction machine while Bond uses it, reducing "the man of action and resource" to "a quivering jelly."

Additionally, while the narration claims the time at the spa got Bond back into fighting trim, the uncertainty about his fitness does not end with the beginning of the mission proper. Bond's weariness is evident in his doubt about there being any point to his following M's hunch. The middle third or so of the book is spent in a frustrated, grasping for clues (like his baiting Largo in the casino, with ambiguous results). His recruiting Domino Petacchi, rather than providing the desired intelligence, gets her into trouble. Afterward, instead of Bond saving her, she has to free herself and come save Bond in the final underwater fight.

The questions raised about Bond's fitness to play the spy game are the more striking because of the unprecedented degree to which Britain's fitness to play it is also questioned. The novel places a new and heavy stress on the treacherous character of the elements with which British intelligence deals, betrayers who in turn betray it when this is convenient. When checking up on Lippe, Bond learns that British intelligence attempted to use his Tong to spy on China (an effort which backfired on it). Ernst Stavro Blofeld, it appears, began his career selling intelligence to both sides from Poland and then later Turkey during World War II, in which not just the Allies but British intelligence itself loaded Blofeld with money and honors. Moreover, British intelligence itself patronized SPECTRE in the past (buying phials from the Czech germ warfare program off the organization). And Giuseppe Petacchi, when he hijacks the Vindicator bomber, was only repeating an earlier action—when, serving aboard a German Condor patrol plane during World War II, he killed his crewmates, handed the plane over to Britain and was hailed a hero for it.

Given this conception of Bond—and Britain—the earlier, symbiotic conception of the Anglo-American special relationship is also problematized. In contrast with the earlier picture of British skill and pluck married to American resources, Britain seems much less skillful and plucky here, ultimately allowing its nuclear bombs to be stolen, and in the process become a danger to the United States and the West. Britain's weakness is the more obvious and troubling for the bomber's having been hijacked at a Royal Air Force base in England itself, and then taken to the Bahamas, unnoticed because Britain lacks even proper radar coverage of its own colony. Afterward, despite British territory being the scene of the subsequent action, it is the American Air Force and Navy which supply the fighter planes and the submarine key to stopping

SPECTRE's plans, while the Americans supply more than hardware this time around. Leiter's recognizing an East German physicist in the company of Largo's people does much to strengthen the case that they have been involved with the bomber's hijacking.

More than before, it might be imagined from this narrative that the Americans do not particularly need Britain after all, and perhaps find it more a liability than asset, which makes Leiter's depiction this time around particularly interesting. He is presented giving a barman grief over watered-down martinis, spewing expletives, complaining about the "wild goose chase" that the job seems to be and boasting about the technical wonders of the *Manta* at every opportunity—an exceptionally graceless presence (an unhappy echo of Milton Krest).

Amid all this it seems telling that for the first time in the Bond novels the Chief Villain survives to fight another day, Blofeld getting away. (By contrast, even Klebb got captured as a result of her attempt on Bond's life.) The result is that despite the disruption of SPECTRE after their failed blackmail attempt, the possibility of his reemerging remained. Both the greater doubtfulness about British prowess (highlighted by its vulnerability to betrayal), and the survival of Blofeld to menace the world again—not only reappear in subsequent James Bond adventures, but do much to define their trajectory.

The Spy Who Loved Me (1962)

The next Bond tale to appear was not another novel about SPECTRE, but a shorter piece published in the *Sunday Times* in which Bond was given a job in Berlin, "The Living Daylights." The premise is that a defector is scheduled to cross over to the West, and the Service expects a KGB sniper, code-named Trigger, to target him. Bond is assigned to cover the defection by taking out that sniper on sight. The central twist of the story is Bond's not shooting to kill, but instead targeting the sniper's rifle. This accomplishes the essential task of preventing the sniper from interfering with the defection, but by refusing to kill Trigger he has defied his orders, a fact his colleague Captain Sender makes much of. Comparatively nonchalant, Bond quips that "With any luck, it'll cost me my job."

The themes of counter-assassination and defectors from the East, and Bond's (again) refusing to kill in cold blood, both turn up in the next novel, *The Spy Who Loved Me*. There it turns out that SPECTRE is indeed a going concern, and that the Soviets are still ready to use it, contracting them to kill a Soviet defector living in Toronto—and Bond, again, taking the counter-assassination job. However, the book does not focus on this adventure. In fact, the incident is only related after the fact to the story's actual protagonist, and narrator, Vivien Michel (and might be thought equivalent to Bond's Mexican mission in *Goldfinger*).

The first part of the book is a "confessional" in which she tells her life story, concentrating on her past romantic and sexual experiences. Following the end of an affair, she went on the road in North America, and wound up taking a job at an upstate New York motel—which, as it turns out, mobsters Horror and Slugsy plan to burn down for the insurance money, when Bond comes in. These guys are too small-time to make interesting opponents by Bond's usual standard, but Fleming (again) has his hero performing well below his peak in taking them on in a story (again) pointedly stressing Bond's limitations, rather than exalting his competence.

Taken together these differences are substantial enough to make calling *Spy* a "Bond novel from the girl's perspective" simplistic, the book perhaps Fleming's fullest divergence from the plotting of the prior works yet. However, it also continued the tendencies strongly evident in *Thunderball*, like the less conventional structure that book assumed, the doubtfulness regarding Bond's (and Britain's) prowess, and the stress on America's less attractive features (America the Tacky much in evidence as Vivien goes on the road).

The theme of "America the Tacky" in particular reappeared in the next Fleming short story, "007 in New York," offering an on the whole unflattering portrait of the Big Apple—ironically, given that the piece was supposed to have been written to assuage the feelings Fleming bruised with his earlier unflattering treatment of the city in his travel book *Thrilling Cities*. And the image of Bond at less than his most resolute and competent remained prominent when the series returned to its accustomed focus on espionage action in the next novel, *On Her Majesty's Secret Service*.

On Her Majesty's Secret Service (1963)

Following his battles with SPECTRE in the Bahamas and Canada, Bond is again on their trail in France as the novel opens. He has been assigned to pursue the remnants of the shattered organization, a task at which he has been for close to a year—and he is as displeased about it as if he were stuck back in his office. The mopping-up job seems to him more suited to regular police and intelligence forces rather than the double-o section, and indeed his frustration has driven him to compose a letter of resignation.[5] However, M's decision to send him this way, as always, proves to be the right one in spite of Bond's doubts. It turns out that Blofeld is not a hunted fugitive running to earth, but planning a grand new strike, specifically a bio-weapon attack on British agriculture.

In various aspects of this scenario, be it Bond's frustration in his work or skepticism about M's use of him, the return of SPECTRE, the French and Swiss settings and even Bond's alliance with a criminal against a much more threatening third party (recalling "Risico"), the stuff of the novel is familiar enough. However, again there are significant extensions. This time Bond's battle against Blofeld leads to their first face to face confrontation. Moreover, where Blofeld had escaped the campaign against SPECTRE thus far, here he eludes Bond's personal grasp when he goes to Piz Gloria to capture him—a failure of a kind not seen before in the series.

One can take this as merely a set-up for the next round of the fight, but in light of the increased stress on Bond's exhaustion (for the third book in a row) it seems to be part of a larger pattern, while before the novel's end the fact has important consequences. There is, after all, what readers seem to remember about the book most, namely that this is the one where Bond gets married—to mobster Marc Ange Draco's daughter Teresa "Tracy" di Vicenzo. While less commented upon, it is noteworthy that Fleming set up rather Gothic echoes of Bond's earlier connection with Vesper in those events. Once again Bond is on the job in the vicinity of the Royale-les-Eaux casino when he meets a girl to whom he is attracted, and with whom he quickly becomes involved. Like Vesper, she has some questionable personal connections (being a gangster's daughter, after all), and is troubled to the point of being suicidal. Like Vesper, Tracy shares an adventure with Bond, in the course of which he falls in love with her, decides to marry her—and then loses her.

However, the differences between the two situations are what give the parallels their importance. Rather than the protracted death of the relationship between two people culminating in one of them taking their life, Tracy is abruptly murdered just after her and Bond's wedding, when a bright future might have been hoped for them. Where Vesper's destruction was not the object but just the byproduct of Soviet blackmail, Tracy is felled by the bullets of the wanted enemy who once more eluded him, the professional failure made harrowingly personal. This latest, worse, loss, coming on top of that prior tragedy, in the life of a man a decade of hard living—of damage—older, has a different effect, conveyed in the last paragraphs of the book. As Bold held the body of his murdered wife, a patrolman stopped next to their parked vehicle. Bond

> looked up at the young man and smiled his reassurance.
>
> "It's all right," he said in a clear voice as if explaining something to a child. "It's quite all right. She's having a rest. We'll be going on soon. There's no hurry. You see—" Bond's head sank down against hers and he whispered into her hair—"you see, we've got all the time in the world."

The scene, with its air of shock and even denial, suggests that this time the slipping Bond is not a wounded man who might soon enough recover, but a broken one who might be beyond repair.

You Only Live Twice (1964)

In *Casino Royale* the loss of Vesper left Bond more determined than ever to fight SMERSH. As *You Only Live Twice* opens, however, it appears that Tracy's death did indeed prove too much for him to bear.

Bond's weakened condition, manifesting itself in the poorer quality of his work, seems matched by the weakened condition of his country. While Britain was repeatedly identified as not the biggest or richest power, overt reference to British *decline*, Krest's pointed remarks in "The Hildebrand Rarity" apart, was generally avoided. However, the matter is raised explicitly here. In his briefing M tells Bond that the United States has been disturbed by recent British spy scandals—betrayals in this case involving not dubious foreigners British intelligence tried to use (like Count Lippe), but figures like Head of Station Prenderghast. In response the United States has ceased sharing its intelligence on what goes on in the Pacific region.

The problems of a weakened Bond, and a weakened Britain, intersect when a paternal but frustrated M, wondering how to help Bond (and rectify the loss of American support) sends 007 to Japan to try and secure a compensatory intelligence sharing agreement with his Japanese counterpart, Tiger Tanaka. His idea is that this important, difficult but not dangerous assignment will make him pull himself back together (while making up for what the CIA no longer shares).

As in *Dr. No*, this is supposed to be a "safe," therapeutic mission. Also as in *Dr. No*, the therapeutic job turns into a deadly confrontation with a madman on his own island. However, much more than in that earlier book, the trip to Japan proves to be a test, not only of Bond, but of the British elite that he represents. From the start the Japanese, like the Americans (and as an intercepted communique demonstrates, also the Soviets), are doubtful about the value of a British alliance, and desirous of having Bond prove it to them with a display of personal prowess. The novel, which opens with Bond already in Japan, has 007 trying to do just that in a game of "stone, paper, scissors" in an interesting variant on this element of prior books. Rather than trying to beat an enemy, he is playing to impress an ally.

However, just as was usually the case with the villains the game proves a prelude to something bigger. The real test is Tanaka's challenge to Bond to assassinate Dr. Shatterhand, a wealthy foreigner who has turned his private island into a suicide theme park, the "Garden of Death," which lures the despairing to their deaths (a practice Tanaka's government, of course, wishes to stop). In these circumstances, the Garden is not just the most bizarrely Gothic setting used in the novels yet (Bond himself compares it with "Poe, Le Fanu, Bram Stoker, Ambrose Bierce"), but the strongest evocation of the theme of suicide and death to date, and all the more symbolic given Bond's being at an exceptionally low point. And topping it all off, Shatterhand is really none other than Blofeld.

Bond of course takes up the challenge, preparing for a physically taxing swim-and-kill *Live and Let Die* style in a small village under the tutelage of a local (Kissy Suzuki) and then heading off to do the job for real. On the island he finally faces Blofeld/Shatterhand in a confrontation that comes down to a swordfight. Bond wins, of course, killing Blofeld, and in that one can regard him as having not just exacted revenge for Tracy's death, but redeemed himself, and Britain. However, any such redemption is made less than complete and categorical by his injuries during his escape from the Garden, which leave him living with Kissy as an amnesiac, while officially missing in action and given up for dead by the Service. Moreover, rather than this marking the beginning of some new, peaceful life for Bond, he remembers a place called "Vladivostok," and heads there for clues to his past in a conclusion as much a cliffhanger as Bond's passing out in *From Russia with Love*. Sure enough, his trip to the Soviet city does not work out as he hopes.

The Man with the Golden Gun (1965)—*and After*

At the start of the next and last Bond novel, *The Man with the Golden Gun*, Bond turns up in Britain, seeking a meeting with M. When he gets it, Bond attempts to kill his old boss—the traitor this time not even a Prenderghast type, but 007 himself. Of course, Bond was brainwashed into the act after he was picked up in the Soviet Union. And in British custody again, he is subjected to painful electro-therapy to eliminate his prior conditioning. However, this does not set everything right, Bond still required to redeem himself if he is to escape treason charges.

Once more, much of what follows seems familiar enough. Again Bond's enemy, Francisco Scaramanga, is involved with both Communists and American gangsters (indeed, the Spangled Mob itself is mentioned), scheming to help the Soviets by causing labor problems, and in possession of a miniature train which proves the scene of a deadly confrontation. Again Jamaica will be the scene of the crucial battle.

Still, as in the prior novels, much of what seems familiar is altered in ways that are thematically significant. Where M had given Bond assignments as a way of aiding him in the past, the stakes have never been personally higher, while this time M knows from the start that the mission is dangerous, even suicidal—that theme so prominent in the prior book turning up here again, in a novel that may be even more redolent with death. Bond's assignment is a pure and simple assassination of an assigned target against whom he has no grudge, and which he cannot flub the way he did the counter-sniper job in Berlin in "The Living Daylights." And Jamaica is not the same place it was when Bond came to it in 1954, the country no longer a colony, but an independent nation, and in this way a reminder of British decline.

Again Bond's sad shape makes itself evident in a way familiar from *Spy*—the double-o unable to kill his enemy in cold blood, despite their obvious vileness and the undeniable danger this puts him in, forcing him instead into personal combat. Again Bond is so badly wounded that it seems he may not live. Nonetheless, it seems a matter of things being darkest before the light, not only killing his enemy, but surviving and returning to the good graces of the Service (enough so that he is offered, and refuses, a knighthood), while in the process getting right with himself. He has faced the "spectre" of Blofeld, and the demons raised by life as a man of war, and crushing personal loss, and ultimately triumphed, the resolution of *Golden Gun* bringing to a close the round of professional and personal crisis that began with *Thunderball*, with all that symbolizes.

However, if Bond ultimately recovered, Fleming did not, dying before he could even finish correcting the manuscript (the job of readying it for publication left to Kingsley Amis). As a result the next and final Bond book appearing with Fleming's byline was not a novel, but a new collection, *Octopussy and The Living Daylights*, which brought the new novella "Octopussy" together with the earlier and previously uncollected "The Living Daylights" (and in later editions, "Property of a Lady" and "007 in New York"). Like the earlier "Quantum of Solace," "Octopussy" (1965) uses the Bond adventures as a frame for presenting a drama about an upper-class Briton living in the Caribbean colonies. In the main a character study of retired Marine Major Dexter Smythe, now resident in Jamaica, Bond only appears at the end of the tale to arrest him for a crime he committed many years earlier: murdering a guide in post-war Germany so that he could make off with a cache of Nazi gold. Bond gives him a chance to clear up his affairs before taking him in for court-martial. As an alternative, Smythe ventures into the water to feed his "pet" octopus, and is poisoned by a scorpionfish—an act not unlike that of the visitors to Blofeld's Garden of Death.

After *Octopussy and The Living Daylights*, Fleming's estate enlisted a succession of other writers to continue Bond's adventures, typically picking up where Fleming had left off. Nonetheless, these final years of Fleming's productivity saw the massive success of the Bond series on the screen that made the figure much more identified with the films than the novels. The influence of the films was only to grow in subsequent years, making it only logical to turn to these first.

3. THE JAMES BOND MOVIES, 1962-1967

Looking back on Fleming's novels, one can see that the makings of the screen fantasy are present in the books, with all the essential elements drawn together into a recognizable formula by the time of middle-period novels like *Dr. No* and *Goldfinger*. Caviar and martinis, luxury suites and gaming tables. Larger-than-life villains lurking in hideouts both spectacular and surreal, from which they direct armies of henchmen toward acts of mass murder that would alter the geopolitical landscape. The game-like aspect of the contest, with its theatrical confrontations, elaborate death-traps, unlikely escapes. The shootouts, underwater infiltrations, chases, explosions involving every kind of vehicle on air, sea and land. And of course, the Bond girls. They are all there, and indeed, those formula-oriented, middle-period novels—and even the later *Thunderball* and *On Her Majesty's Secret Service*—were such that the distance between the print and big-screen versions is relatively short.

Still, there is no denying the differences. The Bond of the novels *is* a formidable adventurer who triumphs over long odds time and again while enjoying the good life, which not unsurprisingly made him a fantasy figure not just for his creator, but for much of his audience as well. However, the books of the Bond is much less superman than man, and living in something like the mundane real world. The "two or three times a year that an assignment came along requiring his particular abilities" excepted, Bond's daily life is essentially that of a senior civil servant, putting in bankers' hours at the office.

Additionally, where those assignments are concerned, Fleming is "careful to make Bond's achievements and abilities seem moderate . . . on the heroic secret-agent scale" at any rate.[1] He is better with a deck of cards or a gun than any other member of the Service, an able swimmer and driver, and good at a great many other things besides, but Fleming never lets us forget that he trained long and hard to get that good—showing him practicing for his game with Le Chiffre in *Casino Royale*, on the shooting range at the start of *Moonraker*, being lengthily prepped for the underwater demolitions job that will deliver the coup de grace to Mr. Big in *Live and Let Die*. However, for all that Bond is not always quite good enough, the villains often numbering among them people who can outdo Bond at the particular task at hand, and Bond getting into real trouble as a result (as in the underwater battle at the end of *Thunderball*, which sees Largo get the better of him, and Domino have to come save his life).

Of course, Bond's abilities are not simply a matter of his grab-bag of special skills, but also of that more elusive but not to be slighted quality that gives him such a knack for the game. However, nerve and judgment still do tend to fail him, as when he gets taken in by the fake kidnapping in *Casino*. And the failures of will and judgment, more than those of skill, repeatedly result in Bond's being captured, tortured or injured in ways tough on his pride as well as his body (like Le Chiffre's subsequent use of a carpet-beater).

What can be said of Bond the man of action can also be said of Bond, ladies' man. He is successful with women, including women ordinarily quite resistant to such advances (like Tiffany Case in *Diamonds Are Forever*). There are even ways in which it seems that the sense of sexual wish-fulfillment is taken as far as it can possibly go (in Bond's seduction of Pussy Galore in *Goldfinger*, or Vivien Michel's attitude toward Bond in *Spy*). However, his record is not entirely unblemished by rejections (Loelia Ponsonby, Gala Brand), and his successes are not unalloyed (Bond reflecting in *Casino* on how his affairs end in tears and bitterness).

Moreover, the hard living takes its toll, physically (as Bond's doctor makes perfectly clear in his report in *Thunderball*), but also mentally. Even when he has not just endured Le Chiffre-like torture, Bond gets bored, depressed, ambivalent about the meaning and significance of his work. (In *Goldfinger*, he rationalizes the killing of an enemy with an argument about how everyone alive is, if "only statistically . . . involved in killing his neighbor" through accidents, disease and indirect involvement in industries like H-bomb manufacture.) In the later novels, of course, things get considerably worse than that—and while Bond just manages to pull himself back together by the end of *The Man with the Golden Gun*, the reader can hardly forget his frailties.

One cannot even regard the accommodations Bond enjoys on his rather unusual journey through life as always first-class. While as Fleming says in the opening line of *Live*, "there are moments of great luxury in the life of a secret agent," the shabby and grimy and downbeat appear in his adventures with surprising frequency. In that novel alone there is the "notorious purgatory" of Health, Immigration and Customs at Idlewild International—even if Bond bypasses it—the uninspiring vistas seen from the train as Bond and Solitaire travel south, the "sleazy food-machine" of a Jacksonville diner, the rather sad Saint Petersburg retirement community. Indeed, Jeremy Black has remarked that Fleming's novels are only "superficially more glamorous and less bleak" than those of John le Carré—a thing no one has ever said of the movies.[2]

Bringing Bond to the Screen: Making *Dr. No* (1962)

From the start Ian Fleming's books attracted the attention of the film and television industries, beginning with an early approach regarding *Casino Royale* by Associated British Pictures. By and large, save for the transformation of the book into an episode for CBS' mystery anthology series *Climax!*, these were false starts and dead ends until Albert R. Broccoli and Harry Saltzman purchased a six-month option on Fleming's entire body of work, excepting *Casino Royale* and *Thunderball* (in other hands, as a result of other deals).

With the first Bond novel unavailable, and also the novel which had been most fully developed with an internationally marketable big-screen thriller in mind, Broccoli and Saltzman went with another novel developed for the screen, *Dr. No*, as the basis for their first Bond film. Through the company they jointly set up as their vehicle for making the series, the Piccadilly-based EON Productions, the two men wasted no time getting an actual production going.

Adapting the Story

In making *Dr. No* the filmmakers built on what was most-suited and dispensed with what was least-suited to the side of his work they opted to develop, the fantasy of heroic violence, sex and luxury.

Just like the book, the film opens with the murder of Strangways and his assistant, which results in M sending a recently convalescing Bond to Jamaica to investigate. There he learns of Dr. No, and with the help of Quarrel, goes out to Crab Key to investigate him. On the island he encounters Honey Rider, and the three confront the flamethrower-equipped marsh buggy thought of as "the Dragon." Quarrel is killed in the battle, Bond and Honey captured and taken to Dr. No's underground headquarters, where the bizarre and villainous No wines and dines them and explains his life and his activities—which include the sabotage of American rockets. After dinner, he subjects Bond to the tortures of a gauntlet he is not meant to survive. Bond does so, however, and after emerging from its opposite end, comes after No himself. He kills him, escapes from the facility with Honey, and foils No's plan.

Nonetheless, the film's treatment of this material differs in fundamental ways. Some were merely a matter of the *sixth* Bond novel being positioned as the basis for the *first* Bond film, with an eye to later films down the road. One is the introduction of Quarrel as a character Bond is meeting for the first time (where in the novels Bond had previously met him, and developed a rapport with him, in *Live and Let Die*). Another is the inclusion of American operative Felix Leiter (not actually in *Dr. No*), whose limbs are all intact, and with whom this is a first meeting (the events of not just *Live and Let Die* but *Casino Royale* never having happened).

Additionally, while a brief reference is made to Bond's convalescence, and the failings of his gun as a cause for his injury, no further detail is offered regarding the circumstances (the events of the preceding novel, *From Russia with Love*). There is, too, the presentation of Bond in a casino setting for the first time (also borrowed from *Casino Royale*, though altered to fit the new circumstances).

Other changes, however, are not explicable in such terms. The Service is genuinely alarmed by Strangways' being out of touch, rather than simply thinking that he had "woman trouble"; all the more so because the Service was already investigating interference with American rockets.

Accordingly, there is no thought of Bond's dispatch to Jamaica being a "soft" mission; it is instead deadly serious from the start. Appropriately, despite his recent trauma, Bond does not seem the worse for wear sitting at the baccarat table at Les Ambassadeurs—an impression reconfirmed when Sylvia Trench throws herself at him while he is on his way out of the casino.

Bond (after a little fun with Sylvia) jets off to Jamaica, where the action gets started much more quickly. Leaving the airport, his driver Mr. Jones attacks him, giving the film its first fight scene, and leaving Bond no doubts about the seriousness of the situation—while the assassination attempt is quickly followed up by others. The Three Blind Mice take a crack at Bond themselves, resulting in a car chase. Subsequently No's henchman Professor Dent tries tarantulas, and then having Miss Taro lure Bond into an ambush by sleeping with him.

Of course, Bond sleeps with Miss Taro and then turns the ambush around on Dent, interrogating him at gunpoint. This leads him and Quarrel to Crab Key, where No has a bauxite mine (not guano, eliminating that particular prospect of scatological humor). On the beach, Bond promptly encounters Honey (in a bikini, rather than nude). Events proceed much as they did in the novel after that, but No is not what one might expect: a person of ordinary stature, dressed in a white Nehru jacket, with relatively unostentatious bionic hands rather than hooks. His explanation of his actions also differs in a significant way from what the book posited: he is not working for the Soviet Union, but for an organization named SPECTRE .

No sends Bond into the gauntlet, but it does not contain a giant squid, and at its end, Bond finds the clock ticking down to the sabotage of the next rocket launch. Bond stops it in the proverbial nick of time, then, rather than smothering No under a pile of bird droppings, defeats him in hand to hand combat on a platform above the core of No's nuclear reactor. Bond then rescues Honey (who in the book got away herself), and escapes from the facility with her in a small boat as, due to the disruption of the reactor, the whole thing blows up. Consequently, where in the novel it fell to the Royal Navy to come and mop up, Bond has pretty much singlehandedly finished the job here. The only thing left for him to do is to enjoy Honey's charms as their boat is towed back to land by the belatedly arrived Leiter.

These changes, which even individually are not all minor, have an effect greater than the sum of their parts. In the film's construing the mission as a much more serious thing at the outset, and immediately plunging Bond into danger, it accelerated the pace of the story. So did the multiplication of the incidents of violence (the fights with Jones, the Blind Mice, Dent). The more numerous fight and chase scenes, moreover, turned what had earlier been a thriller containing action into a *showcase* for action. This combination of intensified pacing and stress on set pieces did much to establish the action thriller as we know it, and safely situated the Bond movies within that genre, where they have remained ever since.

There is a comparable change in the sexual content. Its depiction is more restrained (actual nudity elided), but Bond's sexual encounters are more numerous, and more casual, as with his liaisons with Trench and Taro. This set up a pattern in which Bond is with a woman at the start, gets involved with a second woman of doubtful loyalty who is likely to prove a "bad" girl later (the treacherous Taro) and then winds up with a third "good" girl (whom he finally beds at the end of the film).

There is, too, a rethinking of the portrayal of luxury. The shabbier backdrops to the action are upgraded to first class, and the rough edges scraped off, life never less comfortable than it absolutely has to be, or even can be. Kingsley Amis quipped that the Bond of the books never went anywhere near Savile Row—but it is exactly these that Bond identifies as his tailors early in the movie. Equally, Bond seems to experience travel as always comfortable and easy, never having to enduring an Idlewild-like purgatory on the screen.

Reinventing the Character

This selective reorganization and amplification of Fleming's material redefined not just the image of Bond's world, but the character of Bond himself in manifold ways. First and foremost is that in contrast with the physically vulnerable and often damaged Bond of the books, Bond appears unfailingly robust and vigorous, even his near-death leaving no permanent damage. One might add that the smoking and drinking and late nights do not seem to take much toll. (Even such a matter as Bond's being physically sick after his encounter with a tarantula seems exceptional, a rough edge of the adaptation to be smoothed out later.)

In the confidence, even arrogance the character displays on-screen, Bond also seems much more certain of himself than he ever was in the books. This is evident not only at the casino, but back at headquarters. Watching the early scenes the viewer gets no sense whatsoever that Bond spends the vast majority of his working time at a desk in the office. No reference is made to the drudgery of paperwork, the grind of office politics. Bond appears above such things, his whole life seeming to consist almost wholly of the hard work of being a man of war, and hard play like what he engaged in at Les Ambassadeurs.

Indeed, he is so *much* the Strong Individual that other characters regularly appearing in the Bond universe are marginalized. M gives an impression of authority, irascibility, crustiness; but the paternalism he feels toward Bond is absent (quite naturally, given that the concern he showed for Bond in the book has no place here), while there is no occasion to make much of Bond's loyalty to him. Likewise, while the script made a point of writing in Leiter, the figure makes no real contribution to the resolution of the film's events—or even display much in the way of personality.

All that being the case, the Puritan, Spartan side of Fleming's Bond, the self-doubts and recriminations, the fears that he is going soft or slack, the sometimes silly, sometimes morbid ideas to which he becomes prey over the course of the novels, are marginalized, if not totally written out of the story. Indeed, while Bond kills more enemies, they do not weigh on his mind the way they so often do in the books. Rather than a fallible man in a dirty business, Bond comes across as heroic—in his rescuing the girl, in the manner of his fight with No, in his single-handedly shutting down the operation, as well as in the absence of certainty about the rightness of what he is doing. And just as the violence has become less consequential, so has the sex, tears and bitterness are happily absent from these more frequent relations. (Something of this spirit is also apparent in the expansion of Miss Moneypenny's role; minor in the books, the film makes her flirtation with Bond a routine part of his trips to M's office.)

Additionally, even as Bond's life grew more luxurious, its portrayal was, as Jeremy Black has noted, made to seem "cost-free," while the already ambiguous treatment of Bond's social position became more so.[3] The sense of "class" that Bond conveys is "apparently unconnected with money or birth . . . a matter of style, not economics," the references to income (let alone a private income) left out. Additionally, if Bond himself has any opinions about what he is doing, they are rarely (not never, but rarely) expressed.[4] The racialism, the disdain for uppity proletarians and young people, the dislike of the welfare state and decolonization which are overtly, explicitly and at times lengthily present in the books, are generally elided. (Bond's snapping at Quarrel to "Fetch my shoes!" on the beach is a rare exception, and one for which Fleming can hardly be blamed, given Quarrel's much more dignified portrayal in the novels.) The result is that there may be a fair amount of snobbery on display, but Bond's "wisecracks and the absence of pedigree and social stuffiness" made it "possible for 1960s audiences to identify with him and to imagine that he was their type of hero," rather "more a cosmopolitan man than a man of class."[5]

That cosmopolitanism carries over to downplaying the "Britishness" of the Fleming novels (even as Bond became an internationally recognized icon of Britishness), and even their anti-Soviet sentiment. The Cold War remains a major part of the larger context, and there is never any question that Bond is not only fighting it, but regards doing so as his principal task. However, SMERSH is out, and the politically neutral SPECTRE in from the very start this time. Even the rougher edges of the special relationship are softened, Felix Leiter made rather less of a naif, and after the friction of their initial encounter, is on the whole a much more genial figure (never so graceless as he seems in *Thunderball*, for example)—if only because he never gets the chance to be anything else.

Realizing the Fantasy

Ultimately in *Dr. No* EON created from Fleming's material the story of a protagonist apparently living in a world of violence and mortal danger without death, injury, mental trauma or legal reprisal for the hero; of sex without worry about unwanted pregnancy, disease or emotional complications; of indulgence without satiation, addiction, ill health effects or psychological ruin; of luxury without privilege or expense; of travel without tedium and headache; of knowledge without study, skill without training and practice, fitness without exercise. In short, it is a world of extreme experiences, without the troublesome price tags and consequences, all on top of the conventional heroic fantasy of the individual not just mattering, but triumphing, against overwhelming odds, of clear-cut conflicts with recognizable and easily acceptable good guys and bad guys—the stuff of the fantasy Hugh Gaitskell once gushed to Fleming about in a letter rather than grim reality.

Along with the accelerated pace and stress on spectacle, this meant a diminution in the characterization and the irony that mark Fleming's original work—at the price of that earlier aspiration to a thriller designed to be read as literature. Still, if the film displayed less art of that type, it was nonetheless put together with a certain amount of aesthetic flair, including number of small touches that have been customarily repeated in nearly every subsequent Bond film, with which the series as a whole is closely identified, and which in their various ways reflect the sensibility of the production. The most famous of these are the opening shot through a rifle barrel, inside of which the titular secret agent turns to the screen and fires back, underscoring that sense of a world where danger lurks around every corner; the distinctive theme music, which plays over the opening credits; and James Bond's signature introduction of himself to people he meets as "Bond. James Bond," uttered by the character as he smoked at a casino table, with a bravado very different indeed from the character's introduction back in Fleming's first novel.

From Film to Film Series

Dr. No, of course, proved a massive commercial success internationally. This was not only a go-ahead for a sequel, but permitted it to be made with a bigger budget (twice as big this time around), and made it seem logical that it continue in the footsteps of the prior film. This would not only be manifest in the film's following the precedents set in *Dr. No*, but in the kinds of additions later films made to its pattern.

From Russia with Love (1963)

Of course, seen from the standpoint of either, *From Russia with Love* was, as mentioned before, so idiosyncratic that Fleming never really repeated anything quite like it. Moreover, the film was faithful to its source material. Again, the essential plot to entrap, kill and scandalize Bond for retaliation was used with a Soviet defector offering up a Soviet decoding machine. (Interestingly, the "spektor" of the book has here been renamed the "lektor decoder," perhaps to avoid confusion with SPECTRE.) Again, the story opened with scenes conveying something of the villains' plans. However, what could have played on the screen as dry, lengthy exposition was turned into a new feature, the *pre*-credits action sequence (which in this case had "Donovan" Grant kill a target that appears to be James Bond, but turns out to be a man wearing a Bond mask for the benefit of a training exercise).

Moreover, the events of *Dr. No* permitted the adaptation of the plot to involve SPECTRE instead of SMERSH, in line with its precedent. The killing of Dr. No gave the Special Executive for, among other things, *Revenge*, a reason to go after Bond in an action tying in with their broader policy of milking the Cold War for all it is worth. (The British are never meant to get the lektor, Grant instead supposed to recover it when he kills Bond so that SPECTRE can sell it back to the Soviets. Additionally, since the British are meant to think it is the Soviets playing them, Bond's entrapment and murder will turn up the heat on the conflict, which is in itself good for business.) The character of Rosa Klebb is retained, but as a defector to SPECTRE from the Soviet Union (as the novel *Thunderball* informs the reader, one source of their manpower, so this too can be seen as plucked from the books).

The pre-credits scene depicting Bond in a deadly situation, the devotion of the early portion of the film (if a smaller share of it than the book devoted) to the development of the villains' plans, both became series' standards. So did Klebb's final run at Bond in the book, the villains now routinely taking a final swipe at Bond after the failure of their plan.

Other additions, however, were thoroughly the invention of the filmmakers. Bond's briefing at Secret Service headquarters includes the first appearance of Desmond Llewellyn as Q, personally issuing Bond his tools. Additionally, the briefcase Bond uses in the film comes not only with the knife and the gold sovereigns, but also a folding rifle in an early accentuation of his use of special equipment.

The film also uses the space devoted to SPECTRE to develop the image of that organization. With its elaborate training facilities and the large number of personnel seen about them, it appears considerably more impressive than in the books—again, as it must be in order to act in place of SMERSH. The depiction of the organization also extended to the first appearance of its chief, Ernst Stavro Blofeld, and the inauguration of the practice of not showing his face as he sits with a white Persian cat in his lap, tweaks to the character that made him at once distinctive and mysterious.

Less fundamentally innovative, but significant for the development of the series nonetheless, was the investment in bigger action that the larger budget permitted. There was no attempt to repeat the finale of *Dr. No*, with Bond blowing up a villain's base. However, there were opportunities for extra thrills in Bond's stealing the lektor from the Soviet consulate in an elaborate heist scene rather than Tatiana bringing it to him. The confrontation between Bond and Grant is reimagined—with the gimmickry modified to permit hard-edged action. Instead of killing Bond with a gun concealed in a copy of *War and Peace*, he is to strangle Bond with a garrote wire concealed in his watch. However, what results is instead a famous two-minute fight sequence as Bond and Grant punch, kick and chop at each other inside their train compartment until Bond manages to strangle Grant with the wire that had been meant for him.

Additionally Bond's killing Grant does not mark the end of the chase, but caused him to abandon the train while it was passing through Yugoslavia, and cross the Adriatic to Italy. This gives SPECTRE the chance to use a helicopter and then speedboats to pursue him (each a reflection of the organization's greater size and resources). Bond takes out the first of those threats with that folding rifle Q conveniently provided. He takes out the second by dropping fuel barrels off the back of his boat and then, when the pursuing boats are among them, lighting them up with his flare gun—Bond not blowing up any villain's base, but providing the requisite pyrotechnics nonetheless.

Also noteworthy is what the film left out—by and large, material highlighting Bond's vulnerability. Bond's anxiety that he is going soft, his distaste at the killing of Krilencu, and most importantly, Klebb's successfully poisoning Bond, are all deleted, in the process also eliminating the book's cliffhanger ending. Instead Tatiana shoots Klebb, narrowly saving Bond's life, so that the last scene does not show him passing out, but rather enjoying a gondola ride with Tatiana in Venice.

Goldfinger (1964)

From Russia with Love was another, even bigger commercial success, which encouraged the making not only of another Bond film, *Goldfinger*, but the doubling of the budget yet again to $3.5 million.

It also encouraged the filmmakers to continue in their departures from the source material. In line with the practice in the previous films, the Soviets are not the principal villains, Goldfinger's backers instead the Chinese. Additionally, while the villain's plan in the film is somewhat more realistic than in Fleming's original version (notably, his using his atom bomb to irradiate Fort Knox's gold, rendering it unusable, rather than stealing it and shipping it out in a foreign warship), the film also sticks with the more flamboyantly heroic, high-living image established for the character on-screen. Bond is first enlisted to figure out Goldfinger's method of cheating at cards not through a chance meeting as he broods in a Miami airport on his way back home—but while he is receiving a massage from a beautiful blond at the Fountainbleau Hilton hotel. Later he gets his glimpse of the "hood's conference" not working for Goldfinger as a secretary, but by breaking out of his cell and sneaking a peek while his captors think he is safely locked down. And like *Dr. No*, the movie enlarges Bond's role in stopping the villains. Along with his sneaking word of Goldfinger's plans out to Leiter with Pussy Galore's help, Bond winds up in the vault at Fort Knox, handcuffed to Goldfinger's bomb, fighting Oddjob and trying to disarm the weapon as it ticks down to its detonation.

Still, significant differences did emerge out of the elaboration of the novel's ideas, with two items in particular becoming standard within the series. One is Bond's blowing up a heroin warehouse in Mexico, and then avoiding an attempt on his life, before the mission proper begins, which was used for this film's pre-credits sequence, and became a model for subsequent scenes.

The other idea is Bond's reliance on elaborate, specialized electronic and mechanical gadgetry—the Aston Martin he uses to track Goldfinger. And just as in the previous film, what the book provided was elaborated into something more—much more in this case, the Aston Martin now also boasting tire-slashers, wing machine guns and other self-protection devices, all of which come into play in the course of the chase.

Correspondingly the villains, who had usually had the gimmicks on their side, also have more than the usual amount of gadgetry around, like Goldfinger's laser. Besides being of interest in itself, it played a role in lightening the tone of the films as the gadgetry was substituted for violence. In the book Bond's capture, for example, resulted in Oddjob's trying to beat information out of him, and then when that failed, Goldfinger's threatening to cut Bond in two with a buzz saw, groin-first. This time the beating is dropped, and the laser used instead—torture replaced by gimmicky death-traps from which Bond generally emerges unscathed.

Also lightening the tone was an increase in the humor, often blended in with the violence, and rendering the material parodic—albeit in a different way from the books. Where Fleming tended to be ironic and sardonic toward Bond (at times bitterly so), the films permit Bond himself to be sardonic. Indeed, the humor often exaggerates Bond's prowess, both as connoisseur of the finer things (as with Bond's expert identification of a brandy as "a thirty-year old fiend indifferently blended . . . with an overdose of Bon Bois"), and man of action (his coolness under pressure letting him make quips amid mortal danger, electrocuting a would-be assassin and remarking "Shocking. Positively shocking" afterward).

In other cases, what is exaggerated is the menace Bond faces from his enemies (as with Odd Job's imperviousness to being hit in the face with a gold bar). Alternatively the film mines familiar thriller situations in self-aware ways, as in the film's most famous exchange. ("Do you expect me to talk?" Bond asks as Goldfinger's laser threatens to cut him in two. "No, Mr. Bond, I expect you to die!" Goldfinger retorts.) A good many bits of action also cross the line into slapstick (like the ejection seat in the Aston Martin).

While comparatively marginal, the film has two other features which later films regularly emulated. One is that the credits sequence is accompanied by an original song performed by a popular recording artist (Shirley Bassey in this case) which including the movie's title in its lyrics. Another is the treatment of the role of Leiter in this film, here played not by Jack Lord, as in *Dr. No*, but the much older Cec Linder. In contrast with such figures as M, Moneypenny and Q, the recurring character was recast in nearly every movie, a reflection of how much more marginal he is in the films than the books.

The Bond Film Formula, Complete

The result of the foregoing was that by this point virtually all the elements associated with the Bond films, both the contents of the movies as a whole and the structure inside which it is arranged, were in place, so that at this point it seems worthwhile to take a look at that formula in systematic, step-by-step fashion.

1. The Opening Shot

The film begins with a rifled gun barrel projected onto a dark screen as the famous theme music starts up. James Bond becomes visible in the opening of that barrel, which tracks him as he walks across the screen, after which he turns and fires at the camera. Red blood (that of the assassin who had pointed his gun at Bond, presumably) drips down the screen, and then the image gives way to:

2. The Pre-Credits Action Sequence

The sequence is likely to lay crucial groundwork for the film's plot by showing the villains going about their activities (as with Donovan Grant's training exercise in *From Russia with Love*). However, it is also likely to show James Bond in action, perhaps in the course of a mission (as in *Goldfinger*). This may be a self-contained sequence with virtually no bearing on the rest of the film (as in *Goldfinger*), but it might also lay crucial groundwork for the film's plot. It also tends to have Bond in the arms of a woman (again, as in *Goldfinger*).

3. The Opening Credits

The opening credits play with an original song (including the film's title in its lyrics) being sung by a well-known recording artist (like Shirley Bassey in *Goldfinger*). The credits are accompanied by animated imagery in line with the theme of both James Bond films in general (e.g. gunfire, scantily clad women) and the particular film in question (the gold-painted female form in *Goldfinger*).

4. The Exposition

The film turns again to the villains, and provides additional information about their activities, perhaps filling in the audience on crucial details of their plans—perhaps even putting the Chief Villain on-screen (as in *From Russia with Love*). The conveying of this information usually involves some amount of violence, and often a display of considerable organization and technical sophistication (as in the murder of Strangways and his secretary in *Dr. No*, or the view given of SPECTRE's organization in *From Russia*). More modestly, the movie may simply show the villains doing enough to attract the suspicions of Bond or the Service for the first time (as in *Goldfinger*).

5. Headquarters

Bond, perhaps after being contacted in the middle of a tryst (as at the start of *From Russia with Love*), breaks off what he is doing and goes to headquarters. While there he flirts with Moneypenny, gets briefed by M and receives his gadgets from the Service's technical personnel, typically in that order (as in *Goldfinger*, which first introduced the character of Q, and included among the gadgets a modified car). Bond's flirtations with Moneypenny revolve around the idea of her pining for him. M's briefing sets Bond on his mission, which typically begins with Bond being ordered to track down a missing person (like John Strangways in *Dr. No*) or object (like gold in *Goldfinger*) of special significance. And Bond's meeting with Q is likely to take place in Q's lab while he oversees work on gadgets Bond will use. Customarily, Q displays a prickly manner during their conversation. (All of this is seen in *Goldfinger*, when the famous Aston Martin is first presented.)

6. In the Field

Bond travels to the scene of his investigation. This sequence typically includes a shot of an airliner taking off or setting down at an exotic locale. Bond might be met by friends or associates right off the plane, who may represent local stringers for British intelligence (as in *From Russia with Love*). Bond's collection from the airport may also be the occasion of the first attempt on his life (as in *Dr. No*).

7. Meeting the Girls

Once in place, Bond meets a beautiful woman of uncertain loyalty, usually just the first he encounters in the adventure. These women may prove to be allies (like Honey Rider in *Dr. No*), enemies whom he persuade to become allies (like Pussy Galore in *Goldfinger*), or enemies pure and simple until the end of their part of the story (like Miss Taro in *Dr. No*). In any case, Bond will end up with the principal "good" girl at the end of the movie whether she began good (like Honey) or became good (like Pussy). In either case, Bond usually takes some time figuring out which is which, a process that typically entails his sleeping with them.

8. Meeting the Chief Villain

In addition to talking to local contacts, and discerning clues from interactions with the girls he has met—as well as such investigative standbys as surveillance and black bag work—Bond may go straight to the Chief Villain, often as part of a strategy of provocation (as is the case in *Goldfinger*). If he meets him socially, he is likely to engage him in a game of some kind, at which the Chief Villain often cheats, despite which he loses to Bond anyway (again, as Goldfinger does). Bond is also likely to succeed in baiting him into giving away some clue as to his culpability in whatever matter Bond is investigating, after which the villain may threaten Bond to lay off in a scene combining gentility with murderous intent (again, as in the films mentioned, Goldfinger punctuating the point by having Oddjob behead a statue with his bladed bowler hat). Otherwise Bond will meet him later in the film, after he has been captured (more on which below).

9.   Meeting the Senior Henchmen

The Chief Villain typically has a large number of employees, but some are likely to be closer to him than the rest, and receiving their orders directly from him, so that they may be thought of as Senior Henchmen. These tend to be plainclothes personnel (like Strangways in *Dr. No*, or Donovan Grant in *From Russia with Love*), in contrast with the large, uniformed staff typically operating their facilities. Very often one of these is very large, very strong, and visually distinctive, and to kill in an exotic manner (like Oddjob's hat). They also have colorful names (again, like Oddjob). Assuming that the villain has decided to kill Bond early in the film, he usually assigns that task to this henchman.

10. People Start Dying

The villains' various attempts to assassinate Bond do not cause him serious harm. However, some of the people around Bond might be, at least one of his allies—a local contact, for instance—usually being killed by the villain (like Quarrel in *Dr. No*). If it was not that before, the death lends a personal element to Bond's conflict with the enemy, while the circumstances may offer a clue to what is going on (as with the death of Kerim Bey in *From Russia*).

11. Bond Gets Captured

Even as he avoids serious injury, Bond is likely to at some point find himself in a position where he cannot resist capture and live. He may surrender (as in *Dr. No*), or find himself rendered unconscious (as in *Goldfinger*, at the end of the car chase).

This capture is likely to lead to a meeting with the Chief Villain. This may be at the Villain's principal facility, which is likely to be a concealed and nearly inaccessible fortress (as with the underground facility in *Dr. No*). However, the enemy sometimes has multiple facilities, and the one Bond finds himself might later turn out to not be the most crucial (like Goldfinger's Swiss facility). In cases, rather than a fixed facility, a vehicle may fulfill some of these roles (like Goldfinger's private plane).

Like their other meetings, this is likely to combine gentility and murderousness, the latter now more openly expressed as everyone has dropped the pretenses by this point. This may, for example, take the shape of Bond's being treated to dinner while being threatened with a painful death (as in *Dr. No*). The instrument of that death may be an elaborate trap of some kind (like the gauntlet Dr. No runs Bond through), or the Chief Villain's plan itself (like the nuclear bomb to which Goldfinger handcuffs Bond in Fort Knox). During his captivity Bond is likely to learn what he does not already know of the enemy's plot—if not because of the villain's explaining it to him in the confidence that Bond will never be able to use the information, then what he may see or overhear in custody (both of which happen in *Goldfinger*). Alternatively, Bond may simply be captured by a Senior Henchman (as when Donovan has trapped Bond on the train in *From Russia*).

12. Bond Escapes

In either case, Bond escapes, likely with the aid of a gadget, and/or the vulnerabilities latent in a death trap in which the Chief Villain has placed him. Especially if he has been held by the Chief Villain at his principal base, Bond may personally sabotage the enemy's plans (as in *Dr. No*), or arrange outside help for a final assault against the facility (as with the message he gets out in *Goldfinger*).

13. Defeating the Villain's Scheme

In the course of defeating the Chief Villain's scheme, Bond will participate in the film's largest action sequence, fighting both large numbers of nameless uniformed henchmen, and Senior Henchmen, usually inside the fortress, but sometimes at another site where the villain intends to realize their plans (like Fort Knox in *Goldfinger*). Often while Bond is fighting inside the facility, his allies are fighting to get in from outside (as in *Goldfinger*).

Bond may also kill the Chief Villain (in hand-to-hand combat if they can present a physical menace, like *Dr. No*), though they sometimes do escape (as Goldfinger does). In the course of the battle the facility they are in is likely to blow up, as a result of the destruction of key equipment in the fight, whether this was deliberate or accidental (again, as in *Dr. No*).

14. The Last Scene

If they are still alive, the Chief Villain may make a last attempt on Bond in revenge for Bond's disruption of their plans (as *Goldfinger* does). Bond defeats this attempt, and ends up with the principal good girl, often near a body of water (as in all three of the films made up to this point). Belatedly arrived assistance, or simply a search and rescue team, may be looking for them if the manner of the last battle warrants it.

15. The Closing Credits

The end credits roll (with the film's theme playing again), and conclude with a statement that JAMES BOND WILL RETURN IN _____, the next film the producers intend to make filling in the blank. The promise is usually kept.

Years of Bondmania

The near-perfection of the formula by the time of *Goldfinger*, and the balance it struck between fantasy and realism, levity and menace, in combination with the lavishness of the production, give it a special place within the history of the series. Many regard the film as the series' best. However, it seems indisputable that it is the series' most iconic, images from a gold-painted Jill Masterson to the tire-slashers on Bond's Aston Martin having burned their way into pop cultural memory so that they remain easily recognizable a half century later.

Thunderball (1965)

Following the success of *Goldfinger* amid a climate of "Bondmania," the producers turned to *Thunderball*, in collaboration with rights-holder Kevin McClory. In making the film they accentuated the elements the series had successfully highlighted to date and avoided the more idiosyncratic elements—of which there were quite a few. In contrast with the book the development of the story in the film is entirely linear, while any prior connection of Lippe, Blofeld or SPECTRE with British intelligence was completely dropped. (Instead it is the French who are mentioned as having hired SPECTRE to assassinate a scientist who defected to the Russians.)

The downplaying of the element of betrayal, the avoidance of such ambiguities within the film, is also evident in the reconception of the Petacchi siblings, here the Dervals. Domino's brother, Francois, does not perform the hijacking of the bomber, but is murdered by SPECTRE agents who replace him with a double surgically altered to look like him, who carries out the deed. Thus Francois appears dupe and victim, rather than crook.

This fits snugly with the alteration of the early part of Bond's own presence in the novel. Where the book opens with him treating shaving cuts he got as a result of being hung over and generally run-down, in the film the pre-credits sequence had him doing battle with the agents of SPECTRE—not seen in the previous film, but still out there, still a menace. Afterward Bond still goes to Shrublands, but if it is because of an unflattering doctor's report, no mention is made of this; and certainly Bond gives no impression of going soft, or soft-headed, on a regimen of vegetable soup. The episode of the spine-traction machine means that Bond does not altogether avoid looking undignified, but the indignities are nonetheless kept to a minimum.

Still more important, his encounter with Count Lippe is not just an ironic incident. The alterations to the plot fit together so that Bond finds Derval's bandage-covered corpse, which reaffirms the connection of the Shrublands episode to the plot, all the more so because of another alteration for which it sets the stage. Where in the book M concluded that the bomber flew to the Bahamas on the basis of radar telemetry, here M simply had Bond assigned to Canada as his patch of a comprehensive, Service-wide search. It is 007, who recognizing the corpse from the spa in a photo in the file he is given during the briefing (which naturally contained a picture of the bomber crewman Derval), proposes that he go check out Derval's sister in the Bahamas—his intuition, rather than M's, supplying the needed direction. (This, along with the edits to the Shrublands episode, also reinforces the marginalization of M as an actor within Bond's universe, and the existence of any sort of M-Bond dynamic, while aggrandizing the hero.)

Other changes worked in the same way. In line with the tendency to write in "bad girls," SPECTRE No. 6 is converted from a nameless man into Fiona Volpe—the series' archetypal "bad girl," and the film's principal refinement of the formula it inherited. While the novel reveals Blofeld's biography in detail, the film keeps Blofeld a mystery—still a faceless man with a Persian cat in his lap. It is also worth mentioning that Leiter (Rik Van Nutter this time around, the second Leiter in two years) does not come off as nearly so oafish as he seems in the book, but also not as helpful.

And once again the use of gadgetry, the number of violent incidents, the scale of the action are all increased. Volpe does not kill Count Lippe with a tossed hand-grenade, but a rocket-firing motorcycle, while Q (going out into the field for the first time) brings Bond his biggest array of toys yet. Bond's investigation of Largo in the Bahamas much more quickly turns much more violent. And the finale does not have a small team swimming out from a submarine with improvised spears, but shows Aquaparas parachuting into the sea en masse, while warships pursue Largo's yacht with cannons firing. Meanwhile Bond gets aboard the yacht and fights with Largo and his comrades on the bridge, then narrowly escapes with Domino before the yacht runs aground and explodes. Even Bond and Domino's rescue after that entails the use of a gadget, the two whisked out of a rubber raft and into the cargo hold of a plane by skyhook before the credits roll.

These sights, of which the production made the most through the series' first-ever use of Panavision, were recognized by the American Academy of Motion Picture Arts and Sciences with the year's Oscar for best visual effects. They also helped to make *Thunderball* an even bigger hit than *Goldfinger*, earning a then-stunning $141 million at the global box office.

You Only Live Twice (1967)

The success of *Thunderball* encouraged the filmmakers to try and top themselves yet again—an ambition that was somewhat complicated by their choice of *You Only Live Twice* as the next book they wanted to film. The source material of that novel closely followed the events of the preceding *On Her Majesty's Secret Service* (in which Bond first confronts Blofeld, and marries and loses Tracy), which had not yet been filmed, raising continuity problems. Additionally, its depiction of a grief-shattered Bond, and a Blofeld retired to a life of more eccentric but also more modest villainy, was out of line with their images from the EON films.

The result was that the film (scripted by Roald Dahl and directed by Lewis Gilbert) ultimately dispensed with the stuff of the book to an extent not seen in the previous movies. It retained the Japanese setting, and a few of the novel's characters—Tanaka, "Dikko" Henderson, Suzuki, and of course Blofeld. It retained, too, the fact of Bond's working not merely with a local British station, or the CIA, but with a very independent Japanese Secret Service; and the idea of Bond's infiltration into a Japanese fishing village prior to a final assault on Blofeld's fortress.

However, virtually all else is changed. The death and resurrection of Bond referenced in the title come at the start of the story, rather than its conclusion. The Service fakes his death, ostensibly to free him to better perform his next assignment, which M declares "the big one." An American space capsule has been attacked, and the U.S., believing the attack was part of a Soviet plot to dominate space, has threatened all-out war in the event of a repetition—with the launch of its next capsule just three weeks away. British intelligence, however, believes the real culprit was not the Soviets, but a third party operating out of Japan, to which he promptly packs off Bond. There Bond finds that behind it all has been Blofeld—but not as Dr. Shatterhand, just SPECTRE No. 1, with whom he (now) comes face to face for the first time.

As all this suggests, in setting aside the material of the original novel, the filmmakers instead turned to the stuff of the prior films. Again, SPECTRE is targeting the American space program, as in *Dr. No*; again it is playing East and West off each other for a profit, as in *From Russia*; again it appears that China is sponsoring the villainy, as in *Goldfinger*. The film also extended *Thunderball*'s principal innovation, the Fiona Volpe concept repeated with SPECTRE No. 11 Helga Brandt—a briefer and less successful usage in the view of most, but nonetheless an affirmation of this element of the films. Moreover, the organization of the material was a nearly textbook example of the formula established by the time of *Goldfinger*.

Nonetheless, any sense of repetition is submerged in those elements retained from the book that had not previously been used in the films, like Bond's position as a foreign agent working closely with a rather formidable foreign intelligence service on its *own* turf. It helped, too, that the formula was still fresh enough to permit a number of previously untried twists. One was the use of the pre-credits sequence not to show the villain's plans, *or* an action scene involving Bond, but both. The film's pre-credits scene was novel, too, in incorporating Bond's portion of it into the main plot of the film, rather than as merely an entertaining sequence tacked on to the beginning of the movie (the film using it to show the staging of Bond's assassination).

Still other innovations were Bond's briefing taking place not at SIS headquarters, but out in the field, aboard a submarine in Hong Kong harbor; that the "good" Bond girls Bond is paired with are themselves secret agents; that the destruction of the villain's base is not the work of the attackers, but the initiation of a self-destruct sequence by the fleeing villain; and that Bond's intimacy with the girl at the end is interrupted by M—to M's embarrassment, rather than Bond's.

There is also the novelty of Bond's meeting with Blofeld, which plays like a culmination of the events of preceding films. This is reinforced by the scale of the project, both in terms of the plot and the action depicted, funded by the series' largest budget to date ($9.5 million), which permitted the filmmakers to go all-out. If *Thunderball* at times seemed slow because of the copious underwater photography, *You Only Live Twice* often races, Bond bounding from one escape to the next in the three weeks during which the clock ticked down to catastrophe. Along with the action, the gimmickry is more plentiful than ever, epitomized by the autogiro-out-of-a-briefcase in which Bond fights an aerial battle with a squadron of SPECTRE helicopters. And even that pales next to the climax, in which an army of ninjas assaults SPECTRE's volcano crater spaceport mere minutes before the attack that would ignite World War III. Unsurprisingly, if *Goldfinger* is the series' most iconic film, *You Only Live Twice* comes in just behind it as a close second.

4. OF OLD PATTERNS AND NEW

Over time, every series tends to become less innovative and more repetitive, later installments increasingly shaped by the established pattern. The Bond films were no exception. Indeed, more than most series' they created very particular audience expectations, and a Bond film that diverged too far from those expectations tended to suffer for the fact—a fact of which the producers were already well aware when making *You Only Live Twice*.

That same movie also brought the producers to something of an impasse. The film was another, vast commercial success by any reasonable measure—but represented the first drop in grosses to date. Considerable as its $111 million take was, those earnings were less than not just what *Thunderball* made, but also *Goldfinger*. This may have been partly a matter of the delay of the release date, which resulted in Charles K. Feldman's spoof of the series *Casino Royale* (which he made using the rights he purchased to that novel before Broccoli and Saltzman's approach to Fleming) coming out prior to *You Only Live Twice*, and eating into its market. However,

Bondmania, and the broader "Spymania" it had helped foster, had already hit their peak.

Additionally, *You Only Live Twice* itself suggested certain limitations. Where scale of concept and action were concerned, the film not only represented a peak for the series, but also a limit. After taking the story literally out of this world, and making the aversion of World War III the stakes, one could not go bigger plot-wise. Nor did it seem possible to cram any more gadgets, any more action into an even superficially coherent two hour film. Indeed, many a critic regarded *You Only Live Twice* as having gone over that limit—as the Bond film that "jumped the shark"—in such scenes as the plane crash Helga uses to try and dispose of Bond (and Bond's escape).

Between the prospect of falling grosses, and the implausibility of getting much more bang for the buck, the old strategy of "going bigger" seemed to have run its course, resulting in a search for new approaches—and for the first time, lower budgets.

Years of Transition, 1969-1971

The crystallization of audience expectations regarding the Bond films, and the end of the strategy of going bigger, impelled the films toward a strategy of alternation among previously set patterns which largely took its shape in the next two films, *On Her Majesty's Secret Service* and *Diamonds Are Forever*.

On Her Majesty's Secret Service (1969)

On Her Majesty's Secret Service is best remembered as the first EON Bond film after Sean Connery's departure. Indeed, discussions of the film tend to stress the adaptations to the fact, like attempts to link his replacement George Lazenby with the protagonist of the earlier films. They point to, for example, the scene where while resigning from the Secret Service Lazenby cleans out his desk and goes through memorabilia from past missions, with the song from the corresponding film playing in the background as he examines each item.

The focus on casting causes many to overlook other, more fundamental changes in the way that the film was put together. Not the least of these was that with *Secret Service*, the films moved away from over-the-top extravagance, *back* to a more grounded, realistic narrative, a more serious tone. (After Bond's remark that "This never happened to the other fellow" when Tracy steals his Austin in the pre-credits scene, the film dispenses with the movies' style of self-parody.) This helped *Service* make heavier use of Fleming's source material, which was rather more conducive to the established style of Bond film than *You Only Live Twice* had been.

This is not to deny that there were significant adaptations in line with the pattern of the prior films. In the novel Blofeld's biological warfare plot is directed exclusively against Britain; in the film against the world as a whole. Additionally, where in the novel Bond made off with the list of girls Blofeld was using in his attack, so that Bond's return to Piz Gloria was a matter of finally settling things with Blofeld, here he had not done so yet, putting the world in the balance as he undertakes his final assault on the mountain— just as in prior films. Moreover, the figure of Bond is presented as more heroic and aggressive. Where in the novel Bond got tired of chasing Blofeld, and decided to resign if pressed to continue in it, in the film the case is the opposite, the Service losing interest in Blofeld, and Bond, determined to continue the hunt, offering his resignation in protest.

Still, these changes cannot be viewed as the usual amplification of the source material. The germ weapon aspect of the story remains visually low-key. And Bond's aggression in pursuing Blofeld is not simply a case of Bond being less given to world-weariness in the films than in the books. It can seem merely a reflection of the battles he fought against that organization in four of the five previous movies (including the plot directed against Bond himself in *From Russia with Love*), making him especially invested in the fight against this nemesis. Additionally, when Blofeld kidnaps Tracy late in the film (which required only a slight adjustment of the basic narrative), Bond, already more determined in his pursuit, has that much more incentive to act on his own initiative.

More broadly, the filmmakers held back from adding gimmicks the way they had in prior movies. Bond's Aston Martin appears, but in contrast with the two films previously featuring it, the car's special features did not come into play. When it comes time to fight, Bond relies principally on his gun and his fists, while the one "gadget" he relies on is not some deadly toy he carries on his person, but the computer he uses to break into the safe of Blofeld's lawyer. It is worth noting, too, that in contrast with the prior film the impressive set pieces were largely derived from the novel, including the ski chase that made this type of set piece synonymous with the Bond films, the helicopter attack on Piz Gloria, and the bobsled chase. And the film did not alter the book's downbeat ending, in which Bond was left grieving over Tracy's body.

In spite of the waning of the fashion for James Bond-style spies, and the rather sharp change from the previous tack, *On Her Majesty's Secret Service* ended up being one of the more successful films of 1969, taking in an impressive $82 million worldwide—ten times what it cost—and being quite profitable in the end. However, the figure was down yet again from the $111 million take of *You Only Live Twice*, enough so as to compel yet *another* change in course, away from grounded adventure, and back to extravagance and levity.

Diamonds Are Forever (1971)

Of course, extravagance and levity were a bit of a problem with Bond dealing with the death of his wife. One response was to shift the accent from Bond's grief to Bond's revenge, and wrap this all up early in the film—writing something apart from the main plot of *Diamonds*, and tacking it on to the start as its own mini-movie, a practice for which the way had been paved by several preceding pre-credits sequences. In line with his screen image, Bond appears from the first as the determined avenger traveling from one lead to the next and beating information about Blofeld's whereabouts out of them until, by sequence's end, he has caught up with and killed his arch-nemesis.

Still, that was not the only problem. The novels which best fit the screen image of Bond, the middle and later works that lent themselves to comparatively easy adaptation, had already been used up, so that EON was already turning to less and less suitable work, with *Diamonds* no exception. The plot regarding diamond smuggling out of Sierra Leone had become dated, as a result of that country's independence. And at any rate, ordinary diamond smuggling by ordinary criminals was too small-time a sort of crime for the cinematic Bond to deal with, however much M might call it "good, solid work."

The result was that, once again, the screenwriters had to create much more material from scratch—not so much as in *You Only Live Twice*, but still they worked much more in the manner of that film than any other of the preceding series. They also turned to another film for inspiration, namely *Goldfinger*, and to a degree which seems desperate in hindsight. Their original vision of the movie had Goldfinger's twin brother, a Swedish shipping magnate who would have been played by Gert Frobe, mounting a laser—a larger version of the weapon from *Goldfinger*—in the hull of one of his supertankers to do evil on a global scale.

The final version did not go so far as that in its emulation of the prior hit, but the consequences of this thinking are evident. The final script kept the laser, and brought back a favorite old villain— if Blofeld rather than Goldfinger's brother, with the idea of "twins" of this sort retained. As it turned out, what happened in that opening scene was that Bond killed off just one of many doubles of the SPECTRE chief, not the genuine article, while the real thing put a new plan to cause global mayhem into action. And of course, the film brought back Guy Hamilton to direct, Shirley Bassey to sing the theme, and Sean Connery to play Bond.

This did not mark the limit of this derivative approach, however, as where *Diamonds* did not borrow from Goldfinger, it borrowed from that other, most iconic Bond film. The villainous scheme this time around was the use of a laser-armed satellite in a plan to "auction off nuclear supremacy to the highest bidder"— another blend of Blofeld, space weaponry and superpower competition. Blofeld's plan had him taking advantage of the Howard Hughes-like anonymity of billionaire Willard Whyte to channel the resources of his corporate empire into the plan, recalling the role Osato Chemicals played in the earlier movie. And once again the film's climax involved a large assault on an offshore fortress as the clock ticked down to Blofeld's spaceborne weapon staging a major, global havoc-causing strike.

In drawing on these prior examples, the film's makers, convinced they had "to play for something fresh and outrageous" in Guy Hamilton's words, sought to top the earlier movies not by being bigger or more intense, but by being zanier, which meant an unprecedented emphasis on the sorts of broad humor and self-parody *Goldfinger* made a prominent feature of the series. The robust action in the pre-credits sequence, and Bond's fight with Peter Franks in the elevator in Amsterdam, recall the toughness of the films of the '60s, but by the time Bond arrives in Vegas the movie increasingly plays like slapstick, like the chase in which Bond wrecks a squad's worth of police cars. Charles Gray's Blofeld is a flamboyant flop, and the hit men Mr. Kidd and Mr. Wint become comic relief, down to their confrontation with Bond on the cruise line they take back to Britain (much changed from the handling of the original in the book). That same effort to "play for something fresh and outrageous" also gave the film a fair amount of surreal imagery, like Bond running around a mock-up of the lunar surface during a chase, and then stealing a moon buggy with which to flee across the Nevada desert. Even the appearance of Bond in the casinos of Vegas had an element of parody about it—007's white dinner jacket and black bowtie making him look awfully overdressed as casually attired tourists swirl about him.

The Matrix of Change

In the making of *On Her Majesty's Secret Service* and *Diamonds Are Forever*, the filmmakers established two patterns of regular change within the films. The more fundamental of the two was the reuse of elements from the most successful of the '60s-era films. The second concerned the way in which those elements were handled, with the films regularly shifting from a comparatively realistic, serious tone to an over-the-top use of those elements that tended to go with a lighter and typically self-parodying sensibility.

The "Mini-Formulas"

In drawing on the series' two most iconic films, *Goldfinger* and *You Only Live Twice*, *Diamonds Are Forever* set a significant precedent for the films that followed it. Specifically later movies tended to replicate the plot structures of those '60s-era films to varying degrees, down to fairly small features. Indeed, they did so with such regularity that it may be said that the bigger formula perfected in the first films was typically utilized by way of two more precisely arranged "mini-formulas" derived from those movies.

In the *Goldfinger* mini-formula the villain is endeavoring to control the supply of a precious commodity, perhaps as an end in itself, and perhaps to achieve some larger object. (Goldfinger wishes to maximize the value of his stock of gold, while his Chinese associates wish to create economic chaos in the capitalist world by disrupting the gold standard underpinning the American dollar.) Their agenda may be revealed by their engagement in smuggling activities, but this is unlikely to be the end of it. Typically they have enlisted the aid of ordinary criminal elements (Goldfinger having formed an alliance with mobsters), and are planning to make use of a weapon of mass destruction (like Goldfinger's plan to irradiate the

Federal government's gold reserve). Additionally, while the villain may have an elaborate base, it is likely that the final confrontation will take place near their target, which is a key repository or transport route for that commodity (the film's finale occurring in Fort Knox).

As their premises demonstrate, *A View to a Kill* (Zorin sought to corner the microchip market by drowning Silicon Valley), and *The World Is Not Enough* (the Caspian oil supply controlled by cutting off the Black Sea route by irradiating Istanbul with a nuclear meltdown), each utilized the *Goldfinger* mini-formula. And of course, like *Diamonds*, *Die Another Day* wrote smuggled diamonds into a plot involving a space laser.

Other films utilized the structure in more limited ways, *Live and Let Die* seeing Mr. Big trying to corner the heroin market, while Franz Sanchez in *Licence to Kill* convenes a conference with other drug barons in an attempt to organize the narcotics trade surrounding the whole Pacific Rim; *The Man with the Golden Gun* having Scaramanga pursue control of the "Solex Agitator" (and pack a laser of his own); *Octopussy* involving the smuggling of precious art objects out of Russia, a gang of female thieves, a plot to undermine an American prop to world order, Bond stopping the nuking of a U.S. facility with no time to spare; and *Goldeneye* entailing a plan to rob the Bank of England (computers enabling what had been impossible in the case of Fort Knox, with a nuclear device again helping finish the job).

In the *You Only Live Twice* mini-formula, the villains are likely to operate through the vast, widely distributed and opaque operations of a multinational corporate empire (Osato Chemicals). With the help of such assets, they hijack a crucial, high-tech system belonging to a major power, an act which has the potential to result in global havoc of some kind—perhaps intending to "bait and bleed" the major world powers (the theft of American and Soviet space capsules intended to start World War III). Bond is required to hunt down the responsible party, and in the process winds up working with an agent of another power independently investigating the matter (Japan), leading back to what is likely to be the villain's *very* elaborate base, and a massive firefight as his comrades struggle to capture or destroy it.

The most successful use of this mini-formula was in *The Spy Who Loved Me* (ballistic missile submarines instead of space capsules, Bond with KGB agent Anya Amasova instead of a colleague from a more accustomed ally), an effort which even had the director of that earlier film brought back to helm the production. Just like *Diamonds Are Forever*, it in fact became a favored variation, which was closely followed in subsequent films, particularly *Moonraker* (a stolen space shuttle, CIA agent Holly Goodhead), and *Tomorrow Never Dies* (with an Anglo-Chinese confrontation in the South China Sea). Another, limited use of the concept, particularly its "bait and bleed" aspect, appeared in *The Living Daylights* (where Georgi Koskov is involved in faking an aggressive KGB campaign against Western intelligence).

And just as was the case with *Diamonds Are Forever*, many Bond films borrowed elements of both the earlier movies. *You Only Live Twice* was the principal influence on *Spy*; but Stromberg's submarine-swallowing supertanker derived in large part from the earlier attempt to rework *Goldfinger* in the early phase of *Diamonds'* development. Likewise, while the influence of *Goldfinger* prevailed in *Goldeneye*, the film's plot did prominently feature the hijacking of a Russian spacecraft, which was controlled from a vast complex sited in a volcanic crater, which Bond infiltrates in the finale just in time to avert the firing of a nuclear weapon in anger. Similarly *Die Another Day*, for all its resemblances to *Goldfinger*-by-way-of-*Diamonds Are Forever*, also resembled *You Only Live Twice* in having Bond cross paths with a female agent from another agency in pursuit of the same enemy, and eventually work with her to thwart the villain's plan.

On the Edge of Your Seat, or Rolling in the Aisle?

The Bond movies went from *You Only Live Twice* to *On Her Majesty's Secret Service* to *Diamonds Are Forever* within the space of a mere three films, and this was not uncharacteristic of the later films, which shifted among different tones as well as different mini-formulas. Of course, the shifts should be put in perspective. Even the most grounded and serious of Bond films, for example, are far, far less so than, for example, the dramas based on the novels of John le Carré; and the most parodic of EON's Bond films do not go so far in the direction of parody as the Bond film that really was made as a comedy, the Charles Feldman-produced *Casino Royale*.

The question, rather, is will the primary villains look like a large criminal organization (as SPECTRE originally did), or appear to have the resources of a superpower (running the world's most advanced space program out of a secret base in a volcano crater)? Will their objectives make any sense at all? (It is one thing to steal the lektor and sell it back to the Soviets, quite another to start World War III and blow up both superpowers. Yes, you have been paid a hundred million dollars to do it—but what is the value of a hundred million in a Swiss bank under those circumstances?) Will their henchmen be menacing psychotics, or outright superhumans? (Strike us in the face with a gold bar, do we flinch, or just keep on advancing as if nothing happened?) In taking them on, will Bond rely on his fists and his gun, or will it be a matter of working his way through his collection of Q's toys, such that they seem less an adjunct to his personal prowess than a substitute for it? (Captured, for example, will he have to get by totally on his wits, or will he have a rocket-firing cigarette handy?)

Will Bond display a measure of cold-bloodedness, or the consequences of the violence be underlined, or Bond be seen to brood conspicuously? (Will Bond shoot after the enemy has already "had his six," for instance? Will the camera linger on the face of a man he has killed? Will he be seen glowering as he sits on the beach, looking at the waves crashing on the rocks?) Alternatively, how often will the film make us laugh, and why? (If it happens in the middle of an action scene, for instance, will it be at a bit of comic relief, or at the scene itself, the very way in which Bond gets himself out of this latest mess? Does it undermine the intensity of the scene, and the film?)

In short, will it be an adventure in which the villains cook up something a real-life bad guy *might* try, and Bond get by on brain and muscle, facing death and inflicting it himself and making the audience feel that; or will it be a gimmick-crammed, joke-filled, villain-wants-to-blow-up-the-world affair?

Or, as was most common, would there be a blend of the two types of story? Just as the script of *Secret Service* did not wholly leave out self-aware quips ("This never happened to the other fellow"), the most serious of the later films had their lighter elements and moments—sometimes mixed together in the same scene. The pre-credits sequence of *For Your Eyes Only*, for example, opens with Bond standing before the grave of his wife Tracy, recalling her murder—and concludes with Bond dropping a wheelchair-bound Blofeld down a factory smokestack, Blofeld's fall accompanied by a whistling sound effect appropriate to a Warner Brothers' cartoon. Even the famously humorless *Licence to Kill* was not totally without such gags, Pam Bouvier's fooling about with Bond's special Polaroid camera discharging a laser beam while producing an instant x-ray photo of a startled Bond and Q throwing themselves out of its way for dear life. At the same time, just as *Diamonds* had its harder-edged bits, the notoriously broad *Moonraker* had its darker, more brutal moments—Drax setting his dogs on Corinne Dufour, for example.

Accordingly, the more significant adjustments—from a serious film to an over-the-top film, for example—were a matter of "course correction," typically coming after a film's bumping up against one extreme or the other, driving a shift in the opposite direction, especially if this coincided with a disappointing box office take, or the change of lead actor. All three factors were involved in the shift in tone between *You Only Live Twice* to *On Her Majesty's Secret Service*, and then again, the shift between *Service* and *Diamonds Are Forever*.

By contrast, after the comparative success of *Diamonds*, and the replacement of Connery by Roger Moore, the filmmakers continued with the pattern of lighter films, as with *Live and Let Die*. The film had the most scaled-down plot since *From Russia with Love*, but it also had its share of gadgets and over-the-top stunt work, and played much of its material for a laugh (most notoriously, the figure of Louisiana Sheriff J.W. Pepper).

The Man with the Golden Gun had Francisco Scaramanga for its villain, upgraded in respects but no Blofeld-type. It was also comparatively restrained in its visuals. Still, it was even more aggressive in its pursuit of oddities and laughs than the preceding film. The incorporation of kung fu into the film was played for comedy, as was Britt Ekland's turn as the incompetent Mary Goodnight, which even extended to bedroom farce when Bond puts her in the closet, met (and bedded) Andrea Anders. The car chase has Bond stealing a car from a dealer's showroom, with Sheriff Pepper (on vacation in Bangkok) sitting in the passenger seat, and barrel-rolling the car in slow-motion to a kazoo-like sound effect as he jumps a break in a bridge, a feat which proves to have been to no effect when Scaramanga's car *flies away*. Christopher Lee manages to bring a measure of menace to the climactic shootout—but then the movie reverts to broad comedy when Nick-Nack makes a final run at Bond in a scene only slightly less goofy than its send-up in *Austin Powers in Goldmember*. It also proved another box office disappointment, perhaps the series' greatest to date in light of the size of the budget and its performance compared with prior Bond films—and faced the producers with another change of course, with the most extreme possibilities considered.

One was to take the films all the way in the direction of parody, as suggested in Anthony Burgess' screenplay for the next film, in which an organization called CHAOS (Consortium for Hastening the Annihilation of Organised Society) secretly inserts small nuclear devices into the bodies of wealthy visitors to a Swiss clinic. The climax has one such bomb hidden underneath the appendectomy scar of an opera singer, with the bomb to go off as she dances the Seven Veils in a performance of *Salome* at the Sydney Opera House, while Britain's Queen is sitting in the audience—and Bond performing an emergency surgical operation to extract and defuse the bomb.

Representing the other, extreme end was an early Richard Maibaum screenplay, in which SPECTRE came back, but was liquidated by an alliance of the "left" terror groups making headlines in that day—Baader-Meinhof, the Red Brigade and the rest.[1] They then used captured nuclear submarines to attack the oil fields of the Middle East, a scenario which indisputably has its outlandish elements, but which was rooted in the existing political context to an unprecedented extent.

However, course correction prevailed over fundamental change yet again, with the next film ending up with neither a group like CHAOS, nor Baader-Meinhof, as the villains; and the threat neither as absurd as an atom bomb in an appendectomy scar blowing up during *Salome*, nor as plausible as a terrorist attack on Middle Eastern production; but instead Stromberg's scheme to start World War III. In its version of balance between the two modes, the film did not altogether eschew silly gags, and in some respects even escalated them to the sort of thing more characteristic of Feldman's *Casino Royale*, like Bond's riding a camel to a Bedouin tent on his arrival in Egypt; the theme from *Lawrence of Arabia* playing as Bond and Triple-X made their way to the Nile; or the superhuman strength and steel teeth that enable Jaws to tear a van apart with his bare hands, and kill a Great White Shark attempting to make a meal of him. Still, on the whole the action had a harder edge than had been seen in some time. The results proved a considerable commercial success, enough so that the follow-up *Moonraker* had more than a passing resemblance—but which went much further over the top in the most lavishly financed Bond film to date, culminating in laser-packing U.S. Marines assaulting a giant space station.

The result was another commercial success by just about any standard. However, there was also a sense that the film had gone much too far in the direction of the comic and parodic (if not so far as Burgess' script). There was, too, the fact that the budget had been so large, while the earnings were a bit softer than those for *Spy*, and so the films reverted to a much more grounded feel in *For Your Eyes Only*. At least after the opening sequence, the film was a little *too* grounded for some tastes, while the box office earnings continued to drop, leading to a swing back in the opposite direction with *Octopussy*, where Bond let out a Tarzan-like yell as he swung on a vine through the Indian jungle, infiltrated Octopussy's palace inside a crocodile-shaped submersible, hid inside a gorilla costume and disguised himself as a circus clown.

The trend culminated in the *Moonraker*-like silliness of *A View to a Kill*, where Bond snow surfs as a Beach Boys song plays on the soundtrack, and in Max Zorin and May Day, battles enemies who do not merely seem superhuman, but really are the superhuman products of Nazi experiments. With the arrival of Timothy Dalton in the lead role, however, the films got serious again, in *The Living Daylights*, reaching an extreme in *Licence to Kill*, nearly humorless save for incongruous moments like the aforementioned gag with the Polaroid.

Along with the disappointing earnings of the prior film, and the arrival of Pierce Brosnan in the lead, this meant a new approach, never as parodic as the movies of the Moore era, but also never so grim as *Licence*. Still, even here the films ranged from more serious (as with the revenge-soaked *Goldeneye*) to more lightweight (as in the thinly plotted *Tomorrow Never Dies*, with its spectacularly irrational set-up and near-constant chase).

5. KEEPING UP WITH THE JONESES

       If the first five films established the pattern for the Bond films, *On Her Majesty's Secret Service* and *Diamonds Are Forever* developed the practices which enabled the films to continue adhering to that pattern without appearing to simply repeat themselves. The shifting among different formulas and tones from film to film, even if this was within a set range, helped make the films seem more varied than would have been the case otherwise. It seems likely they also helped to keep the attention of a broad audience with differing tastes—both those who preferred their Bond films' light and over-the-top, and those who liked them serious and grounded (relatively), getting something to their taste often enough to keep them interested in the franchise.

       However, formulas are useless without factors which can be plugged into them; and all the attention to tone in the world is meaningless without content to which it can be applied. The Bond films of the '70s developed two strategies for coming up with such material. The first reflected broader changes within filmmaking— ironically, inspired by the Bond films themselves, the rise of the action movie, which began in imitation of the jet-setting spy, but quickly ceased to be his special purview. Other movies, newer and less constrained by precedent, sported more contemporary, fresher ideas—and healthy budgets of their own. A case in point was the contemporary, urban-set crime films in Hollywood, with movies like *The French Connection* and the original *Dirty Harry* becoming huge hits in 1971. Alongside these movies came a more modest but still noteworthy boom in "blaxploitation," which shared the interest in urban crime, but tended to feature African-American protagonists, like *Sweet Sweetback's Baadasssss Song* and *Shaft*—examples not unnoticed when it came time to film the follow-up to *Diamonds Are Forever*, *Live and Let Die*.

Following Rather Than Leading: *Live and Let Die* (1973)

On the face of it the material of Fleming's original *Live and Let Die* was an easy fit with this trend. Bond, going not just into New York, but Harlem, finds himself operating on the mean streets of urban America, against an African-American gangster.

Still, it has to be remembered that *Live and Let Die* was also a Cold War thriller less concerned with Big's criminal operations than his KGB connection. The Bond films had tended to eschew blatantly anti-Soviet plots and conventional counterintelligence themes, and again these were not utilized. However, that left a considerable hole in the plot. This might have been filled by building up his villainy in another direction, much as the diamond smuggling of the original *Diamonds* was built up into Blofeld's space laser plan. However, in line with the urban crime theme, nothing of the kind was attempted. Mr. Big (now the cover under which "two-bit island diplomat" Ross Kananga runs his considerable criminal organization) has no ambitions of the geopolitical kind, just the ordinary business kind, wishing to take over the American heroin market.

In line with this stress on urban crime, there was change in the style of the action, stressing vehicular chases and especially car-centered set pieces of the kind seen in *The French Connection*. Notably Bond's first big action scene had him trapped in an out-of-control car in crowded New York traffic. Additionally, for the first time since *Dr. No*, the climactic battle did not involve large-scale special forces operations or military hardware, Bond instead attacking Kananga's hideout by himself.

Still, there were also real limits to the films' emulation of other crime-themed hits. One had to do with something shared by the crime films *Live* imitated, namely their R-rated violence, sexual content and language (even if the harsher language was implied with em dashes). Fleming's original material was a match for all this, but the Bond films had developed their image in the more sanitized era of just a decade earlier, and a shift away from it to Bond movies with buckets of blood, frontal nudity and four-letter words was a big risk. Not only would it have meant abandoning a substantial audience of families and younger viewers, but it would also have meant alienating older viewers with a fixed idea of just who Bond was, even as they enjoyed such fare in other films. (That Bond yelled "---- you!" at Goldfinger as he was about to be cut in half in the novels did not change the fact that such language seemed out of place in the hero's rarefied on-screen world.) And the producers, playing a defensive game by this point, opted to stay the course.

Moreover, the crime-themed films derived their charge not just from their urban grit, or their violence, sex and language, but the political nerves they plucked—quite contrary nerves, if one compares the Dirty Harry-type cop films with the blaxploitation movies. The former typically spoke to the right-wing populist "backlash" politics of audiences angry over the civil rights movement, the anti-war movement and the counterculture, which were often depicted as having so cowed the authorities that the "few good men" willing to do what it took to protect society had to defy their bureaucratic, PR-minded bosses. *Dirty Harry* in particular was a pointedly *counter*-counterculture film—so much so that its villain, the rather incoherent Scorpio killer, is incomprehensible as anything but an exercise in pushing the audience's buttons so that they cheer the protagonist as he crosses one line after another to fight him. By contrast, blaxploitation films typically had a heavy element of Black nationalism about them.

These could not both be embraced at the same time, or even separately. The populism and nationalism of the crime movies, with their pointedly working-class protagonists, made a tuxedo-wearing Briton an unlikely hero. At the same time, Bond's skin color by itself ruled him out as a blaxploitation movie protagonist. (Indeed, even a *Black* British secret agent would have been a foreigner to America's mean streets, with any other resemblances to Bond likely to diminish his credibility.) In any event, the producers also remained of a mind to stay as apolitical as possible.

The result was that the Bond films could evoke these trends, rather than really partake of them, and this they most certainly did, with the fad for blaxploitation the more conspicuous influence. The Harlem setting and drug trafficking theme aside, there were the fashions worn and the cars driven by Mr. Big's operatives, and the vocabularies they used (the racial slur "honky" directed against Bond); and the inclusion of the series' first-ever African-American Bond girl, Rosie Carver. The use of soul food restaurants inside Big's scheme, and the New Orleans jazz funerals, reinforced the theme.

Apparently, it was enough to give *Live* a helpful boost, as the movie became the franchise's most profitable since the record-setting *Thunderball*. Additionally, even if one could argue that Big's plot was too small-time, "not a Bond caper," as longtime series writer Richard Maibaum (not involved with this particular film) declared, it did suggest that the Bond movies could, without compromising their identity as a series *too* far, seize on prevailing trends to their advantage.

Chasing Trends

In line with *Live and Let Die*'s use of recent trends in Hollywood, its successors regularly drew on cinematic fashions as much as their formulas allowed—a not unimportant qualification.

Airport (1970) and *Towering Inferno* (1974)-style disaster films with their ensemble casts, *Mad Max* (1979)-style postapocalyptic movies where loners navigated desert wastes strewn with the wreckage of civilization, *Conan the Barbarian* (1982)-style sword-and-sorcery adventures, *Die Hard* (1988)-style action movies rooted in a single location, superhero movies about costumed protagonists and people with more-than-human powers like *Batman* (1989) and the *X-Men* (2000), were too great a stretch. Yet just about every other big success registered within the series at some point, so much so that recapitulating the history of the Bond movies can appear a recapitulation of the action movie's history as a whole, while the films seem almost manic as they jump from one bandwagon to the next—or, from another standpoint, play up this or that element in the franchise's past as seems commercially advantageous.

Martial Arts

After succeeding with blaxploitation, EON did not attempt a repeat of *Live and Let Die*. Instead it went for the next fashion in the action film—the Hong Kong-produced kung fu films, the popularity of which exploded with the massive international success of Bruce Lee's *Enter the Dragon* (1973).

A move in this direction was hardly unprecedented for the series. The martial arts had been an influence on the choreography of the Bond films from the start, Bond employing judo in his fight scene with Mr. Jones way back in *Dr. No*. Additionally, the series had previously used East Asian locations, sending Bond to Hong Kong and Japan, and writing Japanese martial arts and even ninjas into the action in *You Only Live Twice*.

However, once again there were limitations, some of them of the same type, the bloodier violence of these movies being outside the range of what a Bond film would depict. There was also no question of Bond being immersed in the kind of strongly localized crime drama the kung fu movies tended to depict. Additionally, while hand-to-hand combat remained part of the films, they had long since been subordinated to larger-scale set pieces and effects. Moreover, this particular film was based on a novel centered on a villain whose prowess in a different area was stressed in the title as well as the plot—gunplay. There could therefore be no question of replacing the car chases and the like with a series of kung fu fights, let alone trading the inevitable shootout between Bond and the titular villain for such a battle.

Indeed, the principal insertion of martial arts into the narrative was not an organic outgrowth of the narrative, but its inclusion within a portion of the formula which easily lends itself to extravagances—the manner in which the villain, having captured Bond, opts to do away with him. In this case, Bond, posing as Scaramanga to win access to Hai Fat's residence, is captured and, instead of being put to death in an elaborate device, dumped in a martial arts school where the other students are instructed to kill him. Bond makes his escape, however, resulting in a street chase during which two high-kicking schoolgirls come to his aid. As such a course of events suggests, the sequence is played principally as slapstick, makes Bond look rather silly, and is not considered a high point of the film, or of the series.

Underwater Adventure

Steven Spielberg's 1975 *Jaws* was the great box office hit of 1975. All too predictably it inspired a rush of other underwater horror-themed films, the more notable of which include, besides sequels to the original, *Tentacles* (1977), *Orca* (1977), and *Piranha* (1978), while the crime thriller *The Deep* (1977) similarly had a strong underwater theme.

The aquatic element, and even the heavy emphasis on sharks, was not new to the Bond franchise, both amply present in *Thunderball* a full decade earlier, while scuba and sharks had figured prominently in a Bond film only recently with *Live and Let Die*. Indeed, Simon Winder has compared the Bond franchise's role in introducing the undersea world to general audiences. Still, the use of them was especially pointed in *The Spy Who Loved Me*, the reuse of the formula from *You Only Live Twice* taking the adventure underwater.

Instead of hijacked space capsules, it is a matter of hijacked submarines, swallowed up by a modified supertanker owned by a wealthy shipping line owner obsessed with the sea, to the point of making his headquarters and his home in an offshore facility, and feeding people who displease him to a pet shark. Bond is also equipped with tools designed to help in an aquatic adventure, namely the Lotus submarine car he drives, and the "wetbike" jet ski on which he rides to Anya Amasova's rescue.

And in case there was any doubt about the reason for the stress on this theme, Stromberg's principal henchman is a giant with metal teeth actually named Jaws, who at the end proves a deadlier predator than the creatures which inspired his appearance, biting to death Stromberg's shark when Bond drops him into its tank. Also like his namesake, this was not his last appearance on the screen, Jaws becoming the only Bond villain since Blofeld to survive the end of the movie and return to menace the hero again—in the next film, *Moonraker*.

Space Spectaculars

Where *Jaws* set the global box office on fire in 1975, in 1977 *Star Wars* became king of the box office. In the process it created a new fashion for big-budget, action-oriented space movies, and once again the Bond films followed suit, the producers setting aside their plans to film *For Your Eyes Only* next in favor of the Fleming title most evocative of an astronomical theme, *Moonraker*. Like *The Spy Who Loved Me* it was a particularly difficult book to adapt into a satisfying Bond adventure. However, the success of *The Spy Who Loved Me* suggested a possible path for the movie, namely reusing the formula of *You Only Live Twice*, which, at any rate, had prominently featured spacecraft.

Still, even if the films had used space vehicles in the past, and more than once (*Diamonds Are Forever* incorporating a space-based laser), the use of a *Star Wars*-style theme could only have been a much more constrained thing than the underwater extravaganza the last Bond film offered. While the films had flirted with the paranormal in *Live and Let Die*, actually introducing aliens, interplanetary travel and the like would clearly have been going too far. For all the series' science fiction trappings, the Bond films still had to be set in something passable as the real, contemporary world, and so the adventure confined Bond to Earth's orbit. Indeed, the film's publicists took pains to stress that the movie was "based on science fact, *not* science fiction."

Nonetheless, the movie did present the spectacle of the hijacking of a space shuttle in its opening scene, for use in a whole fleet of them conveying Drax's population of hand-picked humans to the station he secretly built in orbit. At the climax, it is not Aqauparas or ninjas who aid Bond's attack on the assault, but shuttle-borne, laser-packing space marines, after which Bond and Holly escape in a laser-armed shuttle, which they use to destroy the three nerve gas rounds Drax managed to fire at the Earth before the assault.

In the end, *Moonraker* proved to be the visually most spectacular Bond movie made to date. However, it was also the most expensive Bond movie to date, while the gross, while billed as a new high for the series, was in fact somewhat lower than *Spy*'s.

At the same time, the film is often criticized as a series low, particularly by those who prefer the more serious films, and find the film's gimmickry, slapstick and generally lightweight, over-the-top tone not to their taste. In hindsight, that may have been all too predictable. A Bond movie with death star-like space stations and laser-packing Marines, after all, could hardly have been made with deadly seriousness. And perhaps also predictably, the series never again attempted to go so far in blending the adventures of James Bond with elements from more fantastic genres like the space opera.

H. Rider Haggardesque Adventure

Just as Steven Spielberg's *Jaws* created a fashion for underwater adventures, and George Lucas' *Star Wars* created an even stronger one for outer space adventures, the 1981 Spielberg-Lucas collaboration *Raiders of the Lost Ark* established a new trend—specifically a fashion for period adventures, particularly adventures set in the tropics during the early twentieth century, with ancient treasures like fabled antiquities or precious jewels the MacGuffins.

Once again, there were real limits to the extent to which the Bond films could follow in the wake of that hit. Bond could not go back in time to the 1930s, while bringing the 1930s into the present—for instance, by having Bond go up against a pack of old Nazis—would have seemed similarly questionable. The Bond films of the '60s had avoided the heavy use of Nazi and World War Two elements in the Fleming novels, and the truth was that by the 1980s all of this would have seemed rather tired and implausible.

Likewise, Bond's suddenly turning into an archaeologist would have similarly been jarring, and the same went for his being paired with an archaeologist (whose role in such an investigation would have relegated him to being second banana). And just as it was not plausible to bring aliens into Bond's space adventure in *Moonraker*, there seemed little question of working mystical artifacts into the adventure. Still, something of this intent is apparent in the enlistment of George MacDonald Fraser, writer of the Victorian-set Flashman novels, to work on the script.

On the whole *Octopussy* reflects this direction, not least in its shifting the action to India. (Never used in the films before, the rationale behind the choice is underlined by the fact that the first sequel to *Raiders*, *Indiana Jones and the Temple of Doom*, also used a South Asian setting the following year.) This is all the more so as the movie seems less interested in the India of the present than the India of the past. The idea of a British "imperial policeman" in action in South Asia as Russians intrigue with Afghan princes recalls Rudyard Kipling's *Kim* (1901), especially given how Bond is not working with Indian intelligence in a joint effort, but with members of the Secret Service's own local station.

This evocation of the imperial past also turns up in Octopussy's background, as the daughter of a British officer who "loved India." And just as in *The Man with the Golden Gun* the villains' penchant for devising odd deaths for Bond provided an opportunity to write in the martial arts theme, here Kamal Khan decides to make Bond the target of an old-fashioned tiger hunt, in the course of which Khan, atop an elephant, pursues a safari-clad 007 through the jungle. (In the course of making his escape Bond, like another famous hero of the colonial-era tropical adventure genre, even swings from a vine while letting out a "Lord of the Jungle"-like yell.) There is something of the period adventure genre, too, in the film's drawing on Fleming's short story "Property of Lady," which allots Czarist-era Fabergé eggs a prominent place in the plot.

Paramilitary Action: Rambo and the Special Air Service

Cops remained big on the screen through the 1970s, and the 1980s. However, it could be said that in the 'eighties the backlash-themed action movie was scaled up and internationalized. As Dirty Harry fought the punks infesting American streets, Rambo and Chuck Norris' Colonel James Braddock fought Communists in the Third World. And just as Harry outraged the bureaucratic, PR-minded police captains too cowed by a liberal media to get tough with domestic bad guys, the commandos did their jobs in spite of the bureaucratic, PR-minded foreign policy functionaries too cowed by international opinion to be sufficiently tough with the nation's overseas enemies—for example, too afraid to stand up for American MIAs rotting in Vietnamese prison camps, and so shamefully denying their existence outright until a Rambo or a Braddock brings them home and shoves them in those guys' faces. In the process even the heftiest revolvers were put away in favor of machine guns—and oftentimes, much heavier firepower than that.

First Blood would seem to have anticipated the trend rather than actually got it started, the concept much more fully realized in the sequel, *Rambo: First Blood, Part II* (1985), which went on to far larger success, while the Arnold Schwarzenegger vehicle *Commando* became a hit on a smaller scale that same year. As all this happened, even the crime-themed films increasingly came to involve commando movie-style firepower in the form of more frequent gunplay, automatic weapons and additions like helicopter raids and explosions seen in *Lethal Weapon* (1987) and its sequels, the special case of the Die Hard movies (where a cop is forced by circumstances to *play* commando) and *Tango & Cash* (1989). There was also much of this sort of filmmaking in many of the science fiction-themed hits of the same period, particularly *Aliens* (1986), *Predator* (1987) and *Robocop* (1987). There was even a kids' equivalent, in the G.I. Joe phenomenon (1983-1986), in a Rambo cartoon aimed at children too young for the R-rated originals (1986), in the Disney film *The Rescue* (1988).

Alongside the American fascination with such figures and plots, there was also a parallel British trend—a fascination with the Special Air Service following the massive publicity they received during the hostage crisis at Iran's London embassy. In fairness, it was a comparatively minor phenomenon, confined to British pop culture, and appearing much more prominently in print fiction than film (the principal "SAS movie" the forgettable and now obscure 1982 picture *Who Dares, Wins*). Still, it is reflective of what was in the air at the time, and given the Britishness of the films, should not be overlooked as an influence.

Once again, it did not take much to move the Bond series in the same direction, commando-style action having been a familiar factor in the Bond film formula long before these latecomers appeared on the screen. Additionally, this aspect of the films was already becoming more prominent again in such scenes as Bond's blowing up an aircraft hangar in an unnamed Latin American country and sliding down a bannister blasting away with an AK-47 in *Octopussy*, or escaping Soviet troops through the snow in the opening scene of *A View to a Kill*. (There was also the non-EON Bond *Never Say Never Again*, in which the opening scene has Bond running through a Latin American jungle to rescue a diplomat's kidnapped daughter from rebels—even if it turns out to have just been an exercise—and which ends with Bond leading American special forces out of an American submarine.)

Still, Bond the commando was usually tangled up with Bond the gadget-using and so often self-mocking secret agent. When 007 emerged from the water in the opening scene of *Goldfinger*, he had a fake bird on his head, and underneath the diving suit is dressed for a night out on the town, complete with a red carnation in his buttonhole. And if anything, this was even more the case in those most recent films. In *Octopussy*, when Bond blows up that hangar, it is the work of an anti-aircraft missile pursuing the Acrostar minijet in which he was flying, while Bond conducts his attack on Khan's palace in concert with Octopussy's circus performer-jewel thieves. In *A View to a Kill*, Bond makes his escape from those Soviet troops on a snowboard to the sound of a Beach Boys song, and then sails off in a mini-sub disguised as an iceberg, piloted by a typically Bondian blonde, ready to entertain him in accommodations that look much more like a luxury hotel suite than a compartment aboard a ship of war in enemy waters.

Of course, these extras could be trimmed, and were trimmed, beginning with the introduction of the next Bond, Timothy Dalton. The opening scene of *The Living Daylights* presented Bond, and the rest of the double-o section, participating in a special forces exercise on Gibraltar, which a traitor quickly turns bloody. The rest of the film made conspicuous use of other elements of the paramilitary action genre, like Cold War proxy conflicts in un-touristy Third

World settings, involving Bond with a band of Afghan rebels fighting the Soviet occupation (in this, anticipating the third Rambo film by a year). It is notable, too, that when all is said and done, the villain behind it all is an arms dealer looking to make a big score in the weapons and drug markets, not blow up the planet.

While different in look and feel, *Licence to Kill* also drew on that genre in having Bond defy his boss to go after a Latin American drug lord, an endeavor that brings Bond to the Panama stand-in, "Isthmus." The vile Franz Sanchez, in turns out, has some big plans—creating an alliance among the criminal syndicates of the Pacific Rim, using Stinger missiles to threaten American airliners— but they are much more "ripped from the headlines" than an update of SPECTRE. Additionally, the film cut Bond off from his organization, forcing him to rely on himself, the partner he finds in another target of Sanchez's organization, and a little help from Q, similarly acting outside his official capacity.

Moreover, where the Bond films had largely resisted the trend toward bloodier violence, the Bond films of the late '80s embraced it, with a heavier accent on gunplay, hand-to-hand combat, a bit of blood. *The Living Daylights* just managed to keep it PG, but it was the last such effort on the part of the franchise. *Licence to Kill* was in its original cut R-rated, and only managed to bring the rating down to a PG-13 by trimming such scenes as Felix Leiter's being eaten by a shark, Milton Krest's being blown up in a decompression chamber and Bond burning Sanchez to death.

In the process, the Dalton films lost some of their distinctiveness. In particular *Licence*, with its choice of plot and setting, its harder edge, grimmer tone and more brutal violence (and even its low-key cinematography), looks like a generic '80s action movie. Nonetheless, there was a limit to the extent to which Bond could follow in the paramilitary movies' footsteps. Just as Bond was not going to clean up American streets with a Magnum 0.44, he was hardly going to go to Vietnam to bring American prisoners home; or for that matter, refight the war in the Falklands. Bond's rebellion against M has rather a different tone than comparable scenes in other films—his determination to avenge Leiter a matter not of his sense that M or the state he represents is shirking its responsibilities, but rather a matter of purely personal loyalties that he feels trump his ordinary professional obligations. And Bond certainly was not going to become a musclebound, Spartan—and womanless—warrior in the manner of Rambo and his imitators.

Subsequent films retained the stress on this style of action. *Goldeneye* opens with a black-suited Bond infiltrating a Soviet chemical warfare facility in Archangel. The follow-up, *Tomorrow Never Dies*, has Bond spying on a terrorist arms bazaar in the Himalayas, performing a High-Altitude, Low-Opening (HALO) parachute jump out of an American military aircraft, and concludes with his fighting his way through Elliott Carver's warship with machine gun in hand. Still, the stress on Bond the commando was somewhat less conspicuous in the films that followed, just as it was less conspicuous in film generally, even as the preference for more grounded villains (and PG-13 violence) has remained firmly part of the series ever since.

The Military Techno-Thriller

Alongside the fascination with paramilitary action came an attraction to the plain old military kind. While Rambo was fighting in the jungle, films like *Firefox* (1982), *Iron Eagle* (1984), and the phenomenally successful *Top Gun* (1986), stressed fighter planes and the men who flew them. Often one type of story was bound up with the other, a tale mixing together commando action *and* heavy metal hardware.

Of course, the Bond films had pointedly done that since *Thunderball*, with its bomber hijacking sequence and the final sea chase; and the submarines, warships and missiles of *The Spy Who Loved Me* representing a new peak in this respect. And it was a simple enough matter for those films to renew the stress on this element in the late '80s. *The Living Daylights* had Bond get a Soviet defector into the back of a Harrier jump jet, then threw a battle tank into the pursuit as he raced for the Austrian border. Whitaker made much of the characteristics of the arms he meant to sell the Soviets (like the range and penetrating power of a personal anti-tank weapon on offer). And of course, the climax involves a Soviet air base, a C-130 transport aircraft, and a Soviet column pursuing a band of Afghan rebels.

The storyline of *Licence to Kill* permitted less scope for this sort of action, but the trend went from strength to strength. The early 1990s saw the filming of three of Tom Clancy's Jack Ryan novels—*The Hunt for Red October* (1990), *Patriot Games* (1992) and *Clear and Present Danger* (1994). It also saw the blending of the "Die Hard" formula with military hardware produce successes like *Under Siege* (1992) and *Air Force One* (1997). Something of these elements also turned up in movies like *Crimson Tide* (1995), *Broken Arrow* (1996) and *Executive Decision* (1996), while Harriers were prominently featured in *True Lies* (1994), and F-18 fighters in *The Rock* (1996).

Naturally the Bond films of the next decade took it all a step further. *Goldeneye* wrote in a Tiger helicopter, the destruction of a flight of MiG-29s by an electromagnetic pulse, a chase through the streets of Saint Petersburg in a T-55 tank ending with Bond staring down a missile train, space-based electromagnetic pulse weapons and British spy satellites.

The next film, *Tomorrow Never Dies*, opened with a British destroyer launching a cruise missile at an arms bazaar, an action which forces Bond to steal an L-39 fighter bearing Soviet nuclear torpedoes to get it away from the explosion. Right afterward, Carver's stealth warship, which looks like what was widely advertised at the time as the next generation of naval systems, turned up in the South China Sea, where it launched missiles at a Chinese fighter plane and a British warship. This precipitated an air-sea confrontation between the two countries, which is brought to a close when their military forces, alerted to the existence of Carver's vessel by agents Bond and Lin, collaborate in destroying it. More subtly, the workings of the Global Positioning System, and a secret American military base in the South China Sea, play important roles in Bond's investigation.

The subsequent *The World Is Not Enough* made less use of such elements, but included plutonium filched from an ex-Soviet missile base and a Victor-class nuclear submarine in Elektra's plot to irradiate Istanbul. The next and final Brosnan movie, *Die Another Day*, ramped up the element again with a North Korean plot to clear the way for an invasion of the South by neutralizing the mine fields along the Demilitarized Zone.

Cyber-Crime

The mid-1990s saw an explosion in personal computer use, and the proliferation of Internet connections, turning these into a consumer must-have—and soon, into a mundane essential. Moviemakers saw cinematic potential in the possibility, resulting in a fashion circa 1995 for thrillers involving computer-based criminality, that year seeing the list of major releases include *The Net* and *Hackers*, as well as, in a more futuristic vein, *Johnny Mnemonic* and *Virtuosity*.

Of course, moviegoers were not nearly so interested in seeing computer-themed films as Hollywood imagined, the expected hits never materializing. (The highest earner in the group, *The Net*, was only the thirty-fifth biggest film at the American box office that year.) And the fact does not seem terribly surprising in hindsight. Activities like computer hacking are simply *not* cinematically interesting—the sight of a person sitting in front of a computer, tapping away at the keyboard very far from being the stuff of thrilling celluloid. Additionally, the nerd stereotypes such films traffic in are unappealing to audiences, save as supporting characters at whose expense they might have a laugh.

Goldeneye, while incorporating a substantial computer element for much the same reasons as these other films, benefited from the limited extent to which it incorporated it. Just as the makers of a Bond movie could not abandon its usual shootouts, chases and explosions and become a pure martial arts extravaganza, they could not give them up for two hours of keyboard-pounding. Natalya Simonova and Boris Grishenko fight their battles in cyberspace, but never at the expense of Bond and Alex Trevelyan fighting it out in the real world.

Something of this interest also turns up in *Tomorrow Never Dies*, in the prominent role of hacker Henry Gupta in Carver's scheme, helping stoke international tensions by manipulating navigational satellite signals. It turns up, too, in Carver's status as a media billionaire with a significant stake in software—which it knowingly released with bugs in it to the end of forcing consumers to buy later, "upgraded" versions.

Hong Kong Action—Again

While the earlier fashion for kung fu films waned, the dynamism of the Hong Kong action film continued to attract Western attention. (Indeed, American movies often lifted scenes whole out of their movies, as with the early scene in *Tango & Cash*, where Ray stops two escaping drug dealers coming at him in their big rig—taken from Jackie Chan's 1985 *Police Story*.) The mining of '70s pop culture in the '90s, and the international successes of filmmakers like John Woo and Jackie Chan, soon enough made themselves felt even in the American market. Once again the Bond films responded to the trend, returning Bond to Southeast Asia in *Tomorrow Never Dies*, and, in its reworking of the formula of *The Spy Who Loved Me*, partnering him with Chinese operative Wai Lin, played by Hong Kong star Michelle Yeoh. The movie also played up the martial arts element, giving Yeoh a solo fight scene.

Female Action Heroes

The fall of 2000 saw the film version of *Charlie's Angels* become a blockbuster, and the following summer's *Lara Croft:*

Tomb Raider, went on to comparable success. Both were taken as signifying a new salability for major, contemporary-set Hollywood action movies with female protagonists.[1]

That the new edition of Charlie's Angels reimagined the relatively grounded private detectives of the original series as flashy secret agents, and Lara Croft was a pistol-packing globetrotter, made the prospect of a female Bond-type (an idea floated even before the actual Bond hit the screen) seem a bit more likely. Of course, short of replacing Bond with a female protagonist, there was not much the Bond films could do to follow this trend—and so EON considered the launch of another, parallel series centering on a Bond-style female spy, Jinx Johnson. Intended to crank out films in the "off-years" when no Bond movie was coming out, the plan had their using *Die Another Day* as a platform to launch it by having her partner up with 007 to save the day.

Where *Die* itself was concerned, of course, this did not make a real difference to the pattern of the films, given the long history of Bond's being partnered with female agents, all the way back in *You Only Live Twice*, and especially from *The Spy Who Loved Me* on. What did differ was the *casting* of the role. The Bond films had previously used Hollywood actresses, even fairly well-known Hollywood actresses (for instance, Jill St. John in *Diamonds Are Forever*), but never an expensive A-lister like Halle Berry was during this peak period in her career—a decision clearly motivated by the perceived need for a "bankable" actress to sell the Jinx series.

Of course, *Die* was a major success—the biggest of Pierce Brosnan's tenure in the role. However, the Johnson character was not so well received as had been hoped. And more generally, the fashion for female-centered action movies proved less robust than its enthusiasts imagined. The underperformance of the Charlie's Angels and Lara Croft sequels in the summer 2003 seems to have been something of a final straw, soon enough followed by EON's rather abrupt announcement that the project was canceled (which, it was said, Berry only discovered online).

6. TOPICALITY

The pursuit of fashionability in the Bond films, of course, was not wholly limited to the trends set by other action movies. The songs used in the credit sequences, for example, did not represent an attachment to any established style, but rather a willingness to enlist the popular acts of the moment, from Paul McCartney to Madonna. The casting, too, often included choices reflective of recent sensations rather than the conventions of the films or dramatic need—as with the inclusion of Grace Jones in *A View to a Kill*, or Denise Richards in *The World Is Not Enough*.

However, the effort to keep the films contemporary also compelled the filmmakers to look beyond pop culture, toward current events, and increasingly to rely on the incorporation of topical subject matter in contrast with the earlier, slighter uses. In *Dr. No*, for example, concerns the U.S. space program in having SPECTRE interfere with American rocket launches out of Canaveral, the rockets are not displayed conspicuously, and they play little part in the spectacle. There is no discussion of their workings and significance, while that of No's equipment for sabotaging them is kept to the barest minimum. Indeed, it may be said that all this is mentioned rather than evoked, so that No's plan could easily have been directed against something else without adjusting the film's script to any great degree.

If anything the following film, *From Russia with Love*, was further removed from any seizure on topicality. The Cold War is especially present within the story, and SPECTRE's plan to not just kill but scandalize Bond evoked spy scandals of the era—but on the whole the film feels comparatively backward-looking, its Balkan settings, its ride on the *Orient Express*, bringing to mind the spy stories of a generation earlier that did indeed provide Fleming with crucial inspiration. And so it went in successive films, apart from casual reference to recent events (as with the passing mention of SPECTRE as involved in the 1963 Great Train Robbery in *Thunderball*). However, like other aspects of the series, this was beginning to change by the mid-1970s, and just as *Live and Let Die* established a precedent for imitating movie trends, *The Man with the Golden Gun* established one for more substantive integration of current events into the plots of the Bond films.

The Man with the Golden Gun (1974)

The novel *The Man with the Golden Gun* was, like the two preceding books, very difficult to adapt into an EON Bond film. Its image of Bond at rock bottom, pushed to extremes to get right with himself and the Service, was simply unusable. There was, too, the fact that the Bond films had already made such heavy use of the book's West Indian setting, to which the films returned with the prior *Live and Let Die*. It was therefore predictable that the movie would use little of the source material, and after the success *Live* derived from cashing in on the blaxploitation trend, also unsurprising that the filmmakers would seize on another trend in filmmaking, namely the Hong Kong-style martial arts film.

However, that still left the problem of the villain and his plot. Unlike even Mr. Big, the Scaramanga of the novel was not the head of a criminal syndicate, but a hit man. Granted, he was building up a bigger organization, and connected with the Soviets, making him something more than an ordinary criminal, but this fell short of Bond movie-class villainy—all the more so because, just as with *Live and Let Die*, the Soviet connection was the sort of thing the films tended to sideline.

Some of the adjustments to the material that followed from this were of an already familiar kind. Scaramanga took over the businesses of a private employer, Hai Fat, in the course of the movie, as Blofeld had taken over Whyte's. Additionally, Scaramanga was linked to China. However, even this did not quite fill the gap. Scaramanga's control of Hai Fat's empire is a plot point rather than a real object of the story, its significance for anyone else ambiguous. Additionally, the mention of China seems mainly an excuse to put his island home off-limits to the British government, and force Bond to go face Scaramanga alone in an action his bosses can disavow.

Naturally, the writers did not stop there. They also wrote in the invention of a "Solex Agitator," a technology for producing energy from the sun, the significance of which is explicitly linked to the "energy crisis" of the 1970s, and the encouragement it lent to the search for alternatives to oil as an energy source. Originally a British product, control of it was now up for grabs, and recovering it for Britain actually Bond's initial assignment. That mission is complicated only when he receives one of Scaramanga's "golden bullets," implying that Scaramanga is gunning for him. This proves not to actually be the case at the time, but Scaramanga, like Bond, is seeking control of the Agitator, which not only puts the two men on a collision course, but raises the stakes of their contest considerably.

The Agitator is also prominently depicted at Scaramanga's lair, where the larger solar energy complex of which it is a component powers the laser Scaramanga uses to blow up Bond's seaplane. Following the later climactic battle between the two men, however, Bond grabs the device and takes it with him and Mary Goodnight in the junk in which they flee Chinese territory.

"Ripped From the Headlines"

In contrast with *Live and Let Die*, *The Man with the Golden gun* was a weak performer commercially, and critics have no problem finding explanations, not least that the film went too far in the direction of parody. However, while one could take issue with the movie's development of its theme of a fight for control over solar energy technology, this has generally not been regarded as a liability of the movie—and this turn to topicality was one aspect of the film that was to be imitated time and again. Indeed, the impulse was quite evident in the next film, *The Spy Who Loved Me*.

Dètentè

The Bond films had from the start played down the Cold War element—but the late 1960s saw the superpowers themselves do the same. While the United States and Soviet Union continued to compete in areas like military strength, the exploration of space and the pursuit of client states, and even continued to wage bloody proxy conflicts throughout the "Third World," they also cooperated in many areas. They concluded arms pacts like the Strategic Arms Limitation Treaty; enlarged their trade, the Soviet Union exchanging its oil and natural gas for Western technology; and undertook joint ventures in space, culminating in the 1975 Apollo-Soyuz Mission.

The Spy Who Loved Me extended the pattern by envisioning a more cooperative relationship between British and Soviet intelligence. Despite the film's beginning with the two as competitors for control of the submarine-tracking technology central to the plot, Bond ends up being paired with Soviet agent

Anya Amasova to combat billionaire Karl Stromberg's plan to start a world war.

This is Amasova's only appearance within the films, but her boss, General Anatol Alexis Gogol, becomes almost as much a regular member of the cast as his British counterpart M, appearing in each of the next five Bond films (in the last, as a Foreign Ministry functionary after his retirement from the KGB). Additionally, he consistently appears not just a moderate and a pragmatist, but a genial, good-humored figure quite unlike the stereotyped apparatchik. It might be added, too, that the homage to the famous Russian writer in his name, by evoking the country's literary heritage, is a reminder that there is more to the Soviet Union than caricatured Stalinist monstrousness.

Moreover, while appearing much later, and in quite different circumstances, his successor General Leonid Pushkin in *The Living Daylights* is conceived in the same mold. Senior KGB man that he may be, he is sufficiently removed from the image of the aggressive Soviet militarist to observe Brad Whitaker's fascination with historical conquerors with disgust. (Whitaker exalts them as "surgeons who removed society's dead flesh," but Pushkin regards them simply as "butchers.")

The Space Program

While Gogol put in an appearance in *Moonraker* (spending an evening with his secretary), the Cold War was even more marginal in that film. Rather the film's principal claim to topicality was its reference to the American space program.

Of course, previous Bond films had used space, and especially American endeavors in space. However, *Moonraker* highlighted the technology of the shuttle in a way previous films did not. Where *Dr. No* was very casual in its treatment of American rocketry, Bond discourses on the vehicle's reusability and ability to land like an aircraft in an early dialogue with Goodhead. Additionally, shuttles appear on the screen prominently and lengthily, not just because of the theft in the opening scene, but because of Bond's visit to Drax's California production facility; the mass-launching of shuttles by Drax from his Brazilian base, during which Bond and Holly themselves fly up in a shuttle to his space station; the subsequent attack on the station by another shuttle full of American Space Marines; and then everyone's heading back to the shuttles to flee the station's destruction, during which Bond and Holly use their shuttle's laser cannon to destroy Drax's chemical bombs, and get back to Earth.

Indeed, the film can seem almost like an ad for the Shuttle Transport System, an impression that was all the more striking for what the shuttle was designed and, at the time, still expected, to accomplish. Each shuttle was supposed to be capable of flying as many as sixty a year, while being far more reliable and safer than any launch rocket built before it. In the process, it was supposed to bring down the cost of launching cargo into space by a factor of ten, twenty or more. This kind of regular, reliable, cheap space flight was expected to permit grand space construction projects, as described in serious works like G. Harry Stine's *The Third Industrial Revolution*, or Gerard K. O'Neill's *The High Frontier*.

Of course, in reality the shuttle proved much less robust than hoped; and space flight, not much more affordable or safe than it had been before. However, from the vantage point of the 1970s such elements of the story as Drax's vast space station and the U.S.'s quickly rushing troops into space aboard a shuttle to stop him seemed somewhat less like outlandish science fiction, and more like technical possibilities, than they seem today—the film's space element not just a matter of cashing in on the post-*Star Wars* craze, but also serious talk about where the development of space was headed.

The Second Cold War

Ironically, just as the thaw in East-West relations became a prominent feature of the Bond films in *The Spy Who Loved Me* just as it was coming to an end. The end of the post-World War II economic boom, and the economic doldrums that followed; American defeat in Vietnam, the OPEC oil embargo, and the Portuguese, Iranian and Nicaraguan revolutions all testified to a changing international situation, one in which the West, the United States and capitalism may have been less securely dominant than before.

By and large, the political right was more successful than the left in selling its interpretation of the situation, and its policies, not least neoliberalism in economics, and a much harder line in foreign affairs, widely identified with the ascent of conservative governments in the West, particularly that of Ronald Reagan in the United States. The latter change was evident in a more severe rhetoric (as with the terming of the Soviet Union an "Evil Empire"), but concrete policy actions, like the continuation of the rise in defense spending ongoing since 1979; the deployment of short-range nuclear missiles to Europe; the announcement of the Strategic Defense Initiative; and military exercises in the North Pacific and Europe intended to overawe the Soviets (like the 1983 editions of FleetEx and Able Archer). The period also saw the intensification of American political, financial, intelligence and other support to movements opposed to Soviet-backed regimes, like the Afghan rebellion, or Poland's Solidarity, as well as a greater readiness on the part of the U.S. to intervene abroad with its own military forces, as in Libya (1981, 1986), Lebanon (1982-1985) and Grenada (1983).

Britain also saw a turn to the right culminating in a change of national leadership with the election of Margaret Thatcher in 1979. The realities of Britain's standing as a world power in the 1980s meant that its independent actions within the Cold War were less dramatic in nature, but Thatcher was nonetheless consistently supportive of the American line, not least in hosting American deployments of missiles on British soil.

The Bond films of the '80s reflected this change in the tenor of British and Western politics, starting with *For Your Eyes Only*, which, surprising as it may seem, is actually the first Bond film in which Bond really *is* fighting against East Bloc agents from the beginning of the movie, to the end. The story begins with the sinking of a British spy vessel off Albania, initiating a race between Britain and the Soviets to recover the Automatic Targeting Attack Communicator (ATAC)—a nuclear command-and-control system able to issue orders to Britain's Polaris submarines. And in contrast with that previous Bond film concerned with the sea-based component of Britain's nuclear deterrent, the pursuit of the ATAC was never eclipsed by a larger imperative, like crushing a Karl Stromberg-style plot. Instead it remained the object of the movie's characters all the way down to the end of the film, who even make a joke out of that earlier, more cooperative pattern. When it becomes clear that Bond cannot escape from Gogol and his soldiers with the ATAC, he smashes it against the mountainside to keep it out of their hands and then quips "That's dètentè, comrade. I don't have it, you don't have it."

Gogol has the good grace to laugh and walk away. Still, the change is unmistakable, down to the concluding scene in which Bond receives the praise of a female Prime Minister clearly intended to be taken for Thatcher herself. And indeed, by movie's end, Bond's unceremonious disposal of Blofeld seems symbolic—villains of the sort Blofeld represented, and the lighter tone with which they were associated, wrapped up before getting on to the real story, grounded in geopolitical reality (Maibaum's idea for *The Spy Who Loved Me* utilized in a modified fashion).

Moreover, the stress on the Soviet Union and the dangers potentially coming from it remained prominent through the next three films. To be fair, Gogol remained pragmatic enough, as did his similarly genial General Pushkin. However, those looking to intensify or exploit the situation were not always outsiders like SPECTRE and Stromberg, but often within the Soviet establishment itself. In *Octopussy* the villain attempting to ignite World War III is a senior Soviet officer, General Orlov, whose plan is intended to lead not to the mutual destruction of East and West, but Soviet victory over the West. Specifically, he wanted to detonate a nuclear weapon on an American base in Germany in such a way that it would be thought an accidental explosion of an American weapon. This was to create a political furor that would lead to the United States pulling its tactical nuclear weapons out of Europe, permitting Soviet conventional forces to crush Germany.

Likewise *The Living Daylights* sees arms dealer Brad Whitaker do his share of scheming, but the scheme would be a non-starter without his having a partner in Soviet General Georgi Koskov. In contrast with the fanatical Orlov, his motive is not ideological or nationalistic, but personal, private gain. Still, his scheme entails an old-fashioned defection of the sort that makes it very clear that the ideological contest continues, as does the fact that while Koskov may be a cynic, his henchman Necros still speaks earnestly of his comrades fighting for world revolution. The scheme also assumes that a Soviet campaign of murder against British operatives that "God forbid . . . might lead to nuclear war!"—which Koskov reinforces by evoking the memory of SMERSH for the first time in the films—is surprising, even unlikely, but not inconceivable.

Again, the films went only so far in their image of Soviet aggressiveness—arguably less far than *For Your Eyes Only*—with the rogues Orlov and Koskov both killed on the orders of their own country's spymasters. However, even if cooler heads prevail in the Soviet Union, it does seem a close-run thing. Additionally, the accent on the Cold War is reinforced through smaller details of the plots. Orlov's partner in his scheme is an Afghan prince living in exile in India, while Bond's Latin American adventure in the pre-credits sequence could easily be read as involving if not Cuba, then some fictional equivalent. The less Cold War-centered *A View to a Kill* opens with Bond escaping from icebound northern Russia, and then tangling with billionaire Max Zorin, a KGB agent—a connection that the early films wrote out of their depictions of wealthy businessmen like Goldfinger and Hugo Drax (even if the attack on Silicon Valley is a matter of his, again, going rogue).

And of course, *The Living Daylights* has Whitaker selling advanced Western weapons to the Soviet Union, while the Soviet campaign in Afghanistan is a significant part of the backdrop, and Soviet-occupied Afghanistan the setting for a large part of the film. After Koskov's capturing Bond and locking him up on a Soviet air base in that country, Bond makes an alliance with the Afghan rebels the Soviets are fighting. They help him attack the base and destroy a drug shipment from which Koskov and Whitaker hope to make a significant profit, and then as they flee Bond helps the rebels escape a pursuing Soviet column—his unprecedentedly conspicuous bit for the proxy wars.

The Drug War

Of course, by the time of *The Living Daylights*, the situation was already changing, the Second Cold War giving way to glasnost and perestroika under Mikhail Gorbachev. His liberalization of the Soviet system won him points abroad, while he also behaved in a more conciliatory fashion toward the West. His intent may well have been to produce a reformed, more viable Communist system, but in the end he presided over the dismantling of that system, and of the Soviet state itself, so that not only did a phase in the Cold War come to an end, but also the Cold War more broadly.

The result was that policymakers and thriller writers alike turned their attention to new threats—or, if one inclines to a less orthodox perspective, looked for new enemies. One such enemy appeared to be the international drug trade, against which the U.S. was taking the more aggressive and militarized approach of the "Drug War," which EON selected as the context for the next Bond film, *Licence to Kill*.

Of course, Bond had battled drug traffickers before, in the pre-credits scene of *Goldfinger*, in *Live and Let Die*, in *For Your Eyes Only*, and yet again in *The Living Daylights*. However, this time around Bond is not merely fighting a drug lord, but specifically a Latin American drug lord, whose operations were apparently conceived with close attention to the headlines. The imaginary country of "Isthmus" out of which he operates is obviously inspired by the Panama of Manuel Noriega, while his threatened use of Stinger missiles to shoot down airliners if the American authorities did not back off evoked contemporary terrorism (and narcoterrorism). The film also highlights the American Drug Enforcement Agency by depicting Leiter as having transferred to it from the CIA, while also featuring prominently the role of the Coast Guard in interdicting the movements of traffickers—a Coast Guard helicopter facilitating the interception of Sanchez's personal aircraft in the pre-credits sequence.

The Post-Cold War

Prominent as the War on Drugs was in the years following the Soviet collapse, it was far from the only inspiration for the writers of spy tales. The end of the Cold War, after all, proved to be something quite different from what many hoped for in the West. Rather than the Soviet Union painlessly transitioning to capitalist prosperity and Western-style democracy, the country suffered economic collapse and severe political instability. And all of these were read as not just domestic problems, but international ones in ways ranging from the activities of Russian organized crime, to the prospect of Russian nuclear weapons going on the black-market, to the possibility of a new dictatorship which would challenge the West.

All of these figure in *Goldeneye*, where Bond goes to Saint Petersburg (curiously, treated as if it rather than Moscow were the Russian capital). There he meets up with his old acquaintance Valentin Zhukovsky, a former KGB officer and present-day mobster who points him toward underworld figure Janus, now partnered with an aspiring "next Iron Man of Russia" (Arkady Ourumov) in a scheme that has him stealing nuclear-armed Soviet satellites. *The*

World Is Not Enough sends Bond back to the former Soviet Union, specifically Azerbaijan and Kazakhstan, where again post-Soviet decadence and post-Soviet criminality are on display. And if anything, so is post-Soviet geopolitics, Elektra King's ambition of controlling the flow of Caspian Sea oil is another sign of the times.[1]

Moreover, while the idea of villains stealing the superpowers' nuclear weapons had already been done repeatedly during the series, the idea was newly topical amid fears that post-Soviet Russia would be unable to keep its most powerful weapons secured. Thus did *Goldeneye* revolve around the hijacking of a space-based nuclear weapon, while the idea also appeared, in differing ways, in the next two films. In *Tomorrow Never Dies*, the reason Bond has to steal the jet trainer and take off in it in the pre-credits sequence is because it is carrying nuclear munitions. And in *The World Is Not Enough*, Elektra King gets her hands on stolen plutonium, which she means to use to turn a nuclear sub's reactors into a giant dirty bomb.

Alongside the geopolitical changes, and the implications for nuclear proliferation, the post-Cold War order was also reflected in how the films treated other countries. The dissolution of the Soviet Union left the People's Republic of China the world's greatest non-Western power, with the result that it took the place of the former when the premise of *The Spy Who Loved Me* was updated in *Tomorrow Never Dies*. Likewise, post-Soviet, but still Communist Cuba in *Die Another Day* is depicted as a place where shady individuals unable to travel freely elsewhere might just drop in for high-end medicine.

The War on Terror

As the films shifted away from the Cold War, to other concerns, the Bond movies increasingly wrote international terrorism into the script. An arms bazaar hosting "half the world's terrorists" was the target of the missile strike in the pre-credits sequence of *Tomorrow Never Dies*, while Elektra King's henchman

Renard is also associated with international terrorism in *The World Is Not Enough*.

The same goes for *Die Another Day*'s Zao, to whom the label is also applied. However, in contrast with the vague use of the term in the prior movies, which can easily leave the viewer with the impression that terrorist is just a synonym for "bad guy," the film does supply a broad political context, specifically North Korea's status as a "rogue" state. He is a henchman of the film's principal villain, Colonel Tan-Sun Moon, a North Korean military officer trading in "conflict diamonds" and weapons while pursuing his object of reuniting the peninsula by armed force.

Just as with the Soviet Union in *Octopussy*, cooler heads are in charge, and the villain of the film is a rogue. Nonetheless, that rogue *is* part of the military in a state in conflict with the Western world. Also as in *Octopussy*, the film depicts the military balance between the West and a rival state is presented as shaky, dependent on the retention of a controversial weapon in place. (Here the role of the tactical nuclear weapons of that earlier film filled here by the minefields along the southern edge of the DeMilitarized Zone dividing the peninsula, which is the principal target of Moon's space-based laser.)

In addition to the division of the Korean peninsula, and the prospect of another major war on it, the film also evokes the broader "War on Terror." The term is not used in the film, and nor is explicit reference made to events such as the September 11, 2001 terrorist attacks. However, the use of the word within the context in which the film was released, in which the word "terrorist" was especially charged, and associated with North Korea because of its inclusion in an "Axis of Evil" with Iran and Iraq by U.S. President George W. Bush, was suggestive. So is M's telling Bond that the "world changed" while Bond was in captivity in North Korea, her words an echo of the common refrain that "everything changed" following the attacks (while, perhaps, an implication that had 007 been in action, things might have gone differently).

7. DEEPER CHANGES?

The regular alternation between the mini-formulas offered by the most striking of the '60s-era films, the pendulum-like swings in tone, and the faddish seizure on action movie trends and headlines from film to film, proved sufficient to keep the Bond series popular through four decades. However, alongside this pattern of more or less regular innovation, five long-term trends were also evident in the Bond series' handling of their material: the reduced use of Fleming's original material; an increasingly dark, brutal element within the films; the modification of the depiction of Bond's lifestyle; a corresponding modification of their treatment of gender; and an increasingly aggressive treatment of the world geopolitical situation.

Whither Fleming?

Already at the time when *Diamonds* was written, little of Fleming's remaining material seemed very attractive as a basis for a Bond film. *For Your Eyes Only*, the most solidly Fleming-based of the films made after the '60s, had to combine elements of not just that short story, but also the east Mediterranean setting and smugglers' intrigue of "Risico," and the keel-hauling sequence from the original *Live and Let Die* (but which was left out of the movie version)—material from three different works—while still requiring the plot about the ATAC to produce a full-length film.

Most films settled for evocation of the material rather than its use, with subsequent films doing even this much to a decreasing degree. In *Octopussy* Bond meets not Major Smythe, but his daughter many years after the man's suicide (and the auctioning off of Fabergé eggs play quite a different role from what was seen in the story "Property of a Lady"). In *A View to a Kill*, apart from the broad Cold War theme, the killing of British personnel at the start of the story, the French setting, and the title, virtually nothing of Fleming's work turns up in the film, and the fact that even this much did turn up seems even less evocative than coincidental. *The Living Daylights* has the sniper duel from the short story by that name, complete with Bond's disobedience of his orders, but takes this as the starting point for the adventure, rather than its conclusion.

By the end of the 1980s, even the stock of likely-sounding titles had been largely depleted—only *Casino Royale* (to which EON did not have the legal rights), "Quantum of Solace," "The Hildebrand Rarity" and "007 in New York" remaining. The result was that 1989's film had the Fleming-esque but original title *Licence to Kill*, while largely confining its use of Fleming's work to unfilmed material from *Live and Let Die* (Leiter's being fed to a shark, a vengeful Bond, the warehouse shootout), the inclusion of cruel and vulgar yachtsman Milton Krest from "The Hildebrand Rarity" as a supporting player, and the transference of his use of a stingray tail whip to abuse his woman to Sanchez. And the Pierce Brosnan films did not contain even that much, *Goldeneye* only referencing Fleming's Jamaican estate in the name of the Russian space weapon that is the story's MacGuffin.

Going Dark

Curiously, even as the films ran out of usable material, the movies increasingly reflected aspects of that material which had been previously downplayed, not least Fleming's at times cynical view of Bond's business. *Licence to Kill* was especially striking in this regard. The increased level of violence remained, and moreover, was increasingly directed against Bond.

In contrast with the tendency of villains to put Bond into death-traps from which he escapes unscathed, Bond repeatedly suffers torture in the Brosnan films recalling the experience of the books. Elektra King subjects Bond to a garrote in *The World Is Not Enough*. The scene is brief, Bond promptly freeing himself, but *Die Another Day* goes beyond anything Fleming wrote with Bond's lengthy imprisonment and torture in North Korea which, the flashback scenes imply, traumatizes him.

Moreover, the Brosnan films extended *Licence*'s heavy stress on the theme of betrayal and revenge. In *Goldeneye*, Bond abandons his comrade Alec Trevelyan to complete the mission within the pre-credits sequence—repeating in a small way the British government's betrayal of Trevelyan's people (Cossacks who had sided with the Nazis during World War II) by repatriating them to Stalin. Bond's abandonment of Alec, and Britain's abandonment of the Cossacks, were both motivations for his revenge plot against Britain. And after that, Bond fought Alec again, in a battle to the death.

By film's end, what it all amounted to was the games of state, the treacheries involved, triggering a cycle of violence, Bond's readiness to engage in which leads Natalya to tear into him for his coldness. The theme is even more prominent in *The World Is Not Enough*. Kidnapped and ransomed by the terrorist Renard, M, intent on running down Renard, advised her father not to pay the money Renard demanded. This left her with a grudge against both her father, and M, which set her on her own revenge path.

The theme reappeared yet again in the next film, *Die Another Day*. After his capture on a mission to North Korea Bond is left to rot there until a prisoner exchange secures his release, after which M treats him with disdain and suspicion, his boss too ready to believe that he betrayed the Service while incarcerated. And so when Bond goes rogue yet again, it is not on behalf of a brutalized friend, but of himself that he seeks revenge. Of course, his actions are directed not against his own intelligence agency, but his North Korean enemy Zao. Still, Bond's sufferings lend a bit more edge to a virtual reality exercise in which Bond, facing an attack on the Service's headquarters, shoots M in the course of taking down the gunman holding her hostage.

Lifestyle

The word "lifestyle" is used in an overly broad way, now utilized to describe any facet of how people live. It is, for example, often confused with the "way of life" of a whole culture, or the material "standard of living" a person or group enjoy, rather than what it denotes more distinctly and precisely: matters of genuinely *individual* choice, on the part of a person who may be said to have meaningful choices, particularly where choice of activity and consumption goods are concerned. The poor, for instance, cannot really be said to have "lifestyle," precisely because their lack of money is the determining factor in what they do, wear, eat.

However, James Bond most certainly does have a lifestyle, one that can be described as solitary, hedonistic, and oriented toward movement, physical activity and the consumption of luxuries. Bond is single, and for the most part, inclined to remain that way, while also not being terribly social; save when the plot demands it, one hears nothing of his having any friends. (Indeed, his housekeeper May is written out of the films; the old lady would likely cramp his style if she were not.) He is a sportsman, particularly fond of the water and the ski slope, and of course fast cars. However, he also enjoys the gaming table, the luxury hotel suite; enjoys fine food, the high-end alcohol and tobacco he consumes heavily, and (typically brief) sexual relationships with numerous women.

Much of this was not altered over the course of the series. Bond remained solitary, and mobile. He continued to enjoy expensive cars and expensive suites and expensive clothes, albeit with an occasional updating of the brand names. (In *Goldeneye*, for example, the Aston gave way to a BMW, the Savile Row suits to Brioni.) Bond even put in appearances in the casino. Thus he retained an image of hedonism—though this reflected a more health-conscious age. Back when *Thunderball* was made into a movie, the doctor's report, M's alarm at it, were completely left out of the script, while Bond's time in the spa was made much less parodic. However, the later movies went far beyond having a character criticize Bond's less responsible habits to having him moderate or even give up those habits. So did it go with his smoking. (By *Tomorrow Never Dies* he could remark "filthy habit" while taking out an enemy smoking a cigarette.) As Jeremy Black remarked, were it not "for his association with the trademark 'shaken, not stirred' line, he probably would no longer drink" either, and as it is he may be drinking less.[1]

Perhaps most significantly, Bond bedded fewer women, while the tone of the relationships was different. The Timothy Dalton years were a period of comparative restraint, *The Living Daylights* involving Bond with only one woman after the pre-credits scene, Kara Milovy. (She was, of course, a "good girl," no bad girl or any other girl coming along.) Moreover, the relationship between them stressed romance over lust, while it was only implicitly consummated after the closing credits. *Licence to Kill* had Bond with two women, and Bond's early sex scene in the speedboat with Pam Bouvier had something of the older films about it. However, both women are again firmly part of the plot, and there is no question of no-strings-attached sex enabling him to avoid emotional entanglement. The three of them form a triangle, complete with jealousy and anger on Pam's part, expressed in some rather PG-13 language. *Goldeneye* was a return to form, though on the whole the casual dalliances (like Cecile Thomsen's Inga Bergstrom in *Tomorrow Never Dies*) continued to fall off in frequency.

Like Bond's giving up smoking, this, too, has often been attributed to changes in ideas about health, and particularly an upsurge in anxiety about sexually transmitted disease (of which the AIDS epidemic is only the most prominent part). However, it would be simplistic to completely attribute the change to this, changing attitudes toward gender also playing their part.

Gender

The sexual fantasy of the Bond films did not stop at the hero's having casual sex with desirable partners. There was a broader sense of his living in a whole world of available, willing pulchritude, evident not just in the women with whom Bond became involved, but the women seen in the credits, the women who filled out scenes as eye candy.

To be sure, strong female characters were by no means absent from the early films, even Honey Rider qualifying as such; while women who were presented as equal partners to Bond in his endeavors, or formidable villainesses, were routine before the end of the 1960s (as figures like Kissy Suzuki and Fiona Volpe demonstrate). However, the films also contained women like Sylvia Tench, Tatiana Romanova, Jill Masterson. Fair maidens in need of rescue, admiring and grateful and supportive; women who switched their sexual orientation when he came along if they had been previously averse to men; women who breathily said "Oh, James."

However, just as concessions to health-consciousness led Bond to give up smoking, concessions to feminism changed this aspect of the films, altering both the depiction of the "Bond girls," and Bond's relations with them. The Trenches, Romanovas, Mastersons, the bevies of essentially decorative beauties, the alluring women whose role seemed to be to fill out the image of Bond's world as a world of sexual fantasy, disappeared from the scripts—perhaps the last purely casual fling Kell Tyler's Linda at the start of *The Living Daylights*. Past that point, even the dalliances marginal to the plot gave the women a substantial reason for being there, and usually an impressive-sounding job too—like Bond's psychiatrist in *Goldeneye*, Professor Bergstrom in *Tomorrow Never Dies*, or Dr. Molly Warmflash in *The World Is Not Enough*, who does not regard this as a casual dalliance at all, applying physical pressure to an injured Bond to make him promise to "call her."

There was, too, a change in the presentation of the Strong Bond Woman, who was apt to be not just Strong, but more than before, competitive, abrasive, aloof, difficult; to challenge Bond, to one-up him, to give him grief, as with an Anya Amasova in *The Spy Who Loved Me*, or Holly Goodhead in *Moonraker*. Of course, even after that, the formula imposed certain boundaries. There remained the expectation that they would meet conventional standards of physical attractiveness, that they would be sexual beings, and that this would extend to their having sex with Bond by film's end. There remained the expectation that Bond, and not they, would remain the center and prime mover of events, the dominant figure within the narrative and on the screen. Still, exceptions to this became regular occurrences, Grace Jones' May Day, for example, by no means a conventional choice of Bond heroine, an unconventionality that extended to her bedroom scene with him in *A View to a Kill*. And along with women like Pam Bouvier, Wai Lin and Jinx Johnson, she upstaged Bond at various points through the film. In *Goldeneye*, the occupant of M's post became an older woman whose age, authority and general presentation, down to her flinging the words "sexist, misogynist dinosaur" in his face in their first scene together, made her, at the very least, an unlikely figure in such a film.

There was at times even a sense of overcompensation, Deborah Lipp remarking that in *Licence to Kill* Bouvier "opens with more-macho-than-thou sarcasm, then goes straight for strident feminism" of a kind that "substitutes stridence" for feminism, with a "forced and artificial" result. Over

> a decade after *The Spy Who Loved Me* . . . by now we all know that Bond can accept and work successfully with a strong woman. At this date, having a bossy American woman shout "Why can't you be *my* executive secretary?" is thick-headed.[2]

Something of this may have been the case with M as well, following the assumption of the role by a woman. In contrast with the earlier marginalization of M, the makers of the later Bond films at times seemed to strain to give her as much screen time, as much dialogue, as possible. More importantly, where the hard, callous side of M (which famously incurred Kingsley Amis' dislike) was treated in a restrained manner in the films, now it was played up, whether she is chewing out 007 for his well-known antics, or playing the tough-minded spymaster, ever ready to sacrifice her people for raison d'etat. *The World Is Not Enough*, for example, entailed much of both. It is also likely no accident that the first villain to get the upper hand over M, to expose her vulnerabilities; or to personally inflict physical torture on Bond rather than threaten injury or death; is not a man but the series' first female Chief Villain, Elektra King.

In his time among all these women, Bond is so often challenged, one-upped, given grief that, far from appearing to live out the ultimate male fantasy, he appears to be living out a certain male anxiety, and a much less formidable figure for it—the butt of a joke, rather than a conquering figure. And he is expected to be a good sport about it, the sort of remarks that Fleming's Bond normally made about such women (or even the subtler displeasure that the '60s screen Bond would have conveyed) never escaping his lips, even when they made a point of being difficult—Bond all charm and smiles in the face of Holly Goodhead's antagonistic manner. Indeed, film critic Vicky Allan has described the films as having undergone a lengthy "feminization" from the Connery era forward, with the Bond of the Brosnan era rather thoroughly feminized.

Geopolitics

The changed depiction of Bond's lifestyle, and the treatment of gender, suggest a more "politically correct" Bond. However, the opposite was the case with the films' treatment of the political context in which Bond operated. Reflecting some of the trends it chased (like the '80s action movies), the pursuit of topicality (with their invocation of current issues), and the broader turn of politics to the right (making stances on those issue appear less forbiddingly provocative), the films were not only more overtly related to the international political situation of the moment, but more hawkish.

This was particularly the case with the '80s films, and the use they made of the "Second Cold War." That Bond really is fighting the Soviets in *For Your Eyes Only* is entirely unremarked within the film itself, the situation seen as "normal," and along with the Prime Minister's comical but not unfavorable presentation with the film, the decision can be read as an embrace of the right-wing politics of the period.

If anything, this became more pronounced in the next two films. In *Octopussy* not only is the question of the military balance in Europe invoked, but the film takes at face value the claims that tactical nuclear weapons were vital to counterbalancing Soviet military might—the point given visual resonance by Orlov's computerized simulation of a successful attack before Russia's high command, and the implication that the anti-nuclear movement are the dupes of Moscow.

Never before had the series taken such a clear and provocative stance on such a controversial issue, the comparison with the stance of just a few years before striking. Screenwriter Maibaum remarked that Albert Broccoli gave as a reason for the abandonment of the terrorist plot for *The Spy Who Loved Me* fear of alienating young people sympathetic to groups like Baader-Meinhof—a much smaller risk than alienating sympathizers with the then-burgeoning protests against the nuclear arms race.[3]

The emphasis on Soviet villainy continued in both *A View to a Kill*, and still more strongly, *The Living Daylights*, with its spy vs. spy game, and Afghan scenes. Additionally, while the villain in each of the latter three films was a rogue acting on his own, in opposition to the authorities in Moscow, it is notable that the rogues always came from that side. None of the Bond films, for example, had an American, British or other Western fanatic threatening world peace by some scheme to attack the Soviet Union. And even Whitaker does not rise to that level, and at any rate, he was a reject, having been kicked out of West Point for cheating, and rather pathetically overcompensating for his underwhelming career as a soldier through his idolization of great captains and his tabletop war games. Moreover, while *Daylights* did not lionize the rebels in the way that, for example, the next year's *Rambo III* (1988) does (a note on-screen at film's end dedicating it to them), it makes it very clear that these rather rough, drug-trafficking folks are the good guys here, the Soviets the bad.

The more hawkish tone remained in subsequent films. *Licence to Kill* leaves no question that a militarized response toward the drug trade is appropriate. Similarly *Goldeneye* opened with Bond bombing a massive facility inside Soviet territory and killing a large number of Soviet soldiers on a vague pretext—the Cold War, apparently, thought enough to explain such an action—and presented Bond as still regarded as an enemy by the Russian state during the post-Cold War main story. Those who would turn back the clock were shown to be still worse villains, with brief reference made to General Ouromov as having aspirations to being the next "Iron Man" of Russia—an evocation of Stalin.

Tomorrow Never Dies was more ambiguous in its treatment of China, which was not painted as a default enemy. (Indeed, reflecting China's rapprochement with the West in the 1970s, the country had not figured in the films as an enemy since *The Man with the Golden Gun*.) Still, the film presented Bond as fighting international terrorism (however vaguely defined), and treating it as normal that Britain should unilaterally use military force against terrorists, regardless of the sovereignty of the countries in which they happened to be.

A similar attitude to the subject remained in the next film *The World Is Not Enough*, while the treatment of North Korea (and the terrorism with which it was associated) in *Die Another Day* evoked and exceeded the treatment of the Soviet Union in the films of the '80s. Again, the principal villainy is wrought by a rogue, and implicit comparison made with a more senior, more moderate figure—Colonel Moon's own father, General Moon. However, Moon in his brief screen time never approaches the character development of the Soviet Union's General Gogol or Pushkin, while his image is compromised by the fact that he is personally responsible for Bond's imprisonment and torture. And rather than Moon appearing the face of the North Korean establishment, it is he who is the exception by film's end, hard-liners who think more like the Colonel having staged a coup.

Naturally, in contrast with the help the Soviets extended Bond and the West in stopping Stromberg by way of an Anya Amasova-type, or their killing Orlov or Koskov themselves, none of the North Koreans render meaningful assistance in stopping Colonel Moon; this is entirely a job for the U.S. and Britain working together, with Bond killing the Colonel himself. And of course, where Bond stopped Orlov's nuclear bomb from going off in the nick of time, Moon's laser is shown blasting American forces from space. Indeed, one can make a plausible argument for *Die Another Day* as the most hawkish Bond film made to date.

Of course, this hawkishness may appear to be complicated somewhat by the darker view of espionage taken in the Brosnan-era films. However, the darker take never appears to be a questioning, critical take. Actions like Bond's may involve betrayals, blowback and other ugly things—but there is never a suggestion that Bond is part of the problem. Instead that ugly side is "the real world," and you had simply better "get used to it." One could call it cynicism without critique.

8. REBOOT

The battery of strategies EON pursued with the Bond films contributed to their enjoying a remarkable run: twenty major feature films in forty years, every one of them profitable, and the vast majority ranking among the top-grossing films of their year. *Die Another Day* was no exception, not just the highest-grossing of Brosnan's films, but the highest-grossing Bond film since *Moonraker*; while the idea of launching a Jinx Johnson spin-off franchise for the series' off-years remained a possibility afterward. Still, as one might expect given the length of the films' run, and the consistencies of the series' over that run, the series was showing its age, both creatively and commercially.

The Long Decline

While the foundations of the Bond films were clearly established in the '60s, and the pattern of tweaking them was largely in place in the early '70s. All the same, innovation did not entirely cease, as flattering imitation demonstrates: *G.I. Joe: The Rise of Cobra* (2009) for instance, borrowed heavily from *The Spy Who Loved Me*, having for its villain a madman (Destro) in an undersea fortress visually reminiscent of Karl Stromberg's aquatic facility in the Bond film, whose plan is to launch stolen weapons of mass destruction at both Moscow and the United States, then build a new order in the aftermath. The writers even decided to make Duke and the Baroness lovers on opposite sides of the secret war between their organizations (spies who love each other?), though the move had no basis in the history of either of these characters. And while *G.I. Joe* did not use it, *Spy*'s pre-credits ski chase remains heavily imitated to this day.

Still, on the whole the battery of changes in choice of formula and tone, the faddish use of trend and headline, resulted in slighter and slighter innovation. The repeated reuse of formula and mini-formula made their limits very clear over time, not least in the repeated plugging of the same factors into them. And the shifts in tone became smaller—the Brosnan films avoiding both of the extremes to which earlier films were prone.

The newer ideas taken from other action movies, or from world events, could not conceal the fact that in seven of the twenty movies, the villains' plots prominently feature the use of rockets or spacecraft; while the same number involve their use of nuclear weapons of various kinds, and on more than one occasion the two technologies are combined.[1] Four involve laser weapons in various capacities.[2]

Even the smaller details of the films became repetitive. Sixteen of the Bond films include at least one car chase.[3] Five different, conspicuously gadget-loaded Bond cars appear in ten different Bond movies, half of which see Bond cycle through his car's range of features to beat the bad guys.[4] Two films also have the villains operating their own gadget-packed cars (*The Man with the Golden Gun* and *Die Another Day*).

Additionally, at least six Bond films have chases involving boats and ships (*Moonraker* alone has two, in Venice and on the Amazon), and five more, ski chases.[5] Nine have diving sequences.[6] Ten have Bond personally flying aircraft of various types in action, with five of those scenes having him use the aircraft to make his getaway in the pre-credits sequence—with the list considerably longer if one counts parachutes as aircraft.[7] Four have Bond being attacked by a helicopter while he is on the ground, and taking the helicopter down.[8]

Thirteen of the movies have a climax in which Bond races to avert an imminent act of mass destruction, or a triggering of such destruction; while in *Die Another Day* Moon's space-based laser begins blasting the south side of the DeMilitarized Zone before Bond puts a stop to the plan.[9] At least eight of those climaxes have countdowns audible in the background.[10]

Even those movies most reliant on Fleming's original material, and least dependent on the formulas toward which the series tends, reflect the pattern, as *For Your Eyes Only* demonstrates. Just like *From Russia with Love*, it has Bond playing spy vs. spy with the Soviets over a small, secret piece of machinery in the eastern Mediterranean. The heavy underwater theme, complete with diving aimed at recovering a crucial piece of the British strategic nuclear deterrent, evokes *Thunderball*, and still more *The Spy Who Loved Me*, which at the outset also has Bond racing the Soviets for control of a high-tech system relevant to the security of Britain's Polaris missile submarines. The movie features a Central European ski chase, again recalling *Spy*, and before it, *On Her Majesty's Secret Service*. Moreover, the repetition tends to be to diminishing returns. Good as the ski chase in *For Your Eyes Only* is, its details do not stick in the mind to the same degree as in the preceding films. (Indeed, the *MAD Magazine* parody of the film was merciless in its mockery of the movie as an assemblage of familiar parts.) And the problem was the more pronounced as the films progressed, be it in the use of Istanbul as a setting in *The World Is Not Enough*, or the space laser in *Die*.

Ironically, even as the different Bond films came to look too much alike in some respects, they did not look sufficiently alike in others. While writing the later installments of the series, continuity was already a problem for Fleming, not least where Bond's age was concerned. The films were more careful in avoiding references to the character's age, to specific dates, to his past, but after forty years and five actors the strain was far more obvious, such that some viewers theorized that "James Bond" was just a code name utilized by the different agents the different actors were assumed to be playing. Meanwhile, not just the formula and its typical factors, but the essential premise has dated.

Racing Time?

In considering the Bond series one has to remember that the idea did not spring forth fully formed, but distilled an earlier tradition, updating what were already yesteryear's World War I-era clubland heroes for the jet age, atom age, space age; for post-empire, for Cold War; for the Playboy era.

And that all of these things have become quaint.

International jet travel has long ceased to be novel. The atomic and space tech which seemed so cutting-edge in the '60s no longer appear so forty years on. If the idea of a British secret agent keeping the peace of the world already seemed creaky in 1953 (American backing was already an essential part of the update), it seemed far, far more so in 2003.

Additionally, with the British Empire (and the Cold War) each an increasingly distant memory, and nothing quite comparable supplying a new political context for intelligence work like Bond's, the plots seemed the thinner. Already in *Diamonds Are Forever*, Blofeld, in the midst of auctioning off "nuclear supremacy to the highest bidder," could, after attacking the U.S., the Soviet Union and China tell Bond "Your pitiful little island hasn't even been threatened yet." By the time of *Tomorrow Never Dies*, the idea of Britain going to war with China seemed anachronistic to the point of absurdity.

Indeed, even the mad billionaire intent on "taking over the world" has come to appear yesterday's man. One may think of how Number Two berated Dr. Evil at the end of the first Austin Powers film, uttering a line that transcended lightweight parody to become meaningful commentary on the course of the world these last many decades:

> I spent the last thirty years of my life turning this two-bit evil empire into a world-class multi-national. I was going to have a cover story with *Forbes*. But you, like an idiot, want to take over the world. And you don't even realize that there is no world anymore! There's just corporations!

Changing mores even required Bond to rein in his high living, not least where the ladies were concerned, while the rest of the package lost something of its old fascination. Formal evening dress in the casino was already old-fashioned by the time of *Diamonds*. Circa 2000 trips to sunny Caribbean beaches hardly seemed "semi-aristocratness," which may not have been the thing anyway as fabulously wealthy playboys Bruce Wayne and Tony Stark lived it up on the screen.

Diminishing Returns at the Box Office

As has been noted here, the series peaked commercially with *Thunderball*, after which a long downward trend in the grosses set in, through the 1970s and 1980s, by which point real slippage was apparent, not just in comparison with earlier entries in the series, but with other action films.

The American box office, while never the strongest market for the Bond films, is telling. In 1981 *For Your Eyes Only* trailed not just *Raiders of the Lost Ark* and *Superman II*, but two action-comedies: *Stripes*, which featured a van packed with hidden weapons Bond-style, and the car race film *Cannonball Run*, to wind up #8 at the box office. The next film *Octopussy* did better, winding up the year's biggest action hit after *Return of the Jedi* (and #6 overall), but then the competition was weaker that year, as the next film demonstrated. Nineteen eighty-five's *A View to A Kill* only made the #13 position—well behind *Rambo: First Blood, Part II* (which despite its more restrictive R rating made over twice as much), and the *Romancing the Stone* sequel, *Jewel of the Nile*.

The next Bond film, 1987's *The Living Daylights*, was only #19, after *Beverly Hills Cop II*, *The Untouchables*, *Lethal Weapon*, *Predator* and *Robocop*. And the series hit an all-time low with 1989's *Licence to Kill*, which ended up all the way down at #36, after not only summertime box office behemoths like Tim Burton's *Batman*, *Indiana Jones and the Last Crusade* and *Lethal Weapon 2*, but the comparatively modest productions *Tango & Cash* and *Black Rain*.

It took another six years for the next film to appear. *Goldeneye* finally scored the series' first $100 million hit in the American market, long after such grosses had become routine— even requisite—for major action movies. Still, even as the Pierce Brosnan films represented an upswing in the series' commercial fortunes, they only came partway to the successes of prior years, and of other, more recent action franchises.

While making more money than *Goldeneye*, 1997's *Tomorrow Never Dies* was outgrossed not just by *Men in Black*, *The Lost World: Jurassic Park II* and *Air Force One*, but the *reissue* of the original *Star Wars*, to end up the #10 movie of the year. In 1999 *The World Is Not Enough*, a similarly strong earner, was outgrossed not just by the massive events of *Episode I* and *The Matrix*, but by *Austin Powers: The Spy Who Shagged Me*, the James Bond parody making almost twice what the actual Bond movie did, to wind up merely the fourteenth biggest earner of the year (a lower ranking than even *A View to a Kill*). And that highest-grossing movie of the Brosnan era, 2002's *Die Another Day*, appearing in the same year as *Spider-Man*, *The Lord of the Rings: The Two Towers*, *Star Wars: Episode II*, *Men in Black II*—and another Austin Powers sequel— again failed to make the year's top ten, winding up only in the #12 position behind all these films.

As the list of high-earning films makes clear, all of the smaller trends in the action movie added up to two big trends: one toward grittier, more hard-edged movies (like the American crime films, the Hong Kong martial arts films, the '80s-era paramilitary films), and more fantastic films (like the space spectaculars and superhero movies), and even films that partook of both trends, combining R-rated violence with science fiction spectacle (like *Predator*, *Robocop* and *The Matrix*). The Bond films could be seen as not enough of one or the other, leaving them laggards in the race for moviegoers' dollars and affections, even during the upswings in their fortunes.

Reboot

Following *Die Another Day*, four years passed without the release of a new Bond film as the series was, to much fanfare, "rebooted." EON had acquired the rights to *Casino Royale*, and moved to make a new film out of that book—and in the process, reconceive the James Bond films.

Casino Royale (2006)

In *Casino Royale* Bond's mission is to investigate the financing of a terrorist network, a job that initially sends him to Madagascar after a bomb maker. The clue he picks up from his cell phone leads him to the Bahamas, Miami (where Bond stops the bombing of an airliner), and finally Le Chiffre, whom it turns out has been using other people's money to speculate on the stock market, exploiting the impacts of terrorist outrages of which he has foreknowledge. The fact that the targeted airliner did not blow up threw off one such scheme, forcing Le Chiffre to recoup his money in a big game at the "Casino Royale" in Montenegro—the point in the film at which it comes to closely resemble the novel.

Just like in the book, Bond is sent to play the game and bankrupt him, with the help of the British government's own Vesper Lynd, and French agent Rene Mathis; survives assassination attempts intended to keep him from winning his game; loses his stake, but gets back in the game with the help of Felix Leiter's American money, and wins. Afterward, a desperate Le Chiffre stages Lynd's kidnapping to lure Bond into a trap, captures him, tortures him in exactly the manner described in the book in an attempt to make him give up his winnings; Bond is saved when Le Chiffre's own backers come in and kill him; and then Bond undergoes a lengthy convalescence during which he makes plans for a life with Lynd, which all come to naught because of the fact of her betrayal. Bond is angry with her, but even angrier with those who drove her to that betrayal, setting him on a course of revenge.

However, the use of the plot of the original book, with all its idiosyncracies (the centrality of the game, the torture sequence, the romance with Lynd, etc.) as the core of the film's plot is by no means the film's sole distinguishing feature. *Casino Royale* was also conceived as something of an origin story for Bond—a tale of how James Bond came to be James Bond. The movie opens with a black-and-white sequence in which he cold-bloodedly assassinates a traitorous agent of British intelligence, getting his double-o rating, after which he appears to be on his first assignment as a member of that section.

Moreover, the film is peppered with bits about how the character came into his familiar trappings. Craig's Bond gets his first Aston Martin at a gaming table during his time in the Bahamas. Additionally, while he wears the suits, Vesper Lynd gets the impression from the way he wears them that he "didn't come from money," and attended elite schools "by the grace of someone else's charity, hence the chip on [his] shoulder," which is rather conspicuous in the earlier parts of the film. (Indeed, back in the Bahamas, he was at one point mistaken for a beach club's parking attendant, a misconception that led to his taking the proffered keys and using them to crash the car handed over to his care.) He does not even care how his martinis are prepared.

More important, however, is the changed dynamic between Bond and the women on screen, altered even beyond prior concessions to changed ideas about gender. Not only is it the case that the silhouetted women are left out of the opening credits, but the flirtations with Miss Moneypenny (and indeed, Moneypenny herself) are written out, as are the casual dalliances that were a routine feature of the old films, and the bevies of beauties that had still less of a role in the story, but certainly contributed to the atmosphere.

Indeed, even the principal women show little skin. Bond's intimacy with Solange Dimitrios is cut short during preliminary making out before she has slipped off anything but her shoes. And even after Pam Bouvier-style overcompensation has come to seem the norm, Vesper Lynd still manages to stand out, Bond remarking within the script that she is doing exactly that with "masculine clothing" and a "prickly demeanor." When Bond asks her to wear a cleavage-flaunting dress to help distract the other players during the game (not implausibly for the good of the mission), she openly delights in disappointing him. The only female character who wears a bikini or anything else of the sort is in fact Le Chiffre's girlfriend Valenka, though in that too there is a change. Where Le Chiffre is mentioned as having invested in brothels for access to women as well as profit in the book, here he has apparently become a one-woman man, and in contrast with many a previous Bond film, there is no contact between Bond and Valenka—007 never seducing her the way he did Solange, for example.

Indeed, the usual pattern was reversed. In a highly publicized inversion of Honey's first appearance in *Dr. No*, it is Bond who is ogled in his swimsuit by Solange as she stood on the shore; Bond who has his body "objectified" by Lynd's remark about his "well-formed arse" and made to feel "skewered" by her unsolicited assessment of his personality at their first meeting; Bond who is stripped for torture by Le Chiffre.

In addition to the desexualization of the principal Bond girls, the film also downplays the femme fatale aspect of the original Vesper. During their mission, Vesper has occasion to play heroine, using the defibrillator in Bond's car to restart his heart after he has been poisoned. After the mission, Vesper displays none of the romance-killing neurotic behavior she did in the book, their relationship instead presented as idyllic, only the subtlest signs suggesting anything going on beneath the surface bliss, and Bond given no cause to suspect anything until the very end. Then when she finally does die by her own hand, it is not a matter of her overdosing on sleeping pills, but locking herself in the flooded elevator to drown—while the "quantum of solace" between her and Bond is still such that even after her betrayal has become evident, Bond is desperately trying to save her. Bond still utters the line "The bitch is dead," but where in the book it is the last statement uttered by Bond or anyone else, the story's last word on the matter, in the film M (whose callousness might have made one expect her to say "Good riddance" to a traitor) sharply reminds him that Vesper saved his life. The betrayal is softened, her actions made to seem more sympathetic.

There is an alteration to the pattern too in that where once upon a time Bond became involved with a good many women, some of whom ended up dead (typically because of associations, actions and agendas preceding their meeting with him), every woman he kisses in *Casino* promptly ends up dead afterward. In the end, it does not appear excessive to say that the conventional male fantasies bound up with the situation, be it the sexual fantasies to which the series tended, or the macho fantasy of toughness in the face of female manipulation this particular Bond novel derived from the tradition of hard-boiled crime, were not so much discarded as subverted by the movie's makers.

Reboot Oversold?

The novelty of the plot of the source novel, on which the film drew as no Bond film had drawn on Fleming's writing in at least a generation, the younger, coarser Bond, and the rest of these details made for a movie that seemed very far removed from the longtime EON formula. And not only did the producers' publicists trumpet the fact, but so did the entertainment industry press, which largely embraced the film, many a professional critic declaring *Casino Royale* the greatest Bond film ever made, or even the only "true" Bond film made to date.

As might be expected, many a fan of the older films was less complimentary, and the film indeed proved polarizing. (An examination of reader reviews on the Internet Movie Database web site, for example, turned up page after page of ratings of either one star at one end, or eight stars or higher at the other, with very little in between.)

Still, it is arguable that the film was very much in line with the prior pattern of change within the Bond films, both the periodic shifts in the making of new Bond films, and the longer-term trends. With a new actor in the role, coming after a Bond film that was widely criticized as bloated and silly, the filmmakers opted for a more grounded film, which like many of the grounded films, used Fleming's original material—in this case, the previously untapped *Casino Royale.*

Yet, they only went so far in this direction, with the "gritty" plot a case in point. The acknowledgment that Bondian antics like the hero's pursuit of the bomb maker Mollaka onto the grounds of a foreign embassy would create an international incident is a realistic touch. So is the parliamentary committee M has to face afterward. However, while the film is clear that Bond is fighting against "terrorism," the movie is very vague about what this means. It is not at all clear why people are blowing up airliners in the movie (what their ideology is, or what their demands are), or exactly what Le Chiffre's associates hope to gain from financing such actions—so that one can see the film as actually more divorced from real-world politics than *Die Another Day*.

Additionally, one is not quite sure how to take M's contempt-filled rant against the committee before she had to testify. Is it a matter of contempt for democracy, and for all those who would challenge the prerogatives of the security state? Or just the hypocrisy of the "self-righteous, ass-covering prigs" who "don't care what we do, just what we get photographed doing" pretending to go about their responsibilities as elected officials by grilling her? (Given the characterization, and the overall tenor of the film, M the Authoritarian Secret Police Chief seems the more likely, but the point is that there is room for doubt.)

At the same time, the broad trends toward a darker tone of cynicism-without-critique and greater brutality were evident in the harsher view of Bond's work, and Bond's torture by Le Chiffre. One can also say the same of the film's handling of Bond's sex life, and the character of Vesper Lynd—less breaks with the past than extensions of what came before. And even the element of parody that maddened so many a serious fan was not totally absent. The contrast between the "younger," rougher Bond and the established screen image—his "What the hell do I care?" when asked how he likes his martinis—works in this way.

Likewise, in choosing to reboot the series, the Bond films were also seizing on an already ongoing Hollywood trend, pushing the "reset" button to clear the way for remakes of what came before—with the practice successfully demonstrated a year and a half before *Casino*'s release in *Batman Begins*. And in opting for a more serious, grounded style of Bond film, attentive to the "micropolitics" of intelligence work (things like parliamentary oversight and public relations), the movies were not just seeing another swing of the pendulum, but following the trend set by *The Bourne Identity* in 2002, a movie which was only a middling box office hit at the time, but which saw its popularity explode on video, and its sequel, *The Bourne Supremacy*, do much better.

Moreover, such a reading of the film is reaffirmed by the two sequels. Granted, *Quantum of Solace* reflected the renewed accent on Fleming's work, utilizing not just one of his few titles as yet unused by EON, but something of its theme: Bond as an ambivalent agent of British economic interests.

Still, it is worth noting that "Quantum," a short story which spent very little of its time on action-adventure, provided little guidance, and that in developing the film's elements there was again a turn back to the mini-formulas, namely *Goldfinger*—Dominic Greene looking to pull a Bechtel, with the parallel highlighted by agent Strawberry Fields' gruesome death (in a hotel bed, covered in oil, as Jill Masterson was covered in gold). The same goes for Bond's involvement with Camille Montes (even if they never sleep together), the modest retreat from the desexualization of the previous film in Bond's brief dalliance with Fields prior to Greene's murdering her, and the film's conclusion in a battle at the villain's high-tech lair, which, sure enough, goes up in impressive explosions.

Additionally, just like *Live and Let Die* or *Moonraker* it reflected a trend in contemporary cinema, namely that for more critical, questioning spy films like *Syriana* and *Munich*, which had already been an influence on more popular, escapist fare. (The plot of 2006's *Mission: Impossible III*, for example, involved a plan to manufacture a war in the Middle East, evocative of the events of the run-up to the Iraq War.)

The earlier, vaguely conceived Quantum were revealed to be multinational capitalists intent on locking up the world's natural resources, with the water supplies of Bolivia their next target in a story inspired by the Cochabamba Water Revolt. Additionally, in contrast with the billionaire villains of yesteryear they were not looking to wreck the System, but men very much *of* the System, and using their leverage over major Western governments, Bond's own included, to get their way—so that in going rogue this time Bond has American special forces out looking to bring him down.

And of course the limits of the adjustment affirm the old pattern. The conduct of British and American intelligence is here presented as an aberration rather than as the standard operating procedure since time immemorial, with a more ethical norm of conduct restored by the movie's end. Along with the fact that *Quantum* was less well-received than its predecessor by the critics, the producers backed off the idea of making a third Bond movie with the Quantum organization as the villains. Indeed, the next film saw a broader retreat from the direction in which *Quantum* took the films—villains with global ambitions, a stronger connection with contemporary political reality—in favor of a smaller-scale adventure pitting Bond against an ex-Service member intent on personal revenge against M.

Still, *Skyfall*, despite being the first post-reboot film not using a Fleming title, did have something of the books in it, particularly the unexploited aspects of the original *You Only Live Twice* and *Man with the Golden Gun*. Just as in those books Bond was given up for dead, and then came back to a suspicious Service, into whose good graces he has to earn his way back with a dangerous task that requires him to recover a lost edge. There is something of *Golden Gun*, too, in the fact that the redemptive mission has him targeting a specific figure, and at that, a man of Latin background and exceptional handiness with a gun, Silva.

Skyfall also continued the series' attentiveness to action film trends, seizing on one established by that other franchise from whose book the producers had already taken a leaf, the rebooted Batman—with much of the plot structure of *Skyfall* modeled on *The Dark Knight*. The villain Silva was conceived as a Joker to Bond's Batman, a shadow figure intent on pushing him to the breaking point. Additionally, Silva's plan entailed his letting himself be captured midway through the film to the end of giving himself an opportunity to wreak greater havoc.

Also true to past form, the manner in which this was handled repeated the pattern of prior films—interestingly, films far less often treated as a model than the '60s-era selections. Silva evoked the film version of Scaramanga even more than the book version, in his operating out of an island in Southeast Asia, and having in his thrall a beautiful woman who will turn to Bond for protection, which he will fail to provide. It also evoked that film's Chinese connection, Bond having to go to Macao in pursuit of him (even if Silva's relationship with the People's Republic was more antagonistic).

The continuities are particularly apparent in the film's heavy accent on callousness, betrayal and blowback, which strongly recall the Brosnan-era films. M's attitude toward Bond when he comes back recalls not just Fleming's *Golden Gun*, but also *Die Another Day*. Silva's revenge campaign parallels that of *Goldeneye*'s Alec Trevelyan in his being an ex-Service member abandoned to a Communist enemy state who feels a kinship with Bond (in this case, not as a comrade, but a favored brother), and his plan's heavy reliance on a cyber-attack. It likewise reuses an element from *The World Is Not Enough*, Silva bombing Service headquarters early in the film, and then drawing M out in the field, to confront her personally as he holds her in his power, as Bond rushes to the rescue.

More broadly, the delay of the third Daniel Craig movie's production and release to 2012 created a special marketing opportunity in the treatment of a movie put out that year as a fiftieth anniversary event. The result was that where earlier the accent had been on the new films as a fresh start, the filmmakers now endeavored to strengthen the connection of the new Bond films with the old, evoking them at every turn. They wrote in Q and Moneypenny again, and included the old gadget-packed Aston Martin in a twist that was much more nostalgic than logical. At film's end, Moneypenny is not a field agent anymore, but stationed at the desk outside M's office—an old-fashioned wood-and-leather office more evocative of the Connery-Moore films than its sleek modern look in the Brosnan-Craig era, and occupied by an ex-military man once more. Nor was this the only way in which they broke with the pattern of the most recent films, contradicting the impression *Casino Royale* gave of Bond's humbler origins by having him hail from the sort of old Scottish family that would have an estate like the titular "Skyfall." Seen in the context of the film's other more novel elements, these could in fact be seen as part of another, still sharper shift in the films—a quiet reboot of the reboot.

Bond Belongs to the Ages?

In having Bond get knocked down and then get back up again, *Skyfall* was not just a story of regeneration, but an affirmation of Bond's relevance, which made its case for relevancy in very specific ways. Where in earlier films Bond tended to fight his battles abroad, the action rarely touching British soil, the second half of the film is set entirely within Britain, with the fight raging from Westminister Palace, through the streets of London and the Underground beneath it, and even to the Scottish estate on which Bond was raised.

Then, following his triumph, Bond is seen on a London rooftop, surveying the city's skyline much as comic book superheroes do the cities in which they live out their lives and have their adventures—Superman in Metropolis, Batman in Gotham, Spiderman in New York. The shot pointedly includes that icon of London and of Britishness, Saint Stephen's Tower, and a fluttering Union Jack. It is an unprecedented localization of the character, going further than ever to mark Bond—imperial policeman, agent of the Western alliance, anti-Communist Cold Warrior, international counter-terrorist—as above all else the protector and hero of *Britain*. And of course, this historically-loaded, symbol-packed shot suggests Britain not just as a contemporary state or its citizens, but, as the centuries-old domes in the fore suggest, an ancient, enduring *nation*. At the same time the parallel drawn between Bond and the comic book superheroes identifies him with something broader, suggested in M's reading from Tennyson's "Ulysses." A parallel can be drawn between Tennyson's poem's affirmation of an old hero ("that which we are, we are; One equal temper of heroic hearts") and the affirmation of Bond's own continued significance, the more so because of the handling of the climax. Like Ulysses, Bond returns to the family manor after a long absence from it, which turns out to have been in the care of an old loyalist awaiting his return, and almost singlehandedly slays those who had presumed to attack him in it. Bond destroys the manor buildings at film's end, but nonetheless, following the act, following his return to the capital and to the new headquarters (his true home, in a sense), one can see him as having finally "come home" again. Bond as comic book superhero and latter-day Ulysses—especially when he happens to hail from a mist-shrouded wilderness seemingly untouched by the modern world—is an unprecedentedly mythic, universalized, timeless Bond.

Whatever one makes of this image of Bond as both more British than ever before, or more mythically universal than ever before, there is no question that *Skyfall* was a massive commercial success. It did not bring back 60s Spymania, but it made almost as much money as the prior two hits films put together, broke the billion-dollar barrier, and became the series' highest-grossing film, not just in nominal dollar terms, but in *inflation-adjusted* dollars smashing *Thunderball*'s nearly half-century old record. It was similarly successful with critics, receiving five American Academy Award nominations—all in technical areas (score, song, editing, mixing, cinematography), rather than the more prestigious areas of acting, writing or direction, but still a reflection of the critical esteem the film enjoyed, which extended to a tribute to that series at that year's ceremony.

It would be impossible to conceive of a stronger encouragement to EON to stay the course, and so for the first time since the 1980s, the producers had the same director stick around for the next film, Sam Mendes brought back to make 2015's *Spectre*. As of the time of this writing the release of the film is several months away, but one may expect that the pattern will prevail. The films will remain more grounded, darker in tone; still make their concessions to changes in mores. However, in a title indicating that they are bringing back Bond's most famous adversary, it seems the filmmakers will continue to embrace the series' tradition rather than distance themselves from it. Along with the report that the next film will see a terrorist attack in London itself, targeting Big Ben itself; that the film's villain will have a connection with Bond's past (Franz Oberhauser apparently inspired by Hannes Oberhauser from "Octopussy"); it seems plausible that the movement in the direction of a Bond at once more rootedly British and more mythically universal will continue—at least, until the producers see how the audience responds to it.

9. THE POST-FLEMING JAMES BOND NOVELS

The long history of authorized continuations of the James Bond novels can be divided into two periods. The first began with Kingsley Amis (under the pseudonym Robert Markham) in 1968, and continued through the work of John Gardner and Raymond Benson until Benson's final novel, *The Man with the Red Tattoo*. The second may be thought of as having begun with the first authorized new Bond novel, Sebastian Faulks' *Devil May Care*, and continuing up to the present.

Amis, Gardner, Benson

The work of the writers who produced new, authorized Bond novels between 1968 and 2002 was characterized by authors taking Ian Fleming's Bond—the Bond of his novels, with his past, his baggage, his limitations—and continuing his adventures in the present-day world. Amis' *Colonel Sun*, for example, picked up the tale a year after the events of *The Man with the Golden Gun*. Gardner's tenure, which began with 1981's *Licence Renewed*, explicitly situated Bond within the 1980s, while his successor Benson pointedly set his first James Bond adventure, 1997's *Zero Minus Ten*, against the backdrop of Hong Kong's return to China.

Of course, this presented some continuity problems. By 2002, Bond would have been a double-o for a very implausible six decades. These writers usually dealt with the issue by being as vague about the dates of past events (like Bond's battle with Drax or SPECTRE), while making slight concessions to the passage of time. In *Licence Renewed*, for example, Gardner informs the reader that "Minute flecks of grey had just started to show in the dark hair."[1]

Screen Treatment, Novel, or Both?

More fundamental, however, was the problem of keeping the adventures interesting, especially in a context where Bond was so much more defined by the image of the films; and where the films, moreover, had redefined the thriller, in print as well as on screen. The Fleming novels inspired the Bond movies, but the Bond movies created the action film as we know it with their accelerated pacing and plenitude of elaborate set pieces. In their turn, this style of filmmaking shaped the thriller novel, which was also expected to be faster-paced, and to give much more time and attention to scenes of elaborate action, as with the novels of the later Clive Cussler, or the still later Matthew Reilly—next to which Fleming's original novel seem comparatively slow and lacking in action.

This was all less of a problem for Amis, picking up the books shortly after Fleming himself, when all this was much less advanced. Still, the films were certainly a factor in his writing, arguably affecting his handling of the action in the books. Granted, Amis handled it in a brutal, at times gory fashion more like that of the Fleming novels (including Bond's subjection to torture), and avoided the gimmicks and grand scale that increasingly characterized the films. (Like the preceding year's film *You Only Live Twice*, *Colonel Sun* depicted a Chinese plot to bait and bleed the West and the Soviet Union—but one utilizing a trench mortar, not a space program!) Additionally, in contrast with the on-rush of fights, explosions and chases that often strained the structure and plausibility of the films to the breaking point, the book remained a plot-centered thriller with action, rather than a collection of action sequences strung together by a semblance of a plot. Still, that the action got started earlier than is usual for a Fleming novel with the scene in which M was kidnapped from his home, and the relative abundance of the violence from that point on, seem like concessions to the standard set by the movies.

However, by and large Amis reacted *against* the films rather than embracing their style, consistently highlighting those aspects of the books that the movies played down, or entirely elided. *Colonel Sun* actually opens with Bond playing a golf game with Bill Tanner, and wondering if he is not going soft. In line with his personal loyalty to M, now ailing, he then visits him at his home, with his drive over an occasion to display a rather unattractive snobbery. Passing new housing developments on the way over he disdains the "ugly rash of modern housing—half-heartedly mock-Tudor villas, bungalows and two-storey boxes . . . the inevitable TV aerial sprouting from every roof." The sight of a British European Airways jetliner overhead makes him think of "tourists bearing their fish-and-chip culture to the Spanish resorts, to Portugal's lovely Algarve province, and now, as the range of development schemes grew ever wider, as far as Morocco." (The lower orders taking holidays abroad! Horror of horrors!) Bond's age and his Toryism are thrown into still sharper relief by the plot's requiring him to ally with Greek Communist Ariadne Alexandrou in his fight against the titular villain.

This is particularly pointed where the question of Bond as a gadget-using secret agent is concerned. Before he is sent off to Athens, Bond is given a pair of shoes with special heels—one of which contains a transmitter that will enable the Service to track him, while the other has a lock-pick and hacksaw blades he can use to free himself if he is restrained in the other. Low-key as these seem, Bond is dubious about them from the start, and indeed they do not come into play in the novel, even when he actually does get captured and tied up. Lest the reader miss the irony, at the end Litsas jokes that Bond's suit "is full of little radios and concealed cameras and things," giving him occasion to reflect that he "had been right about [the gadgets'] irrelevance, their uselessness when the crunch came."

When it was Gardner's turn to write the Bond novels, he followed a similar pattern, writing thrillers with action for the most part, though the concessions were larger. The first of his novels, *Licence Renewed* strongly recalled the classic films of the '60s— Bond's attempt to escape Anton Murik's estate in his modified Saab 900 recalling *Goldfinger*'s famous car chase, while the foot chase through Perpignan during the festival of Old St. John bringing to mind the Junkanoo sequence in *Thunderball*. Additionally, while few of the books went quite so far in the direction of the films as that, many a bit was written in the same spirit, from Bond's flying combat aircraft in *Win, Lose or Die* and *Cold Fall*, to his one-man attack on a submarine in *SeaFire*. However, his Bond remained more senior civil servant than cinematic superman, with more physical and mental vulnerability than the screen version, and a tendency to make near-fatal errors and wind up enduring terrible tortures.

To a large extent this was also the case with Gardner's successor Benson, though by this point the Bond of the films was clearly getting the upper hand. This was most obviously the case in the increasing depiction of over-the-top action that culminated in *Never Dream of Dying*. However, to some extent it also manifested in alterations to the character, Benson's version somewhat more ruthless in action than his predecessors, certainly where cold-blooded murder is concerned. When Bond kills in this manner, Benson tells the reader in *DoubleShot*,

> He felt absolutely nothing. Bond had once again transformed himself into the blunt instrument of death, something which he had been able to do at will ever since he began his career in government service. When he did it, Bond shut himself

off from every possible emotion and performed the task coldly and objectively.

Benson also had a greater tendency to evoke the films, and not always in the mocking ways to which Amis was prone. In *DoubleShot* Benson describes the Union's conference room as "decorated in reflective sheet metal"—an implausible detail which serves no purpose but to recall SPECTRE's conference room in *Thunderball*.

Keeping Up With the Times: Thriller Trends and Geopolitics

In their additions to the series these later writers not only imitated the films, but in a style similar to that of the movies, drew on contemporary trends in the thriller, and on contemporary headlines for inspiration. The tendency to follow such fashions was primarily evident in Gardner's work. In the early 1980s, with the explosion of video gaming, not just in the arcades but on the movie screens (*WarGames* becoming a major hit, and even the non-EON Bond film *Never Say Never Again* prominently including a gaming sequence), Gardner made the theme central to *Role of Honor*. *Win, Lose or Die*, which had Bond return to duty in the Navy aboard the carrier HMS *Invincible*, clearly drew on the success of *Top Gun* on the big screen, and the popularity of military techno-thrillers. *Never Send Flowers*, which had Bond hunting a serial killer, was clearly a response to the then-recent success of *The Silence of the Lambs*.

More broadly, broadly, Gardner's books from *Nobody Lives Forever* on tended toward smaller-scale plots, often focusing on the assassination or kidnap of public figures, as in *Win, Lose or Die*, *Death is Forever* and *Never Send Flowers*. It was much the same with Benson's work as well. After two plots involving nuclear weapons threats in *Zero Minus Ten* and *The Facts of Death*, his Union trilogy concentrated on smaller-scale villainy—in *High Time to Kill*, a piece of industrial espionage.

However, all three authors were highly attentive to the headlines. Where Fleming had not made serious use of China as a villain within the series, Amis seized on China's rise in *Colonel Sun* to present it as the true threat to peace as relations between the West and the Soviet Union grew more amicable.

Later, Gardner utilized concerns about the safety of nuclear reactors and '70s and '80s-style international terrorism in his earlier books. In *Licence Renewed* he went so far as to present a then-fashionable Carlos the Jackal imitation, "Franco," in the employ of the villainous Murik. Indeed, terrorism took such precedence over the Cold War that Murik's plan was presented as a menace to the Communist bloc as well as the West, an East German power plant being among those targeted by his henchmen.

Moreover, Gardner tended to tie in his resurrected SPECTRE and SMERSH with more contemporary concerns. *Icebreaker*, for example, integrated SMERSH's continued pursuit of Bond with an intrigue surrounding a neo-Nazi terrorist plot; while the revived SPECTRE of Tamil Rahani is linked with leftist and Middle Eastern international terrorism in *Role of Honor*.

As the spectre of such terrorism faded, and the Cold War with it, Gardner set them aside and based his plots on the post-Cold War. The conference in *Win, Lose or Die* was made possible by glasnost. The next novel, *Brokenclaw*, turned its attention away from the Soviets, toward post-Cold War concern with the still substantial military power of China, and the prospect of economic warfare with Japan. *Death is Forever* had die-hard Stalinists contriving to resurrect international Communism, and a climax in the Chunnel; in the wake of German reunification, economic downturn and flaring concern with neo-fascism, *SeaFire* had Bond fighting neo-Nazis again; and *Cold Fall* had Bond doing battle with an American militia.

This even went as far as the incorporation of real-life political figures into the tales, most pointedly *Win, Lose or Die*. The conference aboard the *Invincible* is held not between generic, nameless depictions of the British, American and Soviet leaders, but very specifically Margaret Thatcher, George H.W. Bush and Mikhail Gorbachev, each of whom meets Bond and exchanges a few words with him on their arrival aboard the ship.

In line with the attention to current geopolitics, the later novels also reflected Britain's more modest global profile. Much more of the action took place in Britain itself, as in Gardner's *Licence Renewed, Role of Honor, No Deals, Mr. Bond, Scorpius, Win, Lose or Die, Never Send Flowers* and *SeaFire*. Additionally, Bond's overseas trips tended to be to places closer to home, or last legacies of Britain's imperial history. *No Deals*, for example, has Bond going over the border into Ireland, and then stages the finale in Hong Kong. The final showdown of *Win, Lose or Die* happens on Gibraltar.

Additionally, when Bond went further afield, there tended to be a special reason. A common one was a joint initiative with the United States, as with the joint counterintelligence effort against a Chinese spy in *Brokenclaw*, or the search after the mysterious fate of an Anglo-American spy ring in *Death is Forever*. Otherwise the mission tended to be of a more idiosyncratic nature, as with Bond's trip to Switzerland in *Never Send Flowers* to investigate the death of an agent of MI 5. Characteristically, that assignment did not have Bond freely traveling the Swiss countryside looking for answers and piling up bodies, but rather working closely with the local authorities.

It was much the same with Benson, situating his first adventure against the backdrop of Hong Kong's return to China. Indeed, rather more than Gardner he made a point of incorporating legacies of Britain's earlier great power status into his plots, as in his own use of Hong Kong in *Zero Minus Ten*, and Gibraltar in *DoubleShot*, as well as Cyprus (where Britain retains a base presence) in *The Facts of Death*. Even where Britain no longer had a genuine presence, as in the Indian and Nepali settings of *High Time to Kill*, there was an evocation of the imperial past, of which a present-day legacy was the Gurkha Regiment member Chandra, who accompanies Bond on his mission in that country.

Keeping Up With the Times: Lifestyle

The continuation novels reflected the tendency of the films in another way, their depiction of Bond's lifestyle, Gardner remarking the fact early in *Licence*:

> Bond had even managed to alter his lifestyle . . . drastically cutting back—for most of the time-on his alcohol intake, and arranging with More-lands of Grosvenor Street for a new special blend of cigarettes, with a tar content slightly lower than any currently available on the market.

Later, he gave up smoking altogether, only picking up a cigarette when he felt himself to be under exceptional stress, as in *Cold Fall*. Moreover, the changes were not restricted to his smoking and drinking, but also manifesting in his sex life. Where in *Moonraker* Fleming had given the reader to understand that in between missions this typically meant "making love, with rather cold passion, to one of three similarly disposed married women," *Licence* had Bond looking forward to a weekend with "a girl friend of long standing."

Of course, long association does not necessarily mean monogamy, as demonstrated when Bond visits Q'ute's apartment. With the touch of a button she seems to turn the place into a swinger's pad, and put herself into nothing but a "thin, translucent nightdress" by an elaborate holographic illusion. Bond takes hold of her, kisses her—but she pushes him away and then replies about the "1960s' fantasy: music, lights, the waterbed, scent, and an available bird with very few clothes on" that:

> "I thought you of all people, James Bond, would have got the message. Fantasies should change with the times. Surely

we're all more realistic these days. Particularly about relationships. The word is, I think, maturity."

What follows is hot coffee. (Actual hot coffee, not a euphemism.) The next chapter opens with Bond waking up—alone, and in his own apartment, the scene over at Q'ute's not merely a joke, but a taunt to Bond, and to readers holding certain expectations about what his life ought to be. And of course, being not-quite-legal, Peacock Lavender, the novel's principal Bond girl, can give him no consolation, so that he ends the story womanless. In fairness, he does eventually get Q'ute into bed, sleeping with her early in *For Special Services*, but on the whole he is not the sexual adventurer he once was. Indeed, in *Never Send Flowers*, Bond not only works with a female agent, but begins a relationship with her that makes Bond firmly one-half of a couple through not just the remainder of the book, but the follow-up *SeaFire*, and into Gardner's final novel, *Cold Fall*.

Tied up with this was also a changed attitude toward gender broadly, which manifested itself in ways besides frustrating encounters such as the one just related. When SPECTRE comes back in the next novel, *For Special Services*, it is with Blofeld's own daughter, "Nena Bismaquer," at its head (a female arch-villain for Bond, seventeen years before the movies presented Elektra King). Additionally, that novel's borrowings from *Goldfinger* put a twist on Bond's effect on Pussy Galore—changing the gender of the villain whose attraction to Bond causes them to switch sides, the not entirely heterosexual Markus Bismaquer sabotaging the hypnosis to which his wife Nena subjected Bond, permitting him to save the day. Later, in Gardner's last book, *Cold Fall*, Sir Miles Messervy was replaced by a woman, a pattern Benson continued in his own books.

Self-Parody

Of course, episodes like those involving Q'ute and Markus Bismaquer suggest self-parody. And as might be expected, there was no small amount of that in the books, starting with Amis' own *Colonel Sun*—where the bits of parody are all the more pointed because of Amis' previously having made his opinions clear in the *James Bond Dossier*. Amis frankly disliked M ("a peevish, priggish old monster") and wanted to "take him down a peg" by sticking him in harm's way and seeing him helpless—so he presented him in failing health, getting kidnapped and contributing nothing to saving the day.

In the *Dossier* Amis also took issue with the common charge that the James Bond novels were sadistic, and as if saying "You think that's sadistic? I'll show you *sadistic*," came up with the series' most ostentatiously sadistic villain to date in the titular villain, a devotee of the Marquis De Sade who is prolix about his interests in this area, and whose torturing Bond is not about extracting information he needs from Bond, but *entirely about the pleasure he intends to derive from the torture*. (Indeed, Sun was ordered by his superiors to prise as much information out of Bond as possible before killing him, but chooses to disobey in favor of the chance to explore De Sade's theory about the "uplift" such an experience can produce.) Something of this sensibility is also evident in the abuse inflicted on Ariadne Alexandrou, whose sufferings at the hands of Sun's henchmen extend to rape—a fate never before suffered by a Bond girl during an adventure.

There is, too, the British government's reaction to the kidnapping for comedy in the response of Cabinet Minister Sir Ronald Rideout, and Amis' even more brutal mockery of the Soviets. Out in the field, the principal obstacle to Bond and his allies' stopping the villain's plot is less the evil genius of Sun than the extreme stupidity and equally extreme, conniving careerism of the KGB General who should have been the first to help them— Colonel-General Igor Arenski, who is actually introduced in a chapter titled "General Incompetence." (And while it might be construed as parody of the films rather than of the novels, one can read the uselessness of Bond's gadgets in the same way.)

The plot of Gardner's *Licence Renewed* is, if anything, more parodic than that. The madman Anton Murik, after all, is a nuclear physicist so alarmed by the danger of nuclear meltdowns that he demands fifty billion dollars with which to build a prototype of a new, safe reactor of his design—or his terrorists will promptly engineer meltdowns at several different reactors around the world. And so it goes from novel to novel, from the day-saving twist in *For Special Services*, to the wedding in which Bond is forced to participate while infiltrating a cult in *Scorpius*, to the elaborate deception and counter-deception to which Bond is subject in Italy in *Win, Lose or Die*. Moreover, Gardner often hinted that he was aware of the silliness of his plots. In *Role of Honor*, when Tamil Rahani lets Bond in on his plan, he remarks that

> "We're not talking about stories dreamed up by pulp novelists. No blackmail through concealed nuclear devices hidden in the heart of great Western cities; no plots to kidnap the President, or hold the world to ransom by setting all the major currencies at naught."

Of course, Fleming had already used two of these three scenarios, targeting great Western cities with nuclear weapons in *Moonraker* and *Thunderball*, and attacking the foundation of the free world's monetary system with yet another nuclear bomb in *Goldfinger*. And Gardner himself used the third, the kidnapping of the President, in *Win, Lose or Die*, with the irrationality of the scheme actually acknowledged by Bond's own remarks about it in the book. (Just how was the six hundred billion dollar ransom that BAST demanded to be paid? Bond asks, and never gets an answer.)

Of course, self-parody in the novels did not begin with Amis or Gardner; as shown here, Fleming was prone to this himself, right down to the metafiction, as when he had Bond read the *Mask of Dimitrios* on his flight to Istanbul (a hint that Bond is going to get himself tangled up in a business he should have avoided), or, later in that same novel, Red Grant telling Bond that "No Bulldog Drummond stuff'll get you out of this one."

It might be said, too, that the ironic, sardonic aspect of Fleming's attitude toward his creation was evident in the way they parodied the character. It is not inconceivable that Fleming could have written a character like Colonel Sun, or, in a moment of boredom or frustration with the series, even subjected Bond to the dizzying central plot twist of *Win, Lose or Die*. Still, Rideout and Arenski, and even Ariadne, seem more like the creations of the man who became famous with *Lucky Jim*, and then "turned right."

One can say the same of Gardner, and explain the bits not quite in line with what Fleming did through reference to his blending of book and film in an era when the movies were especially parodic. (Certainly Gardner was not inattentive to these. Aboard an airline flight in *Scorpius* Bond notices that *The Untouchables* is the in-flight movie, and while he had already seen it, "Bond sat through it again," because a "favorite actor of his played a Chicago cop.")

Still, Gardner's comedy also has quirks not attributable to either source, not least in Bond's suddenly becoming a far more cultured individual given to quoting poetry or the Bible, and enough of a theater buff to come up with an on-the-spot parody of Gilbert and Sullivan as guests arrive aboard the *Invincible*. (That Gardner was both an ex-priest, and a former theater critic, would seem to have much more to do with these traits than any interpretation of the character.)

Benson, too, included an element of humor in the books, though in this respect the books again reflected the films more than the writing of his predecessors—as with the farce involving Heidi and Hedy Taunt in *DoubleShot*. At times, Benson even played off of the movies. In *High Time to Kill*, when Bond is summoned to the Situation Room for an emergency briefing, he cynically mutters that "Someone probably lost a contact lens"—an evocation of Bond's quip that "Someone probably lost a dog" in the screen version of *Thunderball*.

Faulks, Deaver, Boyd, and More

As the decades wore on, the strain of continuing the Bond adventures increasingly showed. There was, on the one hand, a resort to heavy repetition of prior elements. Gardner revived SPECTRE and SMERSH, while Benson created a new organization strongly resembling both in his Union trilogy. At times, there were rather close borrowings from the plot structures of earlier Bond books. Featuring a San Francisco Chinatown equivalent of Mr. Big, *Brokenclaw* was an obvious update of *Live and Let Die*, while with its vengeful, damaged Bond trying to clear his name, Benson's *DoubleShot* contained much of *You Only Live Twice* and *The Man with the Golden Gun*.

At the same, such innovation as appeared required the abandonment of all those things that made the Bond adventures distinct. Gardner's *Role of Honor* featured SPECTRE, but with its very public disgrace of the character (even if it is just part of his cover), its months-long mission, and immersion of Bond in the digital age (he even learns to code), it scarcely feels like a Bond novel at all. Indeed, this could be said of most of the books from the late '80s on, whether one is looking at Bond's battle with a chiliastic cult of suicide bombers in *Scorpius*, the Bond-meets-Top Gun of *Win, Lose or Die*, or the serial killers, stage drama-soaked narrative and Euro-Disneyland climax of *Never Send Flowers*. This pattern persisted in Benson's books, like the similarly uncharacteristic mountain climbing-cum-industrial espionage adventure *High Time to Kill*.

Also as happened in the case of the films, the regular production of the novels stopped in 2002, and then resumed several years later—while sharply changing course. The first writer, Sebastian Faulks in *Devil May Care*, took Bond back to the '60s in a period adventure—like Amis forty years earlier, picking up Bond's tale after the battle with Scaramanga in *Devil May Care*. Immediately afterward Jeffrey Deaver swung about in the opposite direction by presenting a 007 born in 1979 and fully a creature of the present, rather than a vaguely ageless version of Fleming's creation. Right after that, William Boyd penned another adventure extending the story of Fleming's original Bond up to 1969.

However, whether the story was set in the 1960s or the 2000s, certain consistencies prevailed. The action varied from author to author, but, Faulks' effort apart, the tendency toward smaller-scale plots more mindful of thriller fashions prevailed. Deaver's Severan Hydt is a businessman in the waste disposal industry who exploits its opportunities for trafficking in intelligence, and dabbling in terror for hire, rather than an aspirant to Blofeld-style villainy. Boyd, in sending Bond to Africa, embroils him in the visceral horrors and shabby oil politics of a Biafra-like humanitarian disaster, with a little drug smuggling thrown in—not altogether unlike the film version of *Quantum of Solace*.

There is, too, the tendency toward cynicism-without-critique so prevalent in the Bond films from the '90s on. *Carte Blanche* depicts Bond as operating within a world of extraordinary renditions and state-sanctioned torture, of Dirty Harry-like disdain for civil liberties and government plants of misinformation in the media, and his Bond (unlike Fleming's) never has any doubts about it. Boyd's *Solo* has its hero simply shrug at the nasty business in which he was caught up.

And of course, there were the changes in the handling of Bond's lifestyle. It is unsurprising, for example, that Deaver's Bond is an ex-smoker who sternly admonishes his colleagues for smoking and drinking on the job. However, the shift back to an earlier period does little to provide *Mad Men*-like relief from the constraints of contemporary health-consciousness and gender politics, with Bond's hedonistic flair suffering accordingly. In Faulks' book Bond turns down an attractive woman's offer to go up to her room early in the book, and then rejects another offer in the Paradise Club. Boyd similarly has Bond celebrate his birthday alone.

So does it go with gender more generally. It may be predictable enough that Moneypenny (identified as a Royal Navy lieutenant) "keeps [Bond] in his place," their relationship friendly rather than flirtatious, and that the same can also be said of Mary Goodnight (not his secretary, but his *personal assistant* now); that Bond only pines for his engaged Ophelia Maidenstone; that the principal "Bond girl," Bheka Jordaan, is thoroughly unpleasant to the hero, and their dining together strictly Platonic; or even that Bond goes out on lousy dates, at the start of the book feeling some relief at being given an out from listening to an artist go on about how underappreciated she is when the office calls and affords him an escape. However, in Faulks' book Scarlett also turns out to be the first woman to join the double-o section (a thing one would imagine unthinkable on old M's watch).

In various ways the authors, again, demonstrated the strain of producing new Bond novels. As Faulks demonstrated, taking Bond back to the '60s (in which May gossips about the Rolling Stones, and M is taking up yoga) does not quite transport him back far enough, the man already out of his time. Treating that decade as a starting point for new adventures is still worse. While previous writers had tended to keep Bond vaguely ageless, Boyd pointedly writes him as a forty-five year-old World War II veteran by having him mark the event with a luxurious hotel stay. (And of course, Fleming offered ample reason to think Bond was rather older than that.)

Deaver's effort indicated another problem, namely the change in the *dimensions* of popular novels. In Fleming's day, 60,000 words was considered a perfectly adequate length for such a book. By the 1980s, this was no longer the case, and Gardner and Benson's somewhat longer narratives reflect the fact. By contrast, *Carte Blanche* is four hundred rather packed pages in the hardcover edition—forcing considerable changes to the style of the plotting. His story involves not one but *two*, separate villainous schemes that turn out to intersect, as well as a smaller, third storyline revolving around an ultimately unrelated vendetta, *and* a mystery which may shed light on the death of Bond's parents. The novel is also heavy on the kind of bureaucratic game play that comprises an increasing share of the spy thriller's content in recent decades, even when the villains are the usual external ones. (Indeed, MI 5 has never before given Bond such grief, for such poor reasons.)

To date none of these authors has produced a second book. Indeed, the zigzags described here, from Faulks' '60s adventure, to the contemporary setting of *Carte Blanche*, to Boyd's return to 1969, give an impression of a franchise searching for a new way to keep itself going, and not quite finding it so far—the print reboot to date less successful than its cinematic counterpart.

Perhaps unsurprisingly in light of such difficulties, the series is at this time changing tacks yet again, not only with respect to author, but to concept. The next book, due out in September 2015, will see Anthony Horowitz write a Bond novel, *Trigger Mortis*—set just two weeks after the events of *Goldfinger*. If those reports are accurate, it takes 007 back to before even that battle with Scaramanga, into the '50s, and hints at an intriguing idea: Bond's being eternally a creature of the era in which he was actually conceived, just as Sherlock Holmes forever walks the gas-lit streets of late Victorian London.

10. ODDS AND ENDS

Simply trying to catalog the history of James Bond in print after Fleming can make one's head spin, especially when one considers spin-offs of the series, and unauthorized work, which extends to parodies actually using the Bond character himself. The first full-length, non-Fleming James Bond novel is not Kingsley Amis' *Colonel Sun*, but Harvard Lampoon's *Alligator* (1962). Not very long after, Bulgarian writer Andrei Gulyashki, reportedly at the behest of the KGB, devoted a volume of his Avakum Zakhov series to a battle with Bond, *Avakum Zakhov Versus 07* (1966), which depicted the titular Zakhov taking on and beating 007.

Also before *Colonel Sun* came along there was a prior effort authorized by Fleming's estate, Geoffrey Jenkins' *Per Fine Ounce* (1967), which was ultimately rejected for publication, and R.D. Mascott's *The Adventures of James Bond Junior 003½* (1967), which *did* get into print. And recent years have seen spin-off series', official and unofficial, acquire the mass of a library in their own right, with works like the young adult *Young James Bond* series, *The Moneypenny Diaries* series, and Mabel Maney's Jane Bond novels, about Bond's hitherto unmentioned lesbian bookstore owner sister, who gets called in because 007 had "gotten sloppy," and similarly has a "way with the ladies."

Managing the history of Bond in other media can be comparably challenging. That a James Bond comic strip ran in *The Daily Express* for twenty-five years is obscure enough information now; that Takao Saito converted four James Bond novels into manga before producing his own massively successful secret agent character (super-gunman Golgo 13) is far more so.[1]

And while the field has long been replete with James Bond parodies, one is not quite sure what to make of works which make one wonder about copyright infringement like 1967's *Operation Kid Brother*—an Italian movie in which the protagonist is not just supposed to be James Bond's kid brother, but is actually played by Sean Connery's real-life younger brother Neil, while also starring the actors who played M, Miss Moneypenny, Tatiana Romanova, Emilio Largo and Professor Dent in the official EON series (Bernard Lee, Lois Maxwell, Daniela Bianchi, Adolfo Celi and Anthony Dawson)? Or Bernard Lee appearing as M and Lois Maxwell appearing as Moneypenny in the 1975 French film *From Hong Kong With Love*? Or for that matter 2012's short film *Happy and Glorious*, a piece of publicity for the London Olympics of that year in which Daniel Craig plays Bond—and Queen Elizabeth plays herself?

Still, even if there is a vast body of marginal work with a connection to the Bond franchise, virtually unknown except to those who make a point of chasing such oddities, there *are* a few works which, because of their official status and special place in series' history, warrant greater attention in a book like this. One is the one-hour version of *Casino Royale* CBS made for American television in 1954. The first-ever translation of Bond to another medium, it is also interesting as an American response to the character.

Another would be the two non-EON Bond films, namely 1967's *Casino Royale*, and 1983's *Never Say Never Again*, each a major feature film legally produced from the original material which went on to be widely viewed. While neither can be said to have really altered the course of the series on screen, it can be said that *Casino Royale* at least *anticipated* some aspects of the films' development in the 1970s, while also having an underrated cultural impact. *Never Say Never Again* also has some interest as a second effort to realize *Thunderball* on screen, while also being notable as an update and Americanization of the material.

Finally, there are the novelizations of Bond films produced by Christopher Wood, John Gardner and Raymond Benson—authorized adaptations of official EON productions by a screenwriter who worked on the films, and two of the authors tasked with writing official continuations to the Fleming books. Christopher Wood's books are of particular interest because they are especially apt to be overlooked, but also because their constituting a "second" *Spy Who Loved Me* and *Moonraker* reflects some of the problems the filmmakers had adapting some of Fleming's material—pointed up by the substantial differences between even these books and the film versions. The novelizations by Gardner and Benson are also of interest as reflecting their takes on the character with which they worked, and the interaction between movie Bond and book Bond, also brought out in the differences between the films and their novelizations.

Casino Royale (1954)

The United States was first exposed to James Bond when Macmillan published Ian Fleming's *Casino Royale* there a year after its first appearance in Britain. The reviews were underwhelming, the sales slow. Still, it was the United States, not Britain, which saw the first screen version of a Bond novel when producer Gregory Ratoff optioned it and used it as the basis for an October 21, 1954 episode of CBS' mystery anthology series *Climax!*

The episode demonstrated the limitations of television—and especially, 1950s-era television—as a medium for telling this story. One reason is the limited scale of the nearly play-like production, which cannot convey those essential traits of a Bond adventure, exotic settings and action. Filmed entirely on a sound stage, the entirety of the episode is set within the grounds of the hotel/casino where Bond confronts Le Chiffre. The attempt by the Bulgarians to kill Bond with a bomb is changed to a failed attempt to shoot him as he enters the complex, and there is no car chase. And of course, one can only convey so much luxury and glamour in this manner.

There was, too, the problem posed by the story's more risqué material, which was largely excised. In place of the original torture scene, Bond is fully dressed in a bathtub (feet excepted) as Le Chiffre tears out his toenails with a pair of pliers—while there is no question of our hero being saved by the killers from SMERSH. Bond manages to get free, get hold of a gun and shoot Le Chiffre (off-screen) to save himself. And of course, it turns out that "the girl" was only pretending to betray the good guys, clearing the way for her and Bond to get a happy ending.

On top of all this, the material is substantially Americanized. Thus the English gentlemanly, martini-drinking James Bond of the British Secret Service is here presented as swaggering, scotch-and-water drinking American "Jimmy" Bond of "Combined Intelligence" (an obvious CIA stand-in), played by Barry Nelson. Meanwhile, Texan CIA agent Felix Leiter is turned into the very English Clarence Leiter of British intelligence, played by Australian actor Michael Pate, who is incidentally quite clueless about baccarat, so that Bond ends up explaining the game to him (though this is, of course, principally for the audience's benefit). Vesper Lynd has become the much more prosaically named American Valerie Mathis (Rene Mathis, or at any rate his last name and his connection with French intelligence, folded into her character), played by Linda Christian. Where the plot is concerned this does not complicate matters very much. However, this reversal of the special relationship's rationale so that instead of having British skill married to American resources, it is British money which backs a "Card-Sharp" American agent makes rather less sense than Fleming's original—while also testifying to Americans' view that they had no need of any "special British prowess" to help them make use of their deeper pockets, thank you very much.

The Non-EON Bond Films

Unsurprisingly, a rendition of James Bond adventure that lacked just about everything that makes James Bond's adventures interesting (whether one is speaking of the books *or* the films) came and went quietly, not even doing very much to help the sale of Fleming's novels in the States. Still, producer Charles K. Feldman took enough interest in the book to buy the film rights in 1956, a move which eventually led to a feature film version of the story. Along with Kevin McClory's work with Fleming on the material from which he derived *Thunderball*, and which resulted in his possession of the film rights, this meant that the rights to two Bond novels were not in EON's hands during the early 1960s. Moreover, as the EON films exploded, both Feldman and McClory sought to make Bond films of their own—efforts which also have their own interest.

Casino Royale (1967)

McClory's collaboration with EON in making the 1965 *Thunderball* resulted in an agreement that he not use his rights for the next ten years. The result was that Feldman was the first to make a Bond film of his own. However, that same commercial success that made a James Bond movie an attractive prospect also made it difficult to produce a competing product. The problem was all the greater, arguably, because of the unconventional nature of *Casino*'s plot, which was a slender basis for a Bond-style feature film.

Ultimately, he went with a much-expanded story in which the elimination of American, British, French and Soviet agents by SMERSH prompts the heads of these organizations to go to the retired Sir James Bond for help. He initially refuses to return to duty. However, M is blown up during the visit, after which Bond ends up head of the Secret Service and forced to take charge of the situation, in which he and his agents (all of them now going by the name James Bond to confuse the opposition) contend with an array of enemies, including not only Le Chiffre, but the megalomaniacal Dr. Noah.

As one might expect, *Casino* goes for wacky comedy over visceral thrills. Moreover, its particular *style* of parody is noteworthy. In its being structured around sketches cramming in the maximum number of visual and acoustic gags, its style of moviemaking can be seen as analogous to the structuring of a film around set pieces that keep the thrills coming thick and fast, doing with comedy what the EON Bond films had just done for action.

In the producer's opting for parody of this type one can see the movie as simply following up Feldman's prior effort, *What's New, Pussycat?*, which featured much of the same cast (Peter Sellers, Ursula Andress, Woody Allen). However, it can also seem a logical result to the position from which he was attempting to launch his film, anticipating EON's later situation. Just as parody seemed to him the only way to compete with the Bond films of the '60s, the series' producers found themselves hard-pressed to do something besides repeat their earlier (and not easily topped) successes, and decided to do so by being "fresh and outrageous."

Moreover, rather than merely imitating Feldman's earlier success with *Pussycat*, *Casino* extended it considerably in a larger, zanier, even more chaotic production. Indeed, while getting little more admiration as a comedy than it does as a Bond film, it may be recognized as having anticipated the larger fashion for gag-based comedies that took off in the 1970s, with such works as Mel Brooks' *Blazing Saddles* and *Young Frankenstein*, and the Zucker-Zucker-Abrahams collaborations on *Kentucky Fried Movie* and *Airplane!* In fact, writing in *Bright Lights Film Journal*, Robert von Dassanowsky declared that

> Monty Python, the subversive parodies of Mel Brooks . . . the Gen X and Y films they inspire . . . [are] all heirs to

Casino Royale. Their creators would have had to invent the film if it hadn't existed.

Indeed, EON's own Bond films embraced the style, in moments like Bond's riding a camel to a Bedouin tent in *The Spy Who Loved Me*.

Never Say Never Again (1983)

The period during which McClory was required to refrain from trying to get a new film made with the *Thunderball* material ended in 1975. Once it was up he wasted no time in attempting to launch another Bond film franchise with a proposed *Warhead* movie, for which Len Deighton was writing a script, and which had Sean Connery attached to star in the lead. No movie by that title was ever filmed, but McClory's continued pursuit of a *Thunderball* remake starring Connery eventually led to the Warner Brothers-produced 1983 film *Never Say Never Again*.

Surprisingly, this later film is more faithful to the original material in key respects. In the movie, as in the novel, M is seen dissatisfied with Bond's current condition, and packing him off to a spa to get clean, with almost the same words. The complications involving SPECTRE's use of a double dreamed up for the film version are discarded. The finale also sees Bond and the team backing him up deploy from an American ballistic missile submarine, while the ensuing battle takes place primarily underwater.

Nonetheless, the broad line of its development is substantially different from both the novel and the 1965 film. Some of this had to do with the updating of the techno-military aspects of the plot. As Britain by this point was no longer using bombers like the Vindicator, the film makes the targeted aircraft an American F-111 strike plane based in England. The method of theft is not an attack on the plane or its crew, but the switching of the dummy missiles it was to carry on a training exercise with live nuclear warheads; and then, following the missiles' launch in the exercise, the electronic hijacking of the weapons so that Largo's divers can recover them. Petacchi's role is to wear a "false eye" that enables him to facilitate the switch from one type of warhead to another before the missiles are loaded on the plane, not to personally take control of the aircraft. Blofeld's extortion threat is broadcast, rather than transmitted in writing. And instead of a hydrofoil, Largo sails about in a luxurious but more conventional super-yacht (Adnan Kashoggi's 281-foot *Nabila*, specifically utilized for the film), '80s luxury chosen over '60s gimmickry.

Additionally, while an old-fashioned baccarat game between Bond and Largo could have served well enough from the standpoint of the plot, the filmmakers opt to heighten the interest of the scene by having it take place over a three-dimensional video game. Topical reference is made to SPECTRE's shipments of arms to Central America and the Middle East. And the organization's target is the oil fields of the latter region, while its financial demands reflect the preoccupation with black gold in these years: they want to be paid ten percent of the value of the oil trade, twenty-five billion dollars.

However, there are other differences which do not, strictly speaking, have anything to do with updating the plot. The portion of the action which occurs in the Bahamas is very limited, written almost as if it were obligatory to make use of that setting. Much more of the story occurs in southern France, and the Middle Eastern location targeted by the first bomb.

The Petacchis are Americanized, with brother "Jack" made a sadomasochist who has simply been seduced by Fatima, while Domino comes off as a comparative innocent among decadent Europeans. At the same time, the coarse Italian gangster Emiliano Largo is reimagined as the smooth Romanian tycoon Maximillian Largo. The Americanization of the Petacchis can seem a logical move, given that the American air force is the target; while the broader choices may reflect a desire to avoid offensive stereotypes about treacherous or thuggish Italians, though the alterations do not stop there. Where in the novel Domino is very clear about her being one in a very long line of women Largo uses and discards, here he appears more emotionally invested in their relationship, driven to personal fury when he realizes she has betrayed him with Bond—and retaliating by selling her to gun-toting, horse-riding desert nomads (that stereotype, apparently, still considered acceptable).

However, the most striking alteration to the characters is the presentation of M, who is reimagined as a prime candidate for the title of Upper Class Twit of the Year. (Indeed, where in the novel it was Leiter who connected widely separated dots in regard to the warhead theft and was dismissed by Bond, it is Bond who hits on the idea of the use of a false eye in the theft, and is dismissed by M for bringing it up—which in the circumstances makes M seem much more stupid.) Rowan Atkinson's Nigel Small-Fawcett is another such caricature. The movie's version of Q (Alec McCowen's "Algernon") does not come off as nearly so foolish, but he does complain long and loudly about the lack of technical resources available to him, saying flatly that if the CIA made him an offer he would be "off like a shot."

Indeed, the British on the whole look a bit shabby and ridiculous. One may take this for American cynicism regarding "the Cousins." (When Ernst Stavro Blofeld announces his ultimatum, an American General actually roars that if British intelligence is aware of the theft of the missiles, then "it's all over the Kremlin!") However, there is enough of such feeling in Fleming's own books that one can read this aspect of the movie as a reflection of the anxieties to which those novels spoke.

The Novelizations

If the post-Fleming novels have often been overlooked, this has been all the more the case with novelizations of the films. After all, movie novelizations tend to be seen as crass exercises in merchandising, and often justify this outlook by being poorly written—frequently giving the impression that the writer simply hastily scribbled down what they saw on the screen.

The interest of the books as books aside, the two novelizations by Gardner (of *Licence to Kill* and *Goldeneye*) and Benson (of *Tomorrow Never Dies*, *The World is Not Enough* and *Die Another Day*) are fairly conventional novelizations. They do contain scenes and details not in the movie versions. In some cases this simply reflects alterations to the films during the drafting phase. (In the book Bond is held by British intelligence not in a ship anchored in Hong Kong, but a mobile medical unit in South Korea.) In others, it is a matter of the writers fleshing out a script into a more satisfactory, novel-length work. (In his novelization of *Tomorrow Never Dies* the principal difference is Benson's opting to flesh out the investigation of the skirmish in the South China Sea from Wai Lin's end, while also filling out Elliott Carver's back story.) In still others, there is an attempt to reconcile awkward differences between the books and the films. (Gardner's version of *Licence to Kill* gave Leiter prosthetic limbs, as a result of his previous subjection to a hungry shark.)

Still, in an introduction at the start of *Licence to Kill* Gardner made clear that he considered the novelization a thing apart from the continuation novels he wrote for Glidrose, and Benson expressed the same assumption in his own interviews. And that seems to be the most plausible way to look at them—as adaptations of the screen versions, rather than evolutions of the series.

Somewhat more complex is the case of the two earlier novelizations by Wood, which evoke Fleming's material to a much greater degree than the films with which they are connected. Wood firmly anchors the print versions of his scripts for *The Spy Who Loved Me* and *Moonraker* within the universe Fleming created, not least by lifting much of Fleming's own prose. His M is pointedly identified as that old sea dog of the "damnably clear grey eyes," and his Bond is Fleming's Bond down to the comma of black hair hanging above his forehead. The block quotation of his doctor's medical report from *Thunderball* even turns up at the start of *Moonraker*, Bond recalling it as he enjoys his fiftieth cigarette of the day.

So does it go with the villains. Wood's Stromberg is an original creation, but in his freakish appearance (Wood's description suggests the figure in Edward Munch's painting *The Scream*), he has more in common with the original Dr. No than any of the villains of the films. His Hugo Drax, moreover, is written much more in line with Fleming's conception, down to the details of his physical appearance (the red hair, the evidence of wartime injury) and his love-hate relationship with things English. And just as the Drax of the original put his private wealth behind the development of a British ballistic missile program, Wood's Drax is footing much of the bill for the American space program.

While the Soviets are not the primary villains of Wood's *The Spy Who Loved Me*, Wood has Anya Amasova working not for the KGB, but specifically SMERSH, which is depicted as loathsome, not least in the person of its chief—rather than the genial Gogol, the disgusting Colonel-General Nikitin. Anya comes off more favorably, but herself can appear a caricature of a Soviet agent (reprimanding herself for not having read more Engels as she suns herself on a balcony in Sardinia). Moreover, while the Soviets are not a significant factor in *Moonraker*, they are much on Bond's mind when he first hears of the shuttle's theft (just as they were when the Vindicator bomber was hijacked in the original *Thunderball*).

As might be expected given such efforts, the action has a somewhat more grounded feel than in those notably over-the-top movies. The book's version of the gondola chase in Venice sees Bond escape his pursuers not by turning the gondola into a hovercraft and driving it into St. Mark's square as pigeons do double-takes, but, in harder-edged fashion. Bond takes his motorized gondola into a cul-de-sac, turns it abruptly in the water, and opens fire with his Walther PPK before the villains can react. The pursuing craft crashes into his gondola as Bond leaps clear of it. There is, too, something of the brutality of the Fleming novels, be it in the gorier descriptions of the killing, or the torture scene in *The Spy Who Loved Me* in which Bond is captured by Amasova's operatives.

Of course, it ought to be remembered that much of what made the novels more reminiscent of Fleming was also what the films dispensed with—like the implausibly freakish Stromberg or deeply anti-Soviet depiction of SMERSH in this version of *The Spy Who Loved Me*, or the anti-envrionmentalism implicit in Stromberg and Drax's schemes. Additionally, that the more brutal or sexually charged material was toned down is unsurprising given the producers' decision to keep the series PG at this point. Still, the two books offer a greater sense of effort to actually adapt the Fleming books for the screen than those two movies give. They also offer the impression that Wood, for his part, would have preferred to keep the films on which he worked more grounded and serious, and more closely connected with the style of the EON films.

CONCLUSION: WHERE TO, FROM HERE?

The Bond series has its roots in World War I-era adventure fiction, but still inspires, and is inspired by, the pop cultural scene of today. All this gives the impression that there is something especially enduring about the character and his adventures. Yet, on closer inspection it is difficult not to be struck by how much Bond was a figure of the period in which he emerged, and by just how transitional that era was, the period that produced Bond, and in which Bond resonated most strongly with audiences in Britain and abroad, one of exceptionally swift, dramatic transition in the life of Britain and the world.

The British Empire may have been in decline for a very long time by 1945, but up until then there was at least the illusion that it was the world's dominant, leading power, and would go on being so for some time to come. However, in the space of a generation Britain was reduced to a mid-sized European country in a world where Europe's position was deeply changed: the European colonial empires were broken up, and the old balance of power game the European powers had played for centuries ended by the continent's dominance by the United States and Soviet Union. At the same time, the realities of the nuclear, missile and space age made war and the idea of war a very different thing from what it had been before—the open, direct use of armed force by one great power against another on any scale nearly inconceivable as a rational, self-interested act.

Additionally, while there is always a tendency to make too much of generation gaps, the cultural changes of the era as experienced in the industrialized world, Britain included, were equally dramatic. The diminished saliency of old-fashioned nationalism and militarism; the experience of an unprecedented economic boom; the advent of the welfare state; the dramatic expansion of higher education; the similarly dramatic expansion of the presence of women in the labor market; the rise of a youth culture; the relaxation of mainstream attitudes regarding sexual matters; also made 1970 a very different place from 1945—indeed, more like 2015 than it was to that earlier and nearer date.

The Bond novels, and the Bond films developed from them, at least in their more distinctive characteristics, lie very close to the far side of that distance, not only in their reflecting the world of the 1950s, but the world of the 1950s as seen by an old Tory a good decade older than his own creation, and in many ways already feeling like he was out of time. Perhaps some part of Fleming thought, as Bond suggested, that "This country-right-or-wrong-business is getting a little out-of-date," but he was attached to that nineteenth century world and the values that prevailed in it all the same.

And updating it all has been a long, arduous task, one that in the end seems to have driven the writers of both the films and the books to simply give up on it, and take another tack. What audiences got with *Skyfall*, and what they seem likely to get with *Spectre*, is a Bond at once more local, and yet more universal.

One may have reservations about the approach. A more parochially British Bond may seem less compelling to the kind of international audience on which the films depend for their financial viability, while also clashing with that aspiration to universalize him. At the same time, it may seem that Bond is not an especially good candidate for mythmaking of this type, too well-known, too bound up with recent history and maybe even too small to properly be the stuff of legend. Still, should *Spectre* prove another major success, the films will likely continue along that path. Should they stumble, their failure will probably be a relative thing, and by no means a series-killer. In today's film industry, a franchise which has been profitable is effectively unkillable, and to date not one has weathered the ups and downs of the box office quite like this one has. The closest thing to a certainty one can say about the future of this series is that JAMES BOND WILL RETURN.

NOTES

1 . THE ORIGINS OF JAMES BOND

[1] Bruce A. Rosenberg and Ann Harleman Stewart, *Ian Fleming* (Boston: Twayne Publishers, 1989), 11.

[2] Andrew Lycett, *Ian Fleming: The Man Behind James Bond* (Atlanta: Turner, 1996), 223.

[3] This particular typo appears on page 185 of the 2003 Penguin USA edition.

[4] After the war the U.S. had an economy five times as big as Britain's, as well as two-thirds of the world's warships, and a monopoly of the atomic bomb. Even where land forces in Europe were concerned, there were three times as many American soldiers on the ground in the theater on V-E Day as there were British and Canadian troops combined. The Soviet Union had the world's second-largest industrial base, and a five hundred division army, while it soon after proved to be the sole country to keep up with the U.S. in the nuclear, missile and space fields.

[5] Andrew Lycett has recounted that traveling in 1959, Fleming was "angered and troubled" by the fact that "with the exception of the British consul in Hawaii, he had not met a single Briton between Hong Kong and New York." An indication of the country's

diminished influence in the world, he resented it, and it seems that this resentment translated to a measure of resentment toward the United States as well. Lycett, 358. All of this makes itself quite strongly felt in *You Only Live Twice*.

[6] Umberto Eco, "Narrative Structures in Fleming," Christoph Lindner, Ed. *The James Bond Phenomenon* (New York: Manchester University Press, 2003), 46.

[7] Julian Symons, *Bloody Murder: From the Detective Story to the Crime Novel*. (New York: Penguin, 1992), 272.

[8] Symons, 273.

2. THE NOVELS OF IAN FLEMING

[1] Eco, 40.

[2] Indeed, the narration claims that "Bond had never killed in cold blood." This would appear to be inconsistent with what the books said about Bond's earlier career. The discussion of Bond's achievement of his double-o rating in *Casino Royale*, particularly his shooting the Japanese cipher clerk, makes it seem certain that he did commit such killings. One can also construe his planting a limpet mine on Mr. Big's yacht in similar terms. Nonetheless, the point is made about Bond's feelings regarding the subject, and he was to have difficulty with pulling the trigger in cold blood again, notably in *The Spy Who Loved Me* and *The Man with the Golden Gun*.

[3] Lycett, 268.

[4] Lycett, 293.

[5] Interestingly, the fact that Bond should be on the verge of retirement from his field duties anyway does not come up, both his aging and the Service's policy unmentioned.

3. THE JAMES BOND MOVIES, 1962-1967

[1] Kingsley Amis, *The James Bond Dossier* (New York: The New American Library, 1965), 18.

[2] Jeremy Black, *The Politics of James Bond: From Fleming's Novels to the Big Screen* (Lincoln, NE: University of Nebraska Press, 2005), 86.

[3] Black, 211.

[4] Ibid.

[5] Black, 212.

4. OF OLD PATTERNS AND NEW

[1] James Chapman, *Licence to Thrill: A Cultural History of the James Bond Films* (New York: Columbia University Press, 2000), 181.

5. KEEPING UP WITH THE JONESES

[1] These were not new, of course. The past decade had seen, for instance, the *La Femme Nikita* remake *Point of No Return* (1992), and the "female Jason Bourne" movie *The Long Kiss Goodnight* (1996). However, such projects consistently performed poorly.

6. TOPICALITY

[1] It might be added, too, that the interest in Caspian oil reflected not just the loss of Russian control of the region, but the hype about the size of the region's oil reserves—dating this plot a bit like the expectations surrounding the space shuttle date *Moonraker*.

7. DEEPER CHANGES

[1] Black, 161.

[2] Deborah Lipp, *The Ultimate James Bond Fan Book* (New York: Sterling & Ross, 2006), 363-364.

[3] Chapman, 181.

8. REBOOT

[1] The rocket-themed films, of course, include *Dr. No, You Only Live Twice, Diamonds Are Forever, The Spy Who Loved Me, Moonraker, Goldeneye* and *Die Another Day*; while one might also count the cruise missile in *Tomorrow Never Dies*. Where nuclear weapon-themed films are concerned, there are *Goldfinger, Thunderball, The*

Spy Who Loved Me, *Octopussy*, *Goldeneye*, *Tomorrow Never Dies* and *The World Is Not Enough* (as Elektra King was going to use her sub's nuclear reactor as a giant "dirty bomb"). Additionally, while it would be a stretch to count them in this way, the prospect of nuclear competition and nuclear war is prominent in *You Only Live Twice*, *Diamonds Are Forever* and *For Your Eyes Only* (the ATAC, after all, controls submarines carrying nuclear-tipped Polaris missiles), while Dr. No also controls American space rockets through an operation involving a nuclear reactor of his own in the film by that name.

[2] Lasers were the villain's principal instrument in *Diamonds Are Forever* and *Die Another Day*, while playing more modest roles in *Goldfinger* (cutting a way into Fort Knox) and *Moonraker* (as Drax's weapon with which to defend his space station against American assault, and as the weapon Bond and Holly use to shoot down the chemical rounds Drax has fired at the Earth).

[3] The sole exceptions are *From Russia with Love*, *Moonraker*, *Tomorrow Never Dies* and *The World Is Not Enough*.

[4] These were the Aston Martin DB5 in *Goldfinger*, *Thunderball* and *On Her Majesty's Secret Service*; the Lotus Esprit in *The Spy Who Loved Me* and *For Your Eyes Only*; the Aston Martin Volante in *The Living Daylights*; the return of the Aston Martin DB5 *and* a new BMW in *Goldeneye*, *Tomorrow Never Dies* and *The World Is Not Enough*; and an Aston Martin Vanquish in *Die Another Day*.

[5] The aquatic chases occurred in *From Russia with Love*, *Thunderball*, *Live and Let Die*, *Moonraker*, *Tomorrow Never Dies*, and *The World Is Not Enough*. One could also count the pursuit of the submarine car in *The Spy Who Loved Me*. The ski chases appeared in *On Her Majesty's Secret Service*, *The Spy Who Loved Me*, *For Your Eyes Only*, *A View to a Kill* and *The World Is Not Enough*.

[6] There is the opening of *Goldfinger*, *Thunderball*, the recovery of Bond from his staged funeral in *You Only Live Twice*, as well as similar scenes in *Live and Let Die*, *The Spy Who Loved Me*, *For*

Your Eyes Only, *A View to a Kill*, *Licence to Kill* and *Tomorrow Never Dies*.

[7] Such scenes appeared in *Thunderball* (jet pack), *You Only Live Twice* (Little Nelly), *Live and Let Die* (glider), *Moonraker* (glider again), as well as *For Your Eyes Only*, *Octopussy*, *Licence to Kill*, *Goldeneye*, *Tomorrow Never Dies* and *Die Another Day*, while in *The Living Daylights* Bond and Kara bail out of the transport rather than fly it. Parachute sequences appeared in *The Spy Who Loved Me*, *Moonraker*, *The Living Daylights* (twice), *Licence to Kill* and *Tomorrow Never Dies*—while in *A View to a Kill* May Day also used a parachute to make her getaway, and in *Die Another Day* Gustav Graves uses one to make a grand entrance (and Bond uses another to force Graves' final exit).

[8] First done in *From Russia with Love*, this happened in each of the first three Pierce Brosnan films.

[9] The twelve are *Dr. No*, *Goldfinger*, *Thunderball*, *On Her Majesty's Secret Service*, *Diamonds Are Forever*, *The Spy Who Loved Me*, *Moonraker*, *Octopussy*, *A View to a Kill*, *Goldeneye*, *Tomorrow Never Dies* and *Die Another Day*.

[10] These are, respectively, *Dr. No*, *Goldfinger*, *You Only Live Twice*, *Diamonds Are Forever*, *The Spy Who Loved Me*, *Octopussy*, *Goldeneye* and *Tomorrow Never Dies*.

9. THE POST-FLEMING JAMES BOND NOVELS

[1] The results were not always consistent or logical. After claiming that Bond had only "minute flecks of grey" in his hair in *Licence Renewed*, Gardner mentioned in *Role of Honor* that Bond had trained back in the Second World War, implying that 007 was about sixty. Still, most readers appear to have taken such errors in stride.

10. ODDS AND ENDS

[1] The four novels Saito adapted were *Thunderball*, *The Man with the Golden Gun*, *On Her Majesty's Secret Service* and *Live and Let Die*.

Interestingly, in the manga Bond looks more than a little like Golgo later would.

SELECTED SECONDARY BIBLIOGRAPHY

Below is a list of secondary sources that were of particular use to me in writing the pieces collected here, divided between works specifically relating to James Bond in print and in film, and more general background works.

WORKS CONCERNING JAMES BOND
Allan, Vicky. "For Your Eyes Only." *Heraldscotland.com*. Oct. 26 2008.

Amis, Kingsley. *The James Bond Dossier*. New York: The New American Library, 1965.

Bennett, Tony and Jane Woollacott. *Bond and Beyond: the Political Career of a Popular Hero*. New York: Methuen, 1987.

Black, Jeremy. *The Politics of James Bond: From Fleming's Novels to the Big Screen*. Lincoln, NE: University of Nebraska Press, 2005.

Brosnan, John. *James Bond in the Cinema*. 2nd ed. London: The Tantivy Press, 1981.

Burgess, Anthony. "Oh, James, Don't Stop." *Life*. Apr. 1987: 114-120.

Chapman, James. *Licence to Thrill: A Cultural History of the James Bond Films*. New York: Columbia University Press, 2000.

Cork, John and Bruce Scivally. *James Bond: The Legacy*. New York: H.N. Abrams, 2002.

_____ and Collin Stutz. *James Bond Encyclopedia*. New York: D.K. Publications, 2007.

Corliss, Richard. "James Bond Meets His Match." *Time*. 1 Nov. 1982: 73.

_____. "We Don't Need Another Heroid." *Time*. 24 Jul. 1989: 53.

D'Abo, Maryam and John Cork. *Bond Girls Are Forever: The Women of James Bond*. New York: H.N. Abrams, 2006.

Duns, Jeremy. "The Secret Origins of James Bond." *Spywise.net*.

Eco, Umberto. "Narrative Structures in Fleming." Lindner, Christoph. Ed. *The James Bond Phenomenon*. New York: Manchester University Press, 2003: 34-55.

Friend, Tad. "Where Have You Gone, Pussy Galore?" *Vogue*. Dec. 1995: 167-169.

"Futile Attraction." *New Statesman and Society*. 12 Oct. 1990: 12-13.

Hibbin, Sally. *The New Official James Bond Movie Book*. New York: Crown Publishing, 1989.

Johnson, Paul. "Sex, Snobbery and Sadism." *The New Statesman*. 5 Apr. 1958: 430-432.

Lane, Anthony. "Of Human Bondage: Ian Fleming, James Bond, and the England That Made Them." *The New Yorker*. 24 Jun. 1996: 148-153.

Leader, Zachary. *The Life of Kingsley Amis*. New York: Pantheon Books, 2006.

Lipp, Deborah. *The Ultimate James Bond Fan Book*. New York: Sterling & Ross, 2006.

Lycett, Andrew. *Ian Fleming: The Man Behind James Bond*. Atlanta: Turner, 1996.

Lyttleton, Oscar. "Skyfail: The 5 Worst James Bond Films." *The Playlist*. 7 Nov. 2012.

Maibaum, Richard. "James Bond's 39 Bumps." *New York Times*. 13 Dec. 1964.

Marche, Stephen. "Why I Hate James Bond." *Esquire*. 1 Nov. 2012.

McGuian, Cathleen. "Bond at 25: Back to Basics." *Newsweek*. 27 Jul. 1987: 56-57.

Pearson, John. *The Life of Ian Fleming*. New York: Bantam, 1967.

Pfeiffer, Lee and Phillip Lisa. *The Incredible World of 007*. Seacaucus, NJ: Carol Publishing Group, 1995.

"The Raymond Benson CBn Interview." *CommanderBond.net* 24 Apr. 2004.

Rayner, Richard. "Of Human Bondage." *Esquire*. Nov. 1995: 72-79.

Rosenberg, Bruce A. and Ann Harleman Stewart. *Ian Fleming*. Boston: Twayne Publishers, 1989.

Rubin, Steven Jay. *The Complete James Bond Movie Encyclopedia*. Chicago: Contemporary Books, 1995.

_____. *The James Bond Films*. Westport, CT: Arlington House Publishers, 1981.

Sragow, Michael. "Heroes We Don't Deserve." *Atlantic*. Oct. 1985: 89-91.

Von Dassanowsky, Robert. "Casino Royale at 33: The Postmodern Epic in Spite of Itself." *Bright Lights Film Journal*. Apr. 2000.

Winder, Simon. *The Man Who Saved Britain: A Personal Journey into the Disturbing World of James Bond*. New York: Farrar, Straus & Giroux, 2006.

GENERAL WORKS

Anderson, Patrick. *The Triumph of the Thriller: How Cops, Crooks and Cannibals Captured Popular Fiction*. New York: Random House, 2007.

Bairoch, Paul. "International Industrialization Levels From 1750-1780." In Patrick Karl O'Brien, ed., *Industrialization: Critical Perspectives on the World Economy*, vol. 2. London: Routledge, 1998: 3-35.

Barnett, Correlli. *Britain and Her Army, 1509-1970: A Military, Political and Social Survey*. London: Allen Lane, 1970.

_____. *The Collapse of British Power*. New York: Morrow, 1972.

_____. *The Audit of War: The Illusion and Reality of Britain as a Great Nation*. New York: Macmillan, 1986.

Bloch, Ivan. *Is War Now Impossible? Being an Abridgment of "The War of the Future in its Technical, Political and Economic Relations."* Trans. R.C. Long. London: Grant Richards, 1899.

Brendon, Piers. *The Decline and Fall of the British Empire, 1781-1997*. New York: Alfred A. Knopf, 2007.

Brode, Douglas. *The Films of the Sixties*. New York: Carol Publishing Group, 1980.

Calder, Angus. *The People's War: Britain 1939-1945*. New York: Pantheon Books, 1969.

Cawelti, John G. and Bruce A. Rosenberg. *The Spy Story*. Chicago: University of Chicago Press, 1987.

Clarke, I.F. *Voices Prophesying War: Future Wars 1763-3749* 2nd ed. New York: Oxford University Press, 1993.

Clarke, Peter F. *The Last Thousand Days of the British Empire: Churchill, Roosevelt and the Birth of the Pax Americana*. New York: Bloomsbury Press, 2008.

Dow, J.C.R. *The Management of the British Economy 1945-1960*. Cambridge: University Press, 1964.

Frank, Thomas. *One Market Under God: Extreme Capitalism, Market Populism, and the End of Economic Democracy*. New York: Doubleday, 2000.

Gibson, James William. *Warrior Dreams: Paramilitary Culture in Post-Vietnam America*. New York: Hill & Wang, 1993.

Harrison, Mark. "Resource Mobilization for World War II: the U.S.A., U.K., U.S.S.R., and Germany, 1938-1945." *Economic History Review* 41.2 (1988): 171-192.

Kennedy, Paul. *The Rise and Fall of British Naval Mastery*. Amherst, NY: Humanity Books, 1983.

_____. *The Rise and Fall of the Great Powers: Economic Change and Military Conflict from 1500 to 2000*. New York: Random House, 1987.

Kindleberger, Charles. *World Economic Primacy: 1500-1990*. New York: Oxford University Press, 1996.

Landes, David. *The Unbound Prometheus: Technological Change and Industrial Development in Western Europe From 1750 to the Present*. London: Cambridge University Press, 1969.

Leigh, David. *The Wilson Plot: How the Spycatchers and their American Allies Tried to Overthrow the British Government*. New York: Pantheon Books, 1988.

Massie, Robert K. *Dreadnought: Britain, Germany and the Coming of the Great War*. New York: Random House, 1991.

McCormack, David and Katy Fletcher. *Spy Fiction: A Connoisseur's Guide*. New York: Facts on File, 1990.

Modelski, George. *Seapower and Global Politics, 1494-1993*. Seattle: University of Washington Press, 1988.

Mordden, Ethan. *Medium Cool*. New York: Alfred A. Knopf, 1990.

Northedge, F.S. *Descent From Power: British Foreign Policy, 1945-1973*. London: Allen & Unwin, 1974.

Parker, John. *Sean Connery*. Chicago: Contemporary Books, 1993.

Paterson, Robert H. *Britain's Strategic Nuclear Deterrent: From the V-Bomber to Beyond Trident*. London: Frank Cass & Co, 1997.

Paxman, Jeremy. *Empire: What Ruling the World Did to the British*. London: Penguin, 2012.

Piketty, Thomas. *Capital in the Twenty-First Century*. New York: Belknap Press, 2014.

Ponting, Clive. *1940: Myth and Reality*. Chicago: Ivan R. Dee, 1991.

Rubenstein, Leonard. *The Great Spy Films*. Secaucus, NJ: The Citadel Press, 1979.

Sinfield, Alan. *Literature, Politics and Culture in Postwar Britain*. Berkley: University of California Press, 1989.

Stafford, David. "Spies and Gentlemen: The Birth of the British Spy Novel, 1893-1914." *Victorian Studies* 24.4 (1981): 489-509.

_____. *The Silent Game: The Real World of Imaginary Spies*. Athens, GA: University of Georgia Press, 1991.

Snyder, William P. *The Politics of British Defense Policy 1945-1962* Columbus, OH: Ohio State University Press, 1964.

Steiner, Zara S. *Britain and the Origins of the First World War*. New York: St. Martin's Press, 1977.

Stross, Charles. "Afterword: The Golden Age of Spying." Stross, Charles. *The Jennifer Morgue*. New York: Ace, 2009: 381-397.

Symons, Julian. *Bloody Murder: From the Detective Story to the Crime Novel*. New York: Penguin, 1992.

Tiratsoo, Nick. *From Blitz to Blair: A New History of Britain Since 1939*. London: Weidenfeld & Nicholson, 1997.

Wood, James. *How Fiction Works*. New York: Farrar, Straus & Giroux, 2008.

INDEX

"007 in New York" (short story), 11, 14, 43-44, 49, 128

Allan, Vicky, 134-135
Amasova, Anya (character), 2, 87, 101, 116-117, 133, 137, 183, 184; See also *The Spy Who Loved Me*
Ambler, Eric, 17-21
Amis, Kingsley, 21, 49, 57, 134, 157-168, 169-170, 173
Ashenden (novel), 15, 18-21
Aston Martin, 64, 65, 68, 72, 82, 146, 153, 192n
Austin Powers (films), 90, 142-143, 144

Bassey, Shirley, 65-66, 67, 84

Benson, Raymond, 157-168, 169, 171, 175, 182
Black, Jeremy, 53, 59, 131, 191n
Blofeld, Ernst Stavro, 8, 10, 12, 39- 40, 41, 42, 44, 45, 47, 50, 53, 62, 72, 74, 75, 76, 81-82, 83, 84, 89, 90, 96, 101, 115, 120, 142, 165, 170, 180, 181
Bouvier, Pam, 89, 131, 133-134, 147
Boyd, William; See *Solo*
Brand, Gala (character), 16-17, 31, 53; See also *Moonraker* (novel)
Britain,
    as power in decline, 8-15, 38-49, 142, 185

"special relationship" with the United States, 13-14, 25, 30-31, 41-42, 46-48, 59-60, 176-177

welfare state, 11, 14-15, 59, 186

Broccoli, Albert R., 2, 54, 79, 135-136

Brokenclaw (novel), 162, 163, 169

Brosnan, Pierce, 92-93, 110, 112, 128, 135, 137, 139, 140, 144, 152, 153, 193n

Burgess, Anthony, 91-92, 195

Carte Blanche, 170-172

Casino Royale (1967 film), 79, 88, 91, 174-175

Casino Royale (2006 film), 145-151, 154

Casino Royale (novel), 9-10, 11, 13, 14, 15, 18, 23, 24-28, 29, 31, 34, 45, 46, 52, 54, 55, 128, 145-150

"Casino Royale" (television episode), 3, 174, 175-177

Chandler, Raymond, 21

"clubland" thrillers, 15-17, 20, 21, 142

Cold Fall, 160, 162, 164, 165

Cold War, 9-15, 25, 33, 59, 61, 96, 106, 114, 116- 117, 118-122, 123, 124, 128, 135, 136, 142, 154, 162

Colonel Sun (novel), 157-160, 162, 166, 168, 173

Connery, Sean, 80, 84, 90, 135, 153, 174, 179

Dalton, Timothy, 92, 106, 107, 132

Death is Forever, 161, 162, 163

Deaver, Jeffrey; See *Carte Blanche*

Devil May Care, 157, 169-171

di Vicenzo, Teresa "Tracy" (character), 45-47, 53, 81-82, 89

Diamonds Are Forever (film), 80, 82-90, 95, 96, 102, 112, 142, 143, 191n, 192n, 193n

Diamonds Are Forever (novel), 9, 10, 21, 32-33, 34, 35, 37, 52, 82-83, 96, 127

Die Another Day, 86, 87-88, 110, 112, 124, 125, 129-130, 137-138, 139, 140, 141, 144, 145, 150, 153, 182, 191n, 192n, 193n

DoubleShot, 160-161, 163, 168, 169

Dr. No (film), 2, 51, 54-61, 63, 64, 66, 67, 68, 69, 70, 71, 75, 97, 99, 113, 117, 147, 191n, 193n

Dr. No (novel), 2, 10, 17, 23, 35-37, 46-47, 51-52, 54-60, 183

Drax, Hugo, 31, 32, 37, 89, 102, 118, 122, 158, 183, 184, 192n

Drummond, Hugh "Bulldog" (character), 15, 16, 21, 168

EON Productions, 2, 54, 60, 75, 80, 83, 100, 106, 112, 114, 12, 128, 139, 145, 149, 155, 161, 174, 175, 177, 178

Facts of Death, The, 161, 163

Faulks, Sebastian; See *Devil May Care*

Feldman, Charles, 79, 88, 91, 177-179

Fleming, Ian,
dealings with film producers, 54, 79, 177
early life, 5-8
literary influences of, 15-21
political views, 11-15, 59, 189-190n
writing of the James Bond series, 23-50

For Your Eyes Only (collection), 23-24, 38-39,

For Your Eyes Only (film), 89, 92, 101, 119, 121, 122, 127-128, 135, 141, 143, 192n, 193n

"For Your Eyes Only" (story), 38, 89, 92, 101, 119, 121, 122, 127-128

From Russia with Love (film), 61-64, 66, 67, 68, 69, 81, 90, 114, 141, 192n, 193n

From Russia with Love (novel), 10, 12-13, 14, 16, 18, 23, 33-36, 48, 55, 190n

Gaitskell, Hugh, 60

Galore, Pussy (character), 37, 53, 64, 68, 165

Gardner, John, 157-168, 169, 171, 175, 182, 193n

Gogol, Anatol Alexis (character), 117, 120, 137, 183

Goldeneye (film), 7, 86, 87, 93, 108, 109, 110, 123, 124, 128, 129, 131, 133, 136, 144, 153, 182, 191n, 192n, 193n

Goldeneye (residence), 5-6, 128

Goldfinger (film), 2, 51, 63-66, 67, 68, 70, 71, 72, 74, 75, 77, 79, 83, 84, 85-88, 106, 121-122, 151, 160, 165, 167, 191n, 192n, 193n

Goldfinger (novel), 2, 10, 14, 23, 37-38, 43, 51, 53, 63-66, 97, 121-122, 172, 193n

Greene, Graham, 15, 17-19, 21

Hamilton, Guy, 83-84

Hammett, Dashiell, 21

High Time to Kill, 161, 163-164, 168, 169

"Hildebrand Rarity, The," (story), 9, 20-21, 38-39, 46, 128

Horowitz, Anthony, 172

Icebreaker, 162

James Bond films (EON film series)
adaptation from the books, 51-77
current events in, 113-125
formulas, 66-72, 74, 76, 85-88, 95, 101-102, 105-106, 111, 127, 133, 139-142, 149, 151; See also James Bond novels (Ian Fleming), formulas
gadgets in, 64-65, 67-68, 71, 74, 80, 82, 90, 106, 140, 153
gender in, 127, 132-135, 147-148
novelizations, 181-184
"reboot," 2, 139-156, 172
self-parody in, 64-65, 81, 84-85, 88-93, 116, 141, 142-143, 150
sexuality in, 1, 52-53, 54, 57-59, 97, 127, 132-135, 147-148, 150-151, 184, 186
use of film trends, 95-112
James Bond novels (Ian Fleming series), 5-50

depictions of America in, 30-31, 43-44
formulas, 23-24, 31-32, 35, 37, 51
gadgets in, 25, 37-38, 64-65
self-parody in, 17-18, 28, 35-37, 40, 65
sexuality in, 17, 25, 33, 43, 52-53, 57-59
James Bond novels (post-Fleming continuation), 157-172
gadgets in, 159-160, 166
self-parody in, 165-168
sexuality in, 164-165, 170-171
Johnson, Jinx (character), 112, 133, 139

Klebb, Rosa, 34-35, 39-40, 62, 63
Krest, Milton (character), 38-39, 42, 46, 107, 128; See also "Hildebrand Rarity, The"

le Carré, John, 53, 88
Le Chiffre (character), 9-10, 18, 25-28, 29, 31, 52, 145, 146, 147, 149, 150, 176, 178
Leiter, Felix (character), 10, 13, 25, 28, 30-31, 33, 37, 42, 55, 57, 58, 59-60, 64, 66, 74, 107-108, 123, 128, 146, 176, 181, 182

Licence Renewed, 157, 158, 160, 162, 163, 167, 193n

Licence to Kill (film), 86, 89, 92, 107-108, 109, 122, 128-129, 131, 133-134, 136, 144, 182, 193n

Licence to Kill (novelization), 182

Live and Let Die (film), 86, 90, 96-98, 99, 100, 102, 114, 115, 116, 122, 128, 151, 192n, 193n

Live and Let Die (novel), 10, 23, 28-31, 32-33, 36, 37, 53, 55, 115, 128, 169, 193n

Living Daylights, The (film), 87, 92, 106, 107, 108, 117, 121, 122, 128, 131, 133, 136, 144, 192n, 193n

"Living Daylights, The" (story), 11, 42, 48, 49, 50, 128

Lycett, Andrew, 7-8, 35, 189n, 190n

Lynd, Vesper (character), 26, 34, 52, 53, 145-148, 150, 176

M (character), 8, 10, 28, 32-33, 35-36, 38, 40, 46, 47, 48, 54, 58, 67, 73, 75, 83, 107-108, 129-130, 134, 148, 149, 150, 153, 159, 166, 171, 174, 177-178, 179, 181, 182-183

Maibaum, Richard, 91, 98, 120, 135-136

Man with the Golden Gun, The (film), 86, 90, 104, 114-116, 137, 140, 193n

Man with the Golden Gun, The (novel), 10, 48-49, 53, 157, 169, 190n, 193n

Man with the Red Tattoo, The, 157

Markham, Robert; See Amis, Kingsley

Mask of Dimitrios, The, 18, 167; See also Ambler, Eric

Maugham, W. Somerset; See *Ashenden* (novel)

McClory, Kevin, 72, 177, 179-181

McNeile, H.C.; See Drummond, Bulldog

Moneypenny, 25, 59, 66, 67, 147, 153, 171, 173-174

Moonraker (film), 87, 89, 92, 101, 102, 103, 117-118, 121-122, 133, 139, 140, 151, 182-184, 191n, 192n, 193n

Moonraker (novel), 7, 8, 10, 14, 20, 23, 31-32, 33, 36, 37, 38, 121-122, 164, 167, 175, 183

Moonraker (novelization), 182-184

Moore, Roger, 2, 90-92, 153

Never Dream of Dying, 160

Never Say Never Again, 106, 161, 174-175, 179-181; See

also *Thunderball* (film); *Thunderball* (novel)

Never Send Flowers, 161, 163, 165, 169

No Deals, Mr. Bond, 163

Octopussy (film), 86, 92, 103, 104, 106, 120, 125, 128, 135, 192n, 193n

Octopussy (story) 23, 49-50, 128, 143, 156

Octopussy and the Living Daylights (collection), 49

On Her Majesty's Secret Service (film), 51, 75, 80-82, 85-93, 95, 141, 192n, 193n

On Her Majesty's Secret Service (novel), 23-24, 44-46, 51, 75, 80-82, 193n

Oppenheim, Edward Phillips, 16-17

"Property of a Lady," 10-11, 49, 104, 128

Pushkin, Leonid, 117, 120, 137

Q (character), 63, 67-68, 74, 89, 90, 153, 181; See also gadgets

Quantum of Solace (film), 151-152, 170

"Quantum of Solace" (story), 18, 20, 38, 49, 128, 151

"Risico," 10-11, 38-39, 44, 127

Role of Honor, 161, 162, 163, 167, 169, 193n

Saltzman, Harry, 2, 54, 79

Savile Row, 57, 131

Scaramanga, Francisco (character), 10, 48, 86, 90, 100, 114-116, 153, 169, 172

Scorpius (novel), 163, 167, 168, 169

SeaFire (novel), 160, 162, 163, 165

Skyfall, 152-156, 186

SMERSH, 12-13, 14, 17, 26, 27, 28, 33, 34, 39, 46, 53, 59, 61, 62, 121, 162, 169, 176, 177, 183, 184

Solo, 169-172

Spangled Mob, 33, 37, 48

Special Executive for Counterintelligence, Terrorism, Revenge and Extortion (SPECTRE), 10, 13, 17, 38-46, 49, 56, 59, 61, 62, 63, 67, 72, 73, 75, 76, 77, 83, 88, 91, 107, 113, 114, 120, 158, 161, 162, 165, 169, 179, 180

Spectre (film), 186, 187

Spy Who Loved Me, The (film), 2, 87-88, 100-101, 101-102, 108, 111, 112, 116-117, 118-119, 120-121, 124, 133, 134, 135-136, 139-140, 141, 179, 191n, 192n, 193n

Spy Who Loved Me, The (novel), 10, 20-21, 42-44 52, 53, 190n

Spy Who Loved Me, The (novelization), 182-184

Symons, Julian, 15-16, 190n

Tanaka, Tiger (character), 11-12, 46-47, 75

Thunderball (film), 2, 51, 54, 72-74, 75, 76, 79, 98, 100, 108, 114, 131, 141, 143, 155, 160, 161, 168, 177, 179, 183, 191n, 192n, 193n; See also *Never Say Never Again*

Thunderball (novel), 2, 10, 13, 14-15, 18, 23-24, 39-42, 43, 49, 51, 53, 54, 60, 62, 131, 167, 175, 177, 179-182, 182-183, 193n

Tomorrow Never Dies (film), 87, 92-93, 108, 109-110, 111, 124, 131, 132, 133, 136-137, 142, 144, 182, 191n, 192n, 193n

Tomorrow Never Dies (novelization), 182

View to a Kill, A (film), 86, 92, 106, 113, 121-122, 128, 133, 136, 144-145, 192n, 193n

"View to a Kill, A" (story), 10-11, 38, 128

von Dassanowsky, Robert, 178-179

War on Terror, 124-125

Win, Lose or Die, 160, 161, 162-163, 167, 168, 169

Wood, Christopher, 175, 182-184

World Is Not Enough, The, 86, 110, 113, 123-124, 124-125, 129, 133, 134, 137, 141, 144, 153, 182, 192n

You Only Live Twice (film), 74-77, 79, 80, 81, 82, 83, 85-88, 90, 99, 100-101, 101-102, 112, 158, 191n, 192n, 193n

You Only Live Twice (novel), 8, 10, 11-12, 13-14, 46-48, 152, 169, 190n

Zero Minus Ten, 157, 161, 163

ABOUT THE AUTHOR

Nader Elhefnawy taught British literature at the University of Miami once upon a time. His prior books include *The Forgotten James Bond*.

Visit him at his blog, *Raritania*.

Printed in Great Britain
by Amazon.co.uk, Ltd.,
Marston Gate.